THE CHRISTMAS MURDER MYSTERY

THE CHRISTMAS MURDER MYSTERY

The third Agatha Aston Mystery

Jack Murray

Kit Aston Series
The Affair of the Christmas Card Killer
The Chess Board Murders
The Phantom
The Frisco Falcon
The Medium Murders
The Bluebeard Club
The Tangier Tajine
The French Diplomat Affair (novella)
Haymaker's Last Fight (novelette)

Agatha Aston Series
Black-Eyed Nick
The Witchfinder General Murders
The Christmas Murder Mystery

DI Jellicoe Series
A Time to Kill
The Bus Stop
Trio
Dolce Vita Murders

Danny Shaw / Manfred Brehme WWII Series
The Shadow of War

Crusader
El Alamein

Copyright © 2022 by Jack Murray

All rights reserved. No part of this publication may be reproduced, distributed, or transmitted in any form or by any means, including photocopying, recording, or other electronic or mechanical methods, without the prior written permission of the publisher, except in the case of brief quotations embodied in critical reviews and certain other non-commercial uses permitted by copyright law. For permission requests, write to the publisher, addressed 'Attention: Permissions Coordinator,' at the address below.

Jackmurray99@hotmail.com

This is a work of fiction. Names, characters, businesses, places, events, locales, and incidents are either the products of the author's imagination or used in a fictitious manner. Any resemblance to actual persons, living or dead, or actual events is either purely coincidental or used in a fictitious manner, except when they really were alive.

ISBN: 9798360438090
Imprint: Independently published

For Monica, Lavinia, Anne and our angel baby, Edward

Married in July, with flowers ablaze,
Bitter-sweet mem'ries in after days. Married in July, with flowers ablaze,
Bitter-sweet mem'ries in after days.

>> Traditional Wedding Poem

1

Ralston House, Betty Simpson's family estate: 21st July 1877

They say time waits for no man but try being a young woman. The saying revealed two injustices in Lady Agatha Aston's book: the relentlessly male purview of language as well as the uncomfortable truth that she was at twenty-seven, and notwithstanding her title, getting dangerously long in the tooth for the rituals required by the mating game.

As much as a young woman may protest, there is a bittersweet feeling to seeing one's best friend standing smiling at the altar, holding the hand of her recently acquired husband. Agatha was aware that her emotions were swirling in a manner that left her perilously close to shedding the tears she swore she would not. Of course, she felt nothing but delight for her dearest friend, Betty Stevens. As was. Her friend was now Mrs James Simpson although neither she nor Betty would ever see her as such. Betty Simpson at a pinch. She felt an ache that was only in part related to the prospect of a house that would no longer have Betty residing with her.

She looked at the young couple standing at the altar, smiles splitting their faces. Had any couple ever been so well-matched? Statistically the answer was probably yes, reflected Agatha, but she had enough romance in her to ignore the cold implacable logic of numbers. No, Betty and James were two peas in the proverbial. They looked like two Labradors, tails wagging in the sunshine. Each had a glorious vigour to the colour of their cheeks which suggested that they'd made an unscheduled start to their wedding festivities after disappearing to sign whatever wedding books cold-hearted legality required.

They marched down the aisle as man and wife. Betty smiled as she passed Agatha. Their eyes did not meet yet, at last, the dam burst for Agatha. The sight of such uninhibited joy on the face of her friend swatted away the last remnants of reserve; Agatha's tears fell freely and unselfishly for her friend.

It was only as she wiped them away the thought struck her that she along with her other great friend from school, Lady Jocelyn Gossage, or 'Sausage' as she was known to her friends and the world at large, would soon be on the receiving end of looks and comments about their unmarried status.

Agatha glanced to her right. Beside her was Sausage. She, too, was crying freely. Unlike Agatha, Sausage had never disguised her desire to marry sooner rather than later. Alas, love had dodged her rather in the manner she had avoided opponents on the hockey field: a feint here, a pass there. Perhaps only Sausage among Agatha's friends matched Betty for bigness of heart, kindness of disposition and unwavering belief that love's light would one day shine in the eyes of a man looking at her.

Agatha had never worried about such things. She was handsome, rich and blessed, or cursed, with an intellect that attracted then put off potential admirers. She had laid waste to many a young man's hopes before the realisation dawned on those same spurned suitors that they had side-stepped a vitriol-tipped arrow from Cupid's malevolent bow.

She professed not to worry about such things but, in truth, a thought had arisen within her mind, unbidden: it had been many months since she had last rejected a proposal. In fact, it was almost the anniversary of her last refusal. Such thoughts, even for the most independent of dispositions, cannot go unacknowledged for long. Not when you have a helpful family for whom such matters are the sole topic of conversation. She avoided going home as much as possible. She much preferred the spacious comfort of her home in Grosvenor Square which had been bequeathed to her by an equally independent great aunt who recognised in Agatha a kindred spirit.

'I say,' said Sausage, who often did.

Agatha waited a moment to see if anything would be added to this. For once, Sausage obliged.

'Betty does look rather wonderful, don't you think? So happy.'

Agatha nodded in agreement. The two ladies watched in pride as their great friend dressed in white silk and lace, swept past them, eyes straight ahead as tradition dictated.

'Yes,' agreed Agatha, 'I've never seen her so radiant.' And Agatha had certainly seen Betty look radiant before, especially after her fourth gin.

Agatha took Sausage's hand, 'Let's go outside.' The two women followed the congregation out of the church to greet the happy couple. As they walked down the aisle, Agatha sensed someone walking alongside her. She turned and saw a man in his mid-sixties with a pockmarked face. Although not tall, he still towered over Agatha who just about made it to five feet. The man nodded to her. His eyes twinkled with enough good humour to suggest he would be good company at that moment.

'Lady Agatha. Lady Jocelyn.'

'Mr Whicher,' replied Agatha with a smile. 'I thought I saw you earlier. Is your lady wife here today?' asked Agatha.

'Alas not. I brought the chief superintendent. Perhaps not quite so attractive,' said Whicher with a hint of a grin. Jack Whicher had retired the previous year from the detective branch of the police following a case in which he had enjoyed the help of both Agatha as well as the services of the groom, James Simpson.

The chief superintendent in question was a man who looked as old as Whicher but was, in fact, fifteen years younger; his thick grey beard rather gave the impression that St Nicholas had been invited to the wedding, or Karl Marx for that matter, thought Agatha.

'Mr Williamson,' said Agatha holding out her hand. There was something reassuring about this man. She liked him and sensed the feeling was reciprocated.

Chief Superintendent Adolphus 'Dolly' Williamson bowed to Agatha and Sausage. Like Whicher, he was a serious man who smiled more with his eyes than his mouth.

'Ladies,' he said, 'I was hoping we would meet again.' He was not the only one. Agatha had missed the excitement of being involved with a case. It had been too long.

The two ladies offered their arms to the former policeman and the current head of the Criminal Investigation Department of Scotland Yard and were escorted from the church.

'Are you coming to the reception?' asked Agatha.

Whicher shook his head and sighed audibly.

'Lady Elizabeth did ask us, but we declined.'

'Pity,' said Agatha and she meant it. The prospect of the reception was a mixed one for her. As much as she wanted to share the joy of the day with her dearest friend, she suspected that her family, particularly Aunt Daphne who was hovering nearby, would do their best to ensure that she was forced to meet members of the dwindling band of eligible young men who were either uncowed by her reputation or had yet to be refused. An afternoon spent with the head of the detective branch and the great Mr Whicher would have been an altogether more enticing way of spending time.

'You will at least stay for drinks, gentlemen,' said Agatha in a firmer tone that the two men recognised so well. It brooked no argument and was matched by a hard glint in her eye. As two married men of many years, they knew that to argue was pointless. They exchanged glances at which point Agatha knew that, for the moment, she had won.

She usually did.

They clapped, waved, and threw rice at the couple who had stepped into an open landau carriage. Although she recognised that this was traditional, Agatha couldn't quite help but wonder about the point of the exercise. The wedding guests watched the carriage drive less than two hundred yards to the front entrance of the manor, Betty's ancestral home. Of course, like Agatha, she was the eldest in the family, but the home would be entailed to her rather dissolute but loveable brother, Rory Stevens.

Agatha and the other wedding guests walked along the path from the small church on the estate towards the manor house. She and Whicher talked of the wedding, but the retired detective suspected that this was just a feint. The assault would happen indoors when he would be armed with nothing more effective than a glass of champagne. In the grand entrance hall, Whicher found himself being firmly led towards a table where champagne was being served. Sausage, unusually quick on the uptake, followed arm in arm with the chief superintendent.

A few minutes later, champagne glass in hand, Agatha was able to discuss the matter uppermost in her mind after, of course, the happiness of her friend.

'Now, doubtless you will know why I have insisted that you stay for a drink,' opened Agatha, fixing her eyes on both men.

Sausage hadn't a clue so said nothing. This was usually the way with Agatha. Sausage's only hope was that something would be said that would shed light on what Agatha was thinking then all would be fine. She smiled keenly; her eyes sparkled with the curiosity of the soon-to-be-informed. Thankfully, it was clear that the two detectives knew what Agatha was referring to. The clue to this, one that even Sausage could spot, was the way both men rolled their eyes although, it must be said, this was not done unkindly. Whicher deferred to the younger man and let Williamson speak first.

'Can I take it, Lady Agatha, that young James has not mentioned anything about the case?'

This was greeted by a shake of the head from Agatha. She did not look too pleased either, noted Sausage. So, it was a case. Sausage was feeling excited now. Even for Sausage, it had been too long.

'I must confess that this is a surprise. Not, I would add, because I think young James is indiscreet. It's more that I have the utmost regard for your ability to, how can I put it?'

'Browbeat a confession?' suggested Agatha.

There was little point in denying this and to do so would only have insulted the intelligence of a woman he admired greatly. His eyes radiated good humour.

'Precisely,' agreed Williamson. He glanced in the direction of James Simpson who worked for the detective branch and now reported directly to Williamson. The look on Williamson's face was a mixture of affection and forbearance, rather like the parent of an amiable but none-too-bright child. Simpson had one arm around Betty's waist, another was holding a glass of champagne and his attention was fixed lovingly on his young wife. Just as it should be, thought Williamson.

He liked Simpson very much. There was so much to recommend him. He was a hard worker, unafraid to risk his body in the line of duty and, crucially, at that moment in the history of the detective branch, he was as honest and trustworthy as any man Williamson had met aside from the great Whicher himself. Was it such a bad thing that he was possessed of no great intellect? Such ambition that he owned up to was in the service of truth and justice rather than personal aggrandisement. Of course, being independently wealthy helped. Lord knows it helped. His attention returned to Agatha and providing an answer to the question she had asked.

'You are referring to Druscovich and Palmer, Lady Agatha?'

'I am referring to Druscovich and Palmer,' replied Agatha.

The names rang a bell for Sausage. She hadn't met them at Goodwood or Cowes. Sausage slowly went through the possibilities. Given that she and Agatha were with policemen, then perhaps they were criminals. Then she remembered: hadn't they met them during the Black-Eyed Nick case? It was difficult to recall. The names were familiar though. Had there been something in the papers about them. Perhaps they'd solved a big case. Sausage turned to Williamson to find out more.

'As you will have seen reported, Chief Inspectors Druscovich and Palmer have been arrested, it is true. I'm sure you'll appreciate that I cannot provide more detail officially.'

Williamson's eyes flitted in the direction of a large, older lady who had emerged from a crowd and appeared to be about to break into their circle. The woman in question was Agatha's Aunt Daphne. She was a woman who had made it her life's vocation to bring young people together in the cause of romance and everything else besides. Seeing her niece chatting happily with men old enough to be her grandfather was too much for this five-foot force of nature. Weddings were spectacularly rich opportunities for young women of means to be seen at their best, assessed by dominant males of the species and caressed gently towards the altar. Neither of the men in Agatha's presence qualified as potential suitors therefore time spent with them, in Daphne's view, was time wasted.

She was just about to make this point through the agency of facial expression and mime when she saw Agatha spin sharply towards her with a set look on her face. Daphne could read her niece like a fashion catalogue. Perhaps she would remind her niece later of the opportunity that these occasions provided: men, mazurkas and marriage.

Agatha spun back towards the two policemen who were impressed by how the young woman before them had warned off the predatory aunt with just a look.

'I love my Aunt Daphne, but she has only one topic of conversation where I am concerned.'

'I'm sure she means well,' said Jack Whicher gently.

A wave of Agatha's hand indicated that the subject was now finished.

'You were going to tell me all about the arrest of Druscovich and Palmer, chief superintendent,' said Agatha.

'Was I?'

'Yes,' said Agatha coldly. 'You were.'

Whicher smiled at his old friend and gave a "I-told-you-so-shrug" of the shoulders. Agatha wondered if a small wager had also been part of the conversation.

Most men reach a point in their lives, hopefully earlier rather than later, when they recognise that the best form of defence against women of decidedly firm opinions is submission rather than opposition. It makes for an easier life. Sometimes even a happy one although this is not guaranteed.

Williamson took a sip of the champagne. He paused for a moment as he realised that it was the best champagne he'd ever tasted. A frown appeared on Agatha's forehead which suggested to him that his appreciation of the alcohol was becoming less appreciated by his audience.

'It is a rather long story,' pointed out Williamson.

'We have time before the wedding breakfast is served.'

Glancing towards Agatha's aunt, Williamson said, 'Are you sure you shouldn't be mingling?'

Agatha had the grace to smile at this but said nothing. This was the chief superintendent's cue to continue.

'Druscovich, Palmer and another officer, Meiklejohn have been arrested for perverting the course of justice. There were some irregularities in the manner in which they conducted a recent investigation.'

'You mean they almost let those confidence tricksters William Kurr and Harry Benson evade arrest?' asked Agatha.

The eyebrows of both Williamson and Whicher rose in unison. The chief superintendent turned in the direction of the newly married Detective Constable Simpson.

'No, James has been remarkably unhelpful on this point,' said Agatha. 'Thankfully, the leak has sprung from elsewhere and a newspaperman of my acquaintance was more than happy to feed my curiosity. I think he felt indebted.'

'Would that indebted newspaperman go by the name of Robbie Rampling?' asked Whicher with a broad grin.

'I couldn't possibly say Mr Whicher,' replied Agatha which the former detective took to mean 'yes'.

The group became aware of a man standing nearby who seemed for all the world to be listening in on their conversation. They turned inward and their voices lowered an octave or three.

'It does not look good for the men,' admitted Williamson, sadly. 'There is evidence that money was exchanged so I fear they will face prison terms. Worse is the damage to our reputation. Druscovich has something of a name, perhaps too much so.'

Agatha nodded and decided to let the matter drop at this point. The two detectives were clearly saddened by the impact of the scandal on the detective branch. There was little point in rubbing salt into these wounds, particularly as they were about to be joined by the happy couple. James and Betty approached them glowing with happiness.

Agatha embraced Betty; they were joined in this hug by Sausage in a manner that recalled their many celebrations back when 'the Invincibles' school hockey team were just that. The men, Simpson, Whicher, and Williamson contented themselves with firm handshakes, even firmer nods and barely audible and certainly inarticulate, mumbles of congratulations.

Sadly, for Agatha, this signalled the point at which the two detectives offered their apologies and left. Her regret was both a sign that she would have enjoyed hearing more about the latest investigations or how Mr Whicher was enjoying his retirement as much as it was the fear that Aunt Daphne would now take matters in hand and recommence her seemingly relentless campaign to find a suitable match for her favourite niece.

Sure enough, the two detectives had barely crossed the doorway for the hall when Agatha felt a firm hand on her elbow. It was Aunt Daphne. As aunts go, Daphne was an interesting outlier of the breed. Her blonde curls, pretty face and seemingly endless ability to chatter about the inconsequential, would have made her a strong candidate to be Agatha's least favourite aunt, in a field of three. In fact, Agatha adored her. Like two warriors, they enjoyed the battle of wills more than the occasional victories. Underneath Daphne's apparent empty-headed appearance was a steely character, with no little shrewdness. She would have prepared her wedding plans to lay siege to Agatha's spinsterhood with a precision which would have put a military planner to shame.

'Come with me,' said Daphne in a voice that had enough edge in it to make even Agatha obey meekly.

2

The hall had filled up since the end of the service. All around were titled nobles, politicians and even some gentlemen from the mercantile class. It was 1877 after all. Things were changing. Surrounding Agatha were women dressed in the latest fashions which required women's bodies to be stuffed into ever slimmer dresses. Bustles abounded much to Agatha's irritation, but she too, had succumbed to a wholly impractical trend with questionable aesthetic value to compensate for its significant practical drawbacks. Daphne had insisted that it was all the rage. Where her aunt was concerned it was best to choose one's battles.

The ground floor of Ralston House, the family home of Betty, had been set aside for the wedding breakfast which was anticipated to last the better part of the day and night. Aunt Daphne hoped it would end up with some dancing in the late afternoon or even into the evening.

It was Daphne's firm conviction that where there was dancing there was romancing. What this proposition lacked in scientific rigour was more than compensated for by Daphne's anecdotal observations over two decades of matchmaking. Agatha was her great challenge. It was the Mount Olympus of challenges. Many of her friends had advised her to give up. She's a lost cause they would say. The subtext of this was, of course, who would have her? Too smart for her own good and Daphne knew this was true. It had taken a while, but the penny had finally dropped.

Agatha had to be matched with someone who was titled. That went almost without saying. However, this immediately presented some challenges. The pool of available men was not large. It had shrunk considerably thanks to a combination of Agatha directly rebuffing them or as a consequence of the unfortunate reputation she had developed which did not so much suggest shrew as scream it from the castle tower.

The pool of eligibility was further diminished by the relatively low number of men who were either as smart as she was or, at the very least, were capable of delivering enough verbal resistance to give her niece some pause for thought. Or...

There was a third possibility that Daphne had only recently begun to consider: a flanking strategy so circuitous, it might have arrived on a second-class tramp steamer from Egypt. The more Daphne considered it, the more its merit revealed itself.

In the past, she had tried to match Agatha with good-looking, titled men. They had quickly been routed by the sharpness of Agatha's tongue. Next she had tried smart, cultured, titled men. This was doomed to failure. Such men, Daphne eventually realised, were often too egotistical or insecure, or both, to accept Agatha as an equal. The ideal candidate had to be someone utterly without ego, yet also titled and, crucially, shrewder than Croesus' bank manager.

Her inquiries on such an individual threw up only one candidate.

By extension, her plan was unlikely to succeed if it were she who was seen to be the prime mover in bringing the pair together. Agatha would immediately be on her guard. This would not do. Not for a moment did Daphne consider the possibility that her target would turn down the chance of being with Agatha. Notwithstanding her reputation for being a trifle too strong of character, too volatile of temper and, worst of all, acerbic of speech; her niece was attractive when she deigned to smile, slender of figure and richer than Midas' rich uncle, Archie. Therefore she had organised an able lieutenant to help.

'Hello,' said Agatha brightly to a tall, rather thin man who approached her with the smile of someone who had had a near miss with her but had thankfully survived and thrived. The two of them were old and very dear friends as much because she genuinely liked him as the fact that he was the brother of Sausage.

Viscount Gilbert Gossage of Ledbury was a friend of all and an enemy of none. His middle name could have been 'Compliance' and it was for this reason that on lonely wet nights in February, Agatha might reflect that she had been a trifle hurried when rejecting his suit. At least, that's what she assumed his stuttering attempts at flattery to be. English gentlemen are not renowned for their mating calls. What in France or Italy sounds like gypsy violins, in England sounds like a faulty church organ: loud notes punctuated by long silences caused by an excess of trapped wind in the pipes.

'Hullo, Agatha,' piped up Gilbert, kissing her and his sister on the cheek. To give credit where it's due, he greeted Daphne as if he hadn't seen her in months rather than just before the service where he had received but one instruction; Daphne couldn't trust men in general and this one, in particular, to remember more than a single order.

'I gather you were out with the groom last night. His last night of freedom.'

'We were,' admitted Gilbert and Agatha detected a faint colouring on his cheeks. This suggested to Agatha that there had been an excessive amount of revelry.

'I trust you enjoyed yourselves,' said Agatha in a tone which had more than the schoolmistress about it. This was an unfortunate habit of which she was not aware, but her many former admirers were.

'Convivial,' spluttered Gilbert, already fearing that Agatha might quiz him more rigorously about what had been, by any standards, a thoroughly drunken affair that ended up with two arrests and a very early morning court appearance for some of the less sensible members of the party. Thankfully, James Simpson's reputation for being able to ship an unholy amount of alcohol without losing his senses remained wholly intact and he made it back to the manor in good enough shape to face the happiest day of his life, match fit.

Gilbert, himself recently married, had retired early from the carousing, and spent the service listening to a report of the night from the man that Daphne had tasked him to introduce to Agatha.

'I'm sure Agatha is not in the least bit interested in such matters,' interjected Daphne, who most certainly was and suspected her niece would be too. The look on Agatha's face confirmed this, causing Gilbert's heart to sink at the prospect of an inquisition from his dear and inconveniently clever friend.

They sat down at a table to enjoy the wedding breakfast, the speeches and, in Daphne's case, wait for the dancing to start. She had already ascertained from Lady Stevens that an orchestra had been hired. Her old friend was as inveterate a matchmaker as she was and also had nieces aplenty in need of a partner for life's perilous journey. Quite why either lady thought that a man was required to help in this mission had never been answered to Agatha's satisfaction, despite her frequent querying on this point. The husbands of the two ladies, like Gilbert Gossage, were remarkable only for their utter acquiescence to anything their commanding officer demanded.

As speech followed speech and course followed course, Daphne's mood of cheerful optimism began to show signs of shredding.

'When are you going to introduce them?' she asked in a voice that was more snarl than whisper.

Gilbert shrugged, as he was wont to do. Pointing out that it was hardly ideal to engineer a meeting mid-speech fell on deaf ears. Daphne had a nagging worry that leaving these things too late was a recipe for disaster.

'I don't want to sound un-Christian, but the man I want Agatha to meet is a walking distillery.'

She was not wrong.

By the third and final dessert course, steam was virtually belching from Daphne's ears, and it was as much for his own safety as Agatha's future happiness that he suggested that they take a stroll around the room. Agatha happily assented to this as she could see the furrowing of Daphne's brow had slowly deepened in direct correlation to the growing snappiness of her manner. Of course, Agatha had guessed immediately why Daphne was becoming so peeved and she assumed that Gilbert was doing the gentlemanly thing: a combination of getting her out of harm's way as well as showing her to the room. Oh yes, Agatha knew the game all right and while she was independent enough not to care about it, she was woman enough to want it all the same.

One never knew who one might meet.

'Betty looked lovely today,' said Gilbert. 'So happy.'

'She did,' agreed Agatha, glancing guiltily back in the direction of Sausage. However, she noted that her friend was walking arm in arm with Daphne, lapping around the other side of the room. Agatha immediately sensed that this had been planned and felt both relief that Sausage had not been abandoned by her brother and now extremely curious to what lay in store.

The first man they encountered was a member of Parliament for Nottingham. John Finch saw Agatha approaching with Gilbert, looked around in panic and realised he was trapped. He stood up and bowed to them. Two years previously he had proposed to Agatha. He'd never actually been turned down, he remembered, but there was something in her laughter and the hug she gave him that suggested he hadn't been quite accepted either.

'Agatha, how wonderful to see you,' said Finch with a nervous smile.

Agatha overlooked this sweet if rather obvious falsehood and chatted briefly with the Parliamentarian about Britain's threat to declare war on Russia if it occupied Constantinople. As Finch had slept through the debate he was a little less informed than Agatha's dog, Talleyrand, on the subject. They did not dwell long with Nottingham's representative before moving on to a succession of men that were all married. This was a deliberate ploy designed by Daphne to lull Agatha into a false sense of security.

And it worked.

Half an hour passed with Agatha and Gilbert chatting amiably with old friends interspersed with a few introductions to carefully selected married men of good, that is to say, compliant, character. At one point a tall, bearded man approached Agatha and Gilbert.

'Augustus,' said Agatha smiling. 'How nice to see you again. Gilbert, may I introduce Mr Augustus Franks, administrator of the British Museum. Augustus is one of the great collectors of this age or any other and he is our foremost expert on the Roman Empire.'

Franks blushed at this but did not deny it. They chatted for a few minutes about a recent find in Witcham of an undamaged Roman helmet.

All in all the wedding breakfast was zipping along pleasantly for Agatha and she was delighted to see, from a safe distance, that Daphne was happily playing Cupid for Sausage. This was a perfect arrangement as Sausage engaged happily with a specially targeted group of men that might otherwise have been foisted on Agatha.

'I must introduce you to Frosty,' said Gilbert as they left yet another couple.

'Who?'

'Frosty. You know, Eustace Frost. Friend of James's. All of us, in fact.'

'I'm not sure I've met him.'

'Stout chap. Lord Eustace Frost.'

'Oh, I think I've heard the name,' said Agatha. 'Does he not live abroad?'

'Yes, he's in the Diplomatic Corps.'

'Unusual for someone like that to work for a living,' observed Agatha drily. Then she felt a twinge of regret as it sounded like an implied criticism of Gilbert who had barely worked a day in his life. Thankfully, the barb passed well over Gilbert's head.

'I wonder where he is,' mused Gilbert scanning the room.

'Good Lord,' said Agatha. 'Look over there.' She pointed to an uncommon sight not thirty feet away.

'What? Where? Anyway, you'd like Frosty. Very much the coming man,' replied Gilbert. Then he spied what Agatha was pointing at. 'Good Lord. Frosty. What are you doing?'

Agatha turned towards Gilbert and then back to the sight that had now attracted their attention.

'Am I to understand that this is Lord Eustace Frost?'

'Yes,' spluttered Gilbert.

'When you said, "coming man", did you mean he had come directly from James's bachelor party?'

Gilbert was at a loss on what to say. Finally, he responded, 'Well, he was with us last night, certainly. He's normally the last man standing on these occasions.'

Agatha and Gilbert stared at the unconscious figure of Eustace Frost lying on the ground still clutching a glass of champagne.

'Not now, apparently,' said Agatha.

3

5 Months Later

Grosvenor Square, London, 14th December 1877

Agatha was not a winter person. It had often been a thought to find a small residence on the continent and winter there. This idea had been shelved when Betty's romance with Simpson had begun. Simpson, as the third son of the Earl of Wister, was required by custom to find a career. That he chose the police and, specifically, the Criminal Investigation Department, presented Agatha and her friends with the exquisite prospect of inveigling themselves onto cases involving Betty's fiancé.

Like Betty, Simpson was stout of build, stout of character and not overburdened intellectually. This charming assembly of personality traits had, hoped Agatha, offered the possibility of his deploying *her* outstanding cognitive capabilities in the cause of catching criminals. Reality had proved disappointing, but Betty was never less than pleased with her acquisition. Occasional pointed references to ongoing investigations from Agatha were certainly picked up by Betty and ignored, while, at the same time, they passed Simpson by completely.

Whatever frustration she felt at this, Agatha kept it to herself. Instead, thoughts once more rose to the surface of how she could spend a few months a year abroad, travelling or ensconced in warmer climes. Another consideration which could not be ignored was that such an enterprise would offer some respite from the ongoing siege warfare waged by Aunt Daphne on her spinsterhood.

Yet the clinching argument was one that Agatha could barely bring herself to acknowledge. The house that once had reverberated to the sound of Betty's laughter was silent. Agatha was comfortable being alone; she welcomed aloneness as a proud sign of her independence, but sometimes an emptiness would assail her that even a dear friend like Talleyrand could not comfort.

Talleyrand sat on the windowsill and looked at Agatha with sad eyes. He often sat at this windowsill as it offered a wonderfully appointed view of Grosvenor Square. From such a vantage point he was able to observe the comings and goings of the well-to-do of London. In particular, the females.

Talleyrand was French in origin, and, like that wonderfully complicated race, he was a romantic, a lover, a *bon vivant* with just the right amount of cad to arouse the interest of the opposite sex. He was, in short, a dog of distinction. A Basset hound, in fact.

Like most canines, Talleyrand had an extraordinary ability to fathom the mood of their owner. It was clear to him that Agatha was at a lower ebb than usual. He was not a man, or dog for that matter, to allow such sadness to infect someone he cared for deeply. Hopping down from the windowsill he pootled over to Agatha and hopped up onto the sofa beside her. He laid his head on her lap and looked up.

The sight of such a sad face never failed to move Agatha. It took her immediately outside of herself. She stroked Talleyrand and they sat in contented silence while the hound worked his invisible spell on the young woman. And work it did.

She began to cry.

This, recognised Talleyrand, was but a stage in her recovery. He knew not what she needed to recover from, but this was not his job. He was not her confessor. She needed him; all else was immaterial. The tears subsided as he knew they would. Energy began to flow once more through Agatha's body and before long her suggestion of a walk was met with Talleyrand's approval. It was around this time that a Poodle of his acquaintance was usually promenading. Perhaps his luck would be in. His relationship with said Poodle was characterised by a certain amount of volatility that their Gallic natures could no more avoid than their evident mutual attraction.

Within minutes, for Agatha rarely stood on ceremony, they were out in the chill December air. And *sacre bleu* was it *tres froid*. Soon the object of his sometime affection hovered into view. A slight tug of the lead was hint enough to Agatha that he could be set free for a little wander on his own.

Dogs are often compared unfavourably to cats intellectually. In Talleyrand's case this was a great injustice. It was easy to be deceived by his looks. He relied on this, in fact. Like his great French political namesake, he was no fool. Day after day, week after week, he had built up Agatha's trust to the point that he would be set loose with no fear that he would wander too far away. This was nothing but a cunning ruse to give him freedom for when serendipity smiled, and the Poodle was similarly free to enjoy a brief tryst while the owners chatted about them.

An assignation was duly achieved and soon, at staggered intervals, the lovestruck canines returned to their unsuspecting owners, from different points in the park. The two lovers then ignored one another to ensure that the romance remained their secret. Unlike Romeo and Juliet or Tristan and Isolde, this was one affair that would flourish away from the unforgiving glare of publicity.

Back at the house, Agatha bent down and planted a kiss on top of Talleyrand's head.

'Thank you old friend, that was just what I needed,' said Agatha taking off her coat. She brushed some snowflakes off the coat and handed it to Flack, her butler.

Flack had been Lady Agatha's butler for over two decades now, girl and woman. She had nabbed him from the family home, and he had followed willingly when she had first moved into Grosvenor Square at the age of twenty-one. He adored her like a grandparent adores small children. In small doses. Thankfully, the presence of a cook and a maid ensured his duties were relatively light. At sixty-four he could no longer run a large house on his own. Retirement was out of the question owing to an unfortunate predisposition towards games of chance combined with a rotten run of luck that had lasted for as long as he had gambled.

'May I have a cup of tea, Flack,' asked Agatha before a thought struck. 'Perhaps a pot of tea for two. Sausage will be along soon. Do you know if Polly has my things ready?'

'I believe so your ladyship,'

Agatha retired to the drawing room to await her friend. She arrived with the tea.

'I say, that was good timing,' said Sausage, holding the door open for Flack who was pushing a trolley. Then she spied the two cups and saucers. 'Ahh. I see you anticipated my arrival.'

Talleyrand greeted Sausage by hopping onto two legs, tail a-wagging. He knew a good source of food when he saw one and there were ham sandwiches on that trolley. When it came to doggy mathematics, Talleyrand was the professor.

'Oh Talleyrand seems happy. You know me, don't you?' said Sausage.

Agatha had a more jaundiced eye for these things and muttered, 'Knows a pushover when he sees one.'

'What's that?' asked Sausage with a wide grin that revealed a healthy set of teeth that reminded Agatha to ask Flack to have the piano tuned. It was playing a little off in G.

'Pour the tea, Sausage. We'll have to be moving soon.'

'What time is the train again?'

'It's the five thirty from St Pancras. We shouldn't leave it too late. The traffic is becoming worse by the week. I've never seen so many carriages. I don't know where people find the money.'

'Well, jolly good for them,' said Sausage who never had a bad word to say about anyone. While she poured the tea, she updated Agatha about the weekend ahead.

'Aside from Pru Parrish obviously you'll know a few of them, Agatha. Should be fun. It looks like snow though. I do hope Gilbert keeps the horses warm.'

Agatha rolled her eyes. Keeping Sausage fixed on one topic during conversation was like trying to catch a butterfly using a doughnut. She was apt to meander from one subject to the next like a traveller exploring a new city. At a certain point she would stop, take stock then ask directions. Agatha waited patiently for the moment when Sausage would realise that she was lost. It came a minute later, mid-reflection on pig farming.

'I say, where was I?'

'You were going to tell me about who would be attending the weekend at Pru's.'

'Oh yes, I remember. Well, Pru obviously.'

'That's where you left it last time.'

'Beefy obviously.'

This was Lord John Parrish who, for reasons that surpassed all understanding given his slender, pleasantly muscular build, was known as 'Beefy' to everyone. He and Pru had married a few months before Betty and James Simpson.

'Two chaps I don't know: Frederick de Courcy and Eustace Frost.'

The latter rang a bell with Agatha, but she was too busy scowling at Talleyrand's shameless and successful attempts to sucker Sausage into parting company with her ham sandwich.

'Who else?' said Sausage, thinking out loud. 'There's Emma and Joanna Potts.'

This was not good news. They were twin sisters who had attended the same school as Agatha, Sausage and Pru, albeit a few years below. Both were notorious practical jokers, a bit like Pru, but, unlike their host, they always took things too far.

'Brother Ernest will be along to keep them under control,' added Sausage, seeing the look on Agatha's face.

'That's a relief,' said Agatha. She quite liked Ernest albeit in small doses. He was as dry as sand and very serious. This was in compensation for two sisters who were as energetic as they were frivolous.

'Difficult to believe they're from the same family,' said Sausage looking at her friend in a way that made Agatha wonder if her thoughts were becoming increasingly transparent.

'Is that it? Anyone else?'

Sausage looked away at that moment as if a banjo-playing cart horse had suddenly captured her attention outside.

'Sausage?'

'Uhhhh. Yes, I think so. Or was it? Actually, there was a mention of a man named Pilbream. Not sure if he's coming or not.'

'The Earl of Gowston's son?'

'Third son, I think,' said Sausage putting sugar into her tea. Sausage didn't usually take sugar. It was clear Sausage had undertaken a little research on this topic, so Agatha let it drop. For the moment. Any young man that set his cap towards one of her friends, or vice versa, would have to undergo a series of forensic evaluations from Agatha before approval would be granted; unless he was a detective, of course. That was a lifetime exemption.

'I think I remember now.'

'Tommy?' responded Sausage.

Agatha was baffled by this initially, but suspected it referred to Pilbream. It was difficult to criticise the practice of the English upper crust to bestow nicknames that always ended in the letter "y" on their friends. She was as guilty as any on that score. Once more she resisted the temptation to comment and continued her train of thought.

'No Eustace Frost. That's the chap your brother was going to introduce me to at Betty's wedding.'

'Why didn't he?'

Agatha smiled and shook her head.

'He was unconscious. Drunk as a sailor,' she announced before breaking off into laughter at the memory.

Sausage began to giggle, 'Oh yes, I remember. I stepped over him at one point. Aunt Daphne wasn't happy, though. In fact, she was furious when she saw him. I'm pretty sure she went back and poured some water over him after we parted.'

'How odd. I wonder why she was so upset. It's not as if she would know him. I gather he spends a lot of time abroad with the Diplomatic Service. Anyway, old girl, get a move on. We should try and arrive early. Better to be one hour early than one minute late as my Uncle Jim used to say.'

The words "get a move on" are one of the ultimate calls to action in the English lexicon. It begs the recipient to expedite rapidly all unnecessary actions while moving at great haste towards an agreed objective. As a rallying cry, it ranks only behind "get your skates on" and the absolute final call in Britain, "chop, chop". What freeborn Englishman can fail to be stirred by Wellington's words at Waterloo as he sat on horseback before his brave men and wagged a finger vaguely at some object in the distance, 'Men, Napoleon is over there. Go on; get a move on. Chop, chop.'

Men and women, however, view these words so differently that one could be forgiven for thinking that one or other was simply missing on the day that the phrase was first taught to eager pupils during a lesson on Physics. You know the sort, 'The act of motion is when a body or matter gets a move on from...'

Twenty minutes after Agatha first urged alacrity, the two ladies and Polly, their lady's maid for the weekend away, were on a landau riding towards St Pancras. Night was falling. So was snow.

'I daresay Pru keeps a warm house,' said Sausage hopefully, as she shivered in the chill of the night air.

Just behind them a hansom cab left at just the same moment as the ladies departed Grosvenor Square. Coincidence it might have been had it not been travelling in exactly the same direction. Nearing St Pancras, a voice from inside inquired.

'Are they still ahead of us?'

'Yes sir,' said the cab driver.

'Overtake them near St Pancras.'

'As you wish sir.'

Two men inside the carriage looked at one another. They felt the carriage speed up. One of the men smiled.

3

St Pancras Station, London – same day

The ladies, along with Talleyrand, arrived in excellent time to discover one of the blights of Britain's transport system. The train was delayed. Snow on the line further up north meant that the train had not yet arrived at the station. Brusque inquiries by Agatha had established that it would be around twenty minutes late but would depart as soon as the people and luggage had been removed from the train. All in all they saw a delay of no more than an hour.

Agatha's next stop was to the telegraph office. A telegram was sent to their hosts Pru and Beefy that they would be an hour late or more. Tasks completed, Sausage and Agatha strode down to the platform with Polly racing to catch up. The two ladies were not of a dilatory bent when it came to perambulations at a station. Talleyrand was already puffing.

Arriving on the platform, Agatha set her small Gladstone bag down while Polly went to check on the main luggage which had been loaded onto a cart fifty yards further up. Given the time of day, the platform was surprisingly empty of people. It seemed the good folk of London preferred to be toasting in front of a warm fire rather than out in the chill.

Agatha looked up and saw a pigeon fly across the cavernous space overhead. The new building with the wrought iron lattice framework roof was certainly an impressive sight. The largest in the world they said. So wonderful that man could create such a wonder. Yet...

Sausage saw a shadow creep over her friend's face. She recognised the sign. Touching Agatha's elbow she asked, 'Is everything all right? You seem a little gloomy.'

Agatha smiled at her friend and nodded towards the soaring roof of the station.

'It's marvellous isn't it?'

'Yes, rather,' agreed Sausage. 'But why does this make you sad?'

St Pancras was one of the marvels of the age. Agatha never felt anything less than proud of her country when she saw the sweeping arch of the roof. That the Romans had mastered such engineering feats over a millennia before was hardly the point. This was the here and now and Britain led the world in so many areas of progress that one could barely keep up. But with this reflection came a sadness too. Her pride for the great advances being made in fields such as engineering, medicine, the natural world and science was tempered by the feeling that such pursuits were denied to one half of the population.

Yes, Ada Lovelace and Florence Nightingale had shown how women could make contributions beyond the arts, but they were the exception. It broke her heart that she and so many others were denied the opportunity. This sadness was not solely rooted in thoughts around her sex. She believed that in blocking women from higher level education and commerce, society was missing out on untold benefits and scientific advance. The distillation of women into the role of mother and homemaker was the great collective shame borne by this nation: an obstacle to its potential, a denial of its humanity.

Agatha regarded her friend for a moment then shook her head, 'Oh, I don't know. I think too much sometimes. Ignore me.'

A whistle of steam and wheels began to grind into action on a nearby platform causing the two women to turn around. There was still no sign of their train so Sausage took the opportunity to freshen up before the journey which would take around two to three hours although there would be one stop en route.

As she left, Agatha heard two men laughing further up the platform. Both were around thirty or perhaps a little older. The younger man was clearly a gentleman, the other was a valet guessed Agatha. The eyes of the younger man hovered over Agatha. Something about him seemed familiar, but it was difficult to tell as he was wearing a hat. He said something to his valet and then, a moment later, his man departed.

Agatha looked away and sensed that the man was about to approach her. She searched her memory for a name. None came. He was definitely moving in her direction. Slowly at first then, much to her astonishment, he began to jog. Then he was sprinting. At this point Talleyrand began barking. Normally he was above such vulgar modes of expression in public. Agatha turned just as another man came from behind her and grabbed the bag she had set down on the ground.

'What on earth?' said Agatha, momentarily shocked by what had happened. Talleyrand gave him a good barking to, but wisely remained rooted to the spot.

'Stop thief,' shouted the man Agatha had spied earlier. He sprinted past her in pursuit of the ruffian who had stolen her bag. 'Stop thief.'

Her Galahad appeared to be gaining on the thief, but then they disappeared off the platform and Agatha was left standing on her own looking around her in disbelief. It was thus that Sausage found her. Polly was also running towards Agatha now, having seen the incident from afar.

'I've just been robbed,' said Agatha in amazement.

'I say.'

This just about summed up the situation. Polly arrived breathlessly having run from the top of the platform.

'Your ladyship, are you all right?'

'Unharmed,' replied Agatha. 'I can't believe it. He's taken my bag.'

Polly pointed to something behind Agatha , 'Look, your ladyship.'

The man Agatha had noticed earlier was walking up the platform. In his hand was Agatha's bag. His face was a little red, but he seemed none the worse for his unscheduled sprint. A minute later he joined the three women.

'Your bag, I believe, madame.'

He set the bag down and removed his hat.

'You are the hero of the day, sir,' said Agatha.

'Hardly,' replied the man. 'The ruffian dropped the bag when he realised I was gaining on him. As much as I would like to say I took him and five of his gang on, it would be something of an exaggeration.'

This made Agatha smile and she studied the man's face more closely. Unusually for men at that time, he was without facial hair. Although not handsome in the classical sense, his face was attractive with a quizzical look around the eyes and a mouth that seemed to arrange itself in a half smile as if he were in on a joke to which you were not party. Nor ever would be.

'Have we met before, sir?'

'I'm sure I would have remembered meeting you, madam,' he said this with just the merest hint of a bow.

'Well, to whom am I indebted?' asked Agatha, some of her old natural irritation resurfacing after her close call with the criminal element.

'My name is Frost. Eustace Frost at your service,' said Eustace. He didn't bother bowing this time.

'Anything to Lord Geraint Frost?' asked Sausage

'Distantly related,' replied Eustace.

'How distantly?' asked Agatha, one eyebrow was now cocked to full mockery.

'He's my father.'

'So you're Eustace Frost,' said Agatha. This appeared to surprise their new acquaintance.

'Have we met?' He seemed genuinely aggrieved that he could not remember who she was.

'In a manner of speaking,' explained Agatha. 'The last time I saw you was at the Simpson wedding in July.'

Eustace's face coloured a little and he smiled self-consciously. He glanced down at Talleyrand who was closely inspecting his footwear.

'Ahh. Yes, I was a little overcome that day. Perhaps it was something I consumed.'

'The fifth bottle of champagne perhaps,' responded Agatha sternly before breaking into a smile. 'James is a good friend of ours. I am Agatha Aston. This is my friend Jocelyn Gossage.'

'Sausage,' said Sausage, with a wide grin. She shifted from one foot to another in a sideways motion that had baffled many an opposing hockey player. 'Everyone calls me Sausage.'

'Then I shall call you Sausage, too,' said Eustace shaking her hand. He was vaguely aware now that Agatha's attention was elsewhere. He looked at her quizzically, but then that's how he looked at everyone. He followed the direction of her gaze to a lone bag sitting fifty yard further up on the platform. One or two men of lower rank seemed to be on the point of claiming it. With a tip of his hat, Eustace said, 'Perhaps, I should retrieve my bag, ladies.'

With that their Galahad departed at a brisk clip which did the trick in ensuring that his bag did not suffer a similar fate to Agatha's.

'I do hope he comes back,' said Sausage. 'Seems a pity to sit apart if we're travelling to the same destination.'

Oddly, Agatha was of a similar frame of mind, but was content to let Sausage deal with the formalities of the arrangement which she did in her usually direct style.

'I say, Lord Eustace, why don't you join us in our carriage?'

This appeared to find favour with Eustace. Soon he was with them again.

'I shall only stay ladies if you call me Eustace. After all, we are to spend a weekend together if my memory serves.'

A few minutes later the locomotive trundled into view. Given how late the train was, it rumbled in at a fairly laggardly pace in Agatha's view. Steam billowed from its sides. Soon after it halted, people began to stream off the train. They looked worn out to Agatha which worried her. Perhaps the snow was a lot worse where they'd come from.

"I say, look at that,' said Sausage suddenly.

Agatha turned around and followed her friend's gaze towards a group of men further up the platform. There were a couple of uniformed policemen plus two plainclothes officers boarding a second-class carriage. It was difficult to see who the prisoner was as they had covered him with a coat. He was half lifted through the door and then he was gone. One of the plainclothes detectives shook hands with the two uniformed policemen. He glanced in the direction and caught Agatha's eye. He frowned and then disappeared into the carriage. The door shut leaving the two uniformed men on the platform. They waved then headed back down the platform, past Agatha, Sausage and Eustace.

It was another half an hour before they were able to set off on their journey to the frozen Fens in the east of the country. Their destination was a manor house near the village of Greater Recton in Norfolk. The ladies, now joined by Eustace, settled down in the carriage for their trip.

'How do you know James?' asked Eustace as the train jerked forward. He had removed his hat and Agatha now had a better chance to assess their new companion. His hair was dark, but his eyes were of a twinkling blue. One eyebrow seemed to be permanently raised giving the appearance that not only did he not believe you, but he couldn't quite believe that you'd said it. Agatha remembered a comment by Gilbert about him.

'He may not appear impressive, but trust me, if we're in ticklish negotiations with a ruffian like Bismarck there's no one I would want more than Eustace facing him at the other end of the table. He's always three steps ahead. Always."

Turning to Sausage, Agatha said, 'Betty, Sausage and I were at school together. Then Betty shared my house in Grosvenor

Square for a couple of years until James came along and swept her off her feet.'

'Ahh, now I remember, James did mention that he'd met someone who'd helped him enormously on a case.'

Agatha nodded. She rarely saw the point in hiding lights under bushels. For good or ill, take responsibility for your actions.

'I must confess,' continued Eustace, 'I was under the impression it was Betty, but am I right in thinking that it was, in fact, you, Lady Agatha?'

'Well we all helped James on the Black-Eyed Nick case.'

'I went undercover,' piped up Sausage proudly.

'You don't say,' said Eustace. 'How exciting. You must tell me all about it. I love reading detective stories and here you've not only been involved, but central to closing the case I understand.'

What young lady can resist the opportunity to talk about her crucial role in solving a murder case? Certainly not two young women brought up reading *penny dreadfuls.* Before long, the ladies were knee deep in the story, taking turns to relate their activities in support of James and the legendary Mr Whicher. All the time, Eustace fed the story with pertinent questions that impressed Agatha with their ability to help shed new light on long forgotten elements relating to the capture of the murderer. They also, Agatha realised after, helped add even greater shine to her own estimation of her achievement, which was not limited by any false sense of humility. When the story had finished, Agatha felt it only polite to ask how Eustace and James had met.

'Like you and the ladies, I met James at school. He was a year or two below me, but we hit it off quite well. He and I used to mitch off at any opportunity. Was never very interested in school. I still come out in a cold sweat when I see algebra.'

'I see,' said Agatha. Gentlemen, whenever a woman says this be on your guard. A rough translation would read something like: *if you are trying to impress me, you have failed. Miserably.*

If Eustace was aware of the danger signs then he gave every indication of not having noticed.

'You were not academic then?' asked Agatha as if to confirm the growing suspicion that Eustace was very much like the rest of the men she knew from the nobility: dim, lazy and entitled.

'Not very,' conceded Eustace. 'Not bad at languages. I suppose that's why I joined the Foreign Office. The rest of it went over my head, truth be told. James wasn't much better. The army was the best place for him.'

'Or the police.'

'Indeed. At least he's honest. More than can be said for those chaps that were arrested.'

'Oh yes, we were hearing about Druscovich and Palmer from Mr Williamson,' said Sausage.

'Of course, you would have met Dolly. My, my. You are very well connected,' said Eustace. 'Good man. I imagine you must have impressed him ladies if he was prepared to accept your consultancy.'

Notwithstanding her doubts about the intellectual horsepower of the man sitting in front of her, it was gratifying for Agatha to be praised for something other than her looks, dress, fragrance or whatever else occurred to a man struggling to converse with a member of the other fifty percent of the population.

The carriage lapsed into a companionable silence. The two ladies decided that a little light reading would be in order.

Agatha took out two magazines and handed one to her friend. The first magazine was entitled *Dr Death Strikes Again*. The cover showed a demonic figure hovering over a young couple. The other magazine was no less literary: *The Hansom Cab Murders*. The cover showed another demonic figure sporting a top hat and a cloak covering face revealing only his eyes.

A smile crossed the face of Eustace which Agatha noted with a frown.

'Do I detect disapproval?'

'Far from it, Lady Agatha. I approve most heartily. As it happens, I am on the board of this publisher. In fact, I occasionally contribute a story.'

Eustace now had Agatha's full and undivided attention. She put the magazine down and studied his face closely for any hint of untruth. Something about his amused disposition suggested to her that he was a man who enjoyed a little sport with the unsuspecting. Eustace read this look in an instant.

'I assure you Lady Agatha I am telling you the truth.'

A moment later he extracted from his bag a magazine with the no less elevating title, *The Sweet Smell of Death and other stories*. He handed the magazine over to Agatha. She studied the cover which showed a middle-aged man holding a diary that seemed to glow malevolently in the dark.

'Shouldn't there be a comma after Death?' asked Agatha.

'Punctuation isn't my strong point,' admitted Eustace. 'But the stories are good. I find most people will forgive the odd slip or two.'

Nothing on Agatha's face suggested that she would be included in this number. She opened up the magazine. There was another illustration, but this is not what drew her attention.

There, underneath *The Sweet Smell of Death* were three words.

By Eustace Frost.

She glanced up at their travelling companion who had the grace not to smile triumphantly. Rather he seemed a little bashful about this revelation.

'This hasn't been published yet. Next day or two if I remember correctly: the Christmas edition.'

'May I?' asked Agatha.

'I would be honoured to hear what you think of it, Lady Agatha,' said Eustace. 'Let me know if you see any punctuation errors. I'm always happy to hear fair-minded criticism from those more gifted in the art of punctuation.'

Agatha glanced once more at Eustace to see if he was making fun of her. She suspected he was. Oddly, she didn't mind.

4

The Sweet Smell of Death

by Eustace Frost

It was the year of our Lord, 18__ and the breath of Christmas hung in the air like a white mist. Mr Dennistoun had undertaken a holiday to the Cotswolds following a recent illness. His trade, if one can call such a high calling a trade, was university lecturer at one of Cambridge's older and more auguste institutions. A lifelong bachelor, his commitment to the study of history from the Stuarts through to the Hanoverians was a passion of such profound consequence that he had chosen to forgo the undoubted joys of married life and the blessing of a family. Not yet fifty, he was most content when perusing, reading, or buying books of particular relevance to the period of interest. Books were his first love, his partner in life, his children.

He was a tall, thin, but not austere, man whose enthusiasm in a book shop was like that of a child when presented with a train or a doll. Every book opened up a world that had physical, emotional and spiritual dimensions. Fiction could transport you to a place that did not exist except in the imagination of the writer and that of the reader. History books were a journey into the past refracted through the prism of the historian's lens. Of equal, if not greater, interest to Dennistoun was the discovery of an old diary. This was living history. Understanding the lives of ordinary people often shed a more brilliant light on a period of history than simply recycling the work of previous historians. This was Dennistoun's speciality: creating an account of ordinary people living ordinary lives of little consequence that were forever destined to leave untroubled the pages of history.

A friend of Dennistoun had recommended the village of Little Winkle, a morning's coach drive north of Bristol, as an uncommonly rich location for his friend to explore as it contained not one, but two, book shops of remarkable interest as well as a number of antique and curiosity shops. In fact, Dennistoun's friend had come away from the village with a splendid haul of half a dozen tomes on the subject of campanology. One of these books was in Latin which presented a delicious translation project for the winter. It must be set down for the record that, like Dennistoun, he was unmarried.

It was with some relief that Dennistoun's coach arrived in the village because night was drawing in bringing with it a malevolently cold wind that suggested snow would follow soon. The innkeeper, Mr Philpott, was a stout man, genial of countenance, deferential in manner, but without being obsequious. All in all, Dennistoun liked him on first acquaintance. A light supper was prepared by Mrs Philpott and the university man retired early for the evening.

The next morning, snowflakes fluttered friskily in the air. The academic pulled his overcoat around him and marched down the street armed with a map of the village. Spotting his first port of call, Dennistoun walked briskly towards it; he was driven as much by excitement at what lay in store as by the fact that his muscles were already cramping in the cold.

Fisher's Booksellers was the largest of the two bookshops, but despite its promising exterior, Dennistoun found it disappointing. The selection of books was tasteful; faultlessly so but lacked a breadth of subject and any hint of a bargain. The choice of product seemed to reflect a desire on the part of Mr

Fisher, an austere man, to please the rich, landowning clientele rather than customers seeking more unusual fare. The two men bid farewell to one another with little regret on either side.

The next stop was more promising.

The imaginatively titled 'Old Curiosity Shop' presented a mixture of antiques, old maps, stuffed animals and some books stacked haphazardly upon a large oak table that might once have been used by Henry VIII to dine on boar. If the name was Dickensian, the owner was more like the less attractive principal in a Mary Shelley novel. A small head was attached to a large, awkward body. His smile seemed to have been stitched together by a seamstress who had succumbed some years past to the lure of gin. The initial promise soon faded for Dennistoun, and he made his escape quickly lest he become like one of the objects created by the owner who had proudly showed off his efforts in taxidermy.

So far so disappointing, thought Dennistoun as he walked towards his next shop, snowflakes now stinging his face. He was somewhat ahead of schedule. Originally he believed the morning would be taken up with one or two of the shops. He had barely been out for half an hour, and he had accounted for two already.

He crossed over a bridge as the village was bisected by a waterway. Below him he saw a man dressed in a dark cloak standing on a punt. He could not see the man's face, but a chill descended on him that may not have been solely due to the intemperate weather. He continued on towards his next destination with diminishing enthusiasm. Arriving at the penultimate shop, he opened the door. A satisfying tinkle of a bell announced his arrival. This was an antiques shop owned by a Mr Padgett. Oddly, he noted that the bookshop across the road was also owned by a Padgett.

The mystery was explained soon after he met the owner. They were brothers who had expanded into two shops, but the business was one. The friendly Pickwickean countenance of Mr Padgett and the presence of many items of interest meant that Dennistoun soon felt a wave of optimism return following his earlier disappointments. The rest of the morning was spent with Mr Padgett who took great pains to understand his new customer's field of inquiry before directing him to objects that would interest him. It was a profitable morning, both for the shop owner and Dennistoun. The academic acquired a musket dating back to the Wars of the Roses and several pistols owned by the defeated Cavaliers. Padgett promised an introduction to his twin brother, after lunch. He would act as a personal guide around the book shop.

A hearty lunch was provided, at Mr Padgett's insistence, by Mrs Padgett. They were joined by his unmarried, bookshop owning brother. The conviviality was such that two hours elapsed before Mr Dennistoun was led, a little unsteadily it must be reported, by Mr Padgett of the bookshop to his final port of call. As he crossed over the road to the shop, he had the unusual feeling that someone was walking behind him. He spun around, but no one was there.

Padgett's Books may have been the name of the shop, but for Dennistoun it may as well have been named, Aladdin's Cave. This was truly the promised land for the academic. All around him were books. Hundreds upon hundreds of books. No gold could have glittered more brightly in Dennistoun's eyes. Even the thick coating of dust added to the allure. Little did he know that each day the clever owner liberally sprinkled dust around the books knowing well that such details matter to those who are bibliophiles. Invariably they were male, not so young, probably unmarried, yet always seeking virgin territory to feed their passion.

The shop's interior was dark. All of the walls were covered with books packed onto shelves. In the middle of the shop were tables with large books disposed haphazardly like confetti at a wedding. Much of the floor space was covered with boxes as newly arrived books clogged up the aisles, waiting for the owner to find a place for them on the already packed bookshelves.

'I think this section will be of interest to you Mr Dennistoun,' said the amiable Mr Padgett. 'A number of the books you will doubtless be familiar with, but there may also be some old maps and diaries, I warrant.'

There were.

After an hour and a half, Dennistoun had already earmarked several books that he would request forwarded to his Cambridge dwelling. An enjoyable afternoon was only slightly marred by the persistent sound of a fly buzzing around the shop. Or perhaps it was a bee, yet Dennistoun could scarcely believe one would be alive at this time of year. Several attempts to locate and dispose of the source of the buzzing met with failure. They gave up when Dennistoun's attention was drawn to a box sitting uninspected under a table.

'And these boxes Mr Padgett? Is there anything that may satisfy a curiosity like mine?'

'Ahh, I suspect the answer is a yes, Mr Dennistoun. These boxes are newly arrived from Colonel Ravel's manor. He left us a few years ago, but much of the estate was subject to a legal dispute as he passed away suddenly without issue. His was an old family who have owned the manor since Tudor times. You may have seen some items at my brother's house. There were old suits of armour and some firearms that the family were keen to sell. Naturally, they contacted my brother and myself and we were most happy to oblige.'

'The misfortune of the colonel appears to have been your good fortune if I may say. I believe I acquired some items from his estate.'

'Misfortune is certainly the word, sir. Colonel Ravel lived a few miles away but was not a social man. In fact, I would go as far as to say he was feared and lost many of his staff for reasons that I know not. There were many suspicious at the time though none would say out loud.'

'When was this?'

'He died ten years ago under highly strange circumstances.'

Dennistoun leaned forward as the bookshop owner's voice had lowered an octave or three. It was as if he did not want the physical or spirit world to hear what he was about to say.

'What happened, sir?'

'Well, the cause of death, I am led to believe, came from a number of bee stings.'

'Bee stings?'

'Bee stings, sir. They covered his entire body. He kept a large apiary and had done so for many years which made his final demise such a surprise.'

'What became of the bees.'

'This is the great mystery sir. They disappeared the day and hour that his body was discovered. It was as if they were running away from a great crime.'

'How odd,' said Dennistoun, shivering involuntarily. 'And you say there are boxes of books from this man's estate.'

Padgett nodded enthusiastically and said the words that were to seal the fate of Mr Dennistoun.

'Indeed sir and there are, I believe, some diaries.'

This was like waving a stick at a dog. Within seconds he was by Padgett, standing over one of the many boxes littering the shop floor. The box was two feet square. The shop owner opened the top to reveal a number of leather-bound books inside. Just at that moment the door opened, and it seemed an ill wind blew. Stray pieces of paper flew across the interior like leaves in autumn. The two men glanced up to view the new arrival.

No one was there.

Padgett rushed to shut the door showing an agility that belied his two score and ten years. He apologised profusely before joining Dennistoun who was busy extracting books from the box. His first glance at the first two volumes raised his hopes enormously. They were journals. The date on the first one indicated it was from 1809. The last entry was in mid 1812. The second volume appeared to pick up where the other had left off before continuing to 1816 where it broke off suddenly.

Dennistoun placed the two journals on a table and glanced at two smaller notebooks. One was an accounts book. A quick read suggested that Ravel had ordered many chemicals. The mystery behind this was explained by the next notebook which contained details of his experiments. Ravel was clearly interested in chemistry. He set it down and looked at the final book inside the box. Whether it was the recent influx of cold air or something else he could not explain, but a chill descended on him. He picked up the book and blew dust off the cover.

This had not been added by Padgett for effect. Opening the book he saw immediately that the book was written in German. This was not unusual, but what surprised him was the nature of some of the engravings illustrating the book. They showed diabolical figures that would have been more at home in Dante's seventh circle of hell.

Dennistoun purchased a number of other books during the next hour, but his fascination with the box was such that he asked if he could take it back immediately while the other books were sent to Cambridge. Mr Padgett was delighted to accede to the request, and they parted with mutual expressions of goodwill and a desire to meet up after the end of Trinity term.

Dennistoun hurried back to his lodgings clutching the box tightly to his chest. It was quite heavy, and the effort left him glowing despite the evident chill of the December air. Back at his room he opened the box and lifted out the first journal. A thin film of dust lay over the sides and he blew this gently away. He opened the first page and began to read.

The Journal of Colonel Laurence Ravel

18th January 1809

It seems strange for a man nearing forty years of age to commence, for the first time, writing a journal. I make no claims on anyone's attention but my own. My sole wish is to lay before posterity a record of a unique experiment that I shall conduct using myself alone.

This was certainly going to be a more interesting read than Dennistoun had bargained for. He read on:

Last summer while travelling in Germany, I purchased an old book from a most extraordinary bookseller in Heidelberg. Its fascination for me was of the most horrific kind for I must confess I have never seen such ugly and disturbing illustrations in any book. The book was written in German so provided an excellent project for translation. My work slowly revealed that the book was quite a find indeed. Initially, I suspected it of being an alchemical manuscript. Closer inspection revealed it to be something else entirely! It was nothing less than a Grimoire: a book of spells.

Of course, as a man of sound mind rooted in rational beliefs, my interest in the writing was purely that of a disinterested scholar, rather than that of Hecate! However, I must confess my interest was heightened when I realised that some of the spells were nothing less than experiments in chemistry. This epiphany has led me to acquire the accoutrements necessary to recreate the experiments described in this Grimoire. I do so not with any expectation of everlasting life or turning lead into gold. This is merely the work of a curious mind wishing to gain an insight into the thinking of men like myself from centuries past.

After such an opening entry to the journal, Dennistoun settled down to what he suspected would be a long and fascinating evening. Time passed; his candle died. As darkness fell on the room, Dennistoun chuckled. He'd truly been lost in the extraordinary mind of Colonel Ravel.

There was no "eye of the newt" in this research. The experiments revealed a man serious in his pursuit of understanding the interaction of chemical elements. However, as he progressed through the diary, the tone appeared to change slightly. Was it Dennistoun's imagination that the writing, originally so neat and precise, became more careless the further he progressed into the diary?

The Cambridge man stood up and looked out of the window. It was dark and a light dusting of snow lay on the ground. Unwilling to part from the extraordinary document, he recognised that he needed some food. He went down to the innkeeper and was shocked to discover that everyone had gone to bed. This was quite a surprise, but he was amused also at what had transpired. Making his way into the kitchen of the inn, he found some bread and cheese and made a light supper with what was at hand. Finishing his repast, he returned to his bedroom and lay down on the bed. He was greeted by a low humming sound, the source of which the professor could not detect. It seemed to be coming from within his room, but from where? He fell asleep before the matter was resolved satisfactorily in his mind.

The next morning he rushed to see Mr Padgett to share what he had found in the diaries. He also wanted to discuss a plan that was forming in his mind.

'Do you think that I could go and visit the manor where Ravel worked? Truly it would bring to life the man and his work.'

For the first time in their short and delightful acquaintance, Padgett's countenance lost its warm geniality.

'Are you sure, Mr Dennistoun? It is a desolate place, and I must confess I was rather glad to leave it. My brother and I felt most strongly that it had an atmosphere. His surviving relatives are desirous to sell, and I can understand why, yet, for the life of me I cannot imagine who would wish to buy.'

Dennistoun was not to be denied. Obtaining directions from Padgett and hiring a pony and trap from the innkeeper, the Cambridge man made the hour-long journey into the country to Ravel's manor. Along the way he stopped to ask directions from locals who seemed perturbed by the idea that he should visit such a forsaken property. Such concerns were ignored by the superior rational mind of Dennistoun as local superstition.

The first sight of Ravel's manor confirmed to Dennistoun that the locals were prey to an ignorance of science and progress. It was a fine old building built in the Tudor style. The half-timber work was impressive and well maintained; large groups of rectangular windows as well as rich oriel windows allowed plenty of light into the interior. The gable ends were high with half a dozen chimneys of various sizes. The house was locked up, but Dennistoun gathered that the real interest lay in the garden and a workshop which was open. There was a perfume in the air that was as subtle as it seemed familiar, but he could not quite place it.

Dismounting from the trap Dennistoun was suddenly aware of a buzzing sound. It flew past his ear. He swatted the air, but the noise disappeared as quickly as it had come. Shrugging the incident off he walked around the side of the manor. Blocking his path to the back was a building that appeared to have been built long after the original house had been constructed. This was the workshop laboratory. Dennistoun approached it with mounting excitement. The chill in the air was forgotten as he pushed the wooden door open.

Inside it was dark with giant cobwebs filling the space making Dennistoun glad that he had a stout walking stick to clear his path. He noted that a number of bees had been ensnared in the cobwebs. The workshop was spacious with large windows that permitted enough light for him to make out a large table in the middle upon which sat glass bottles and test tubes. The contents had long since evaporated. Dust was everywhere. It felt as if he was the first person to inspect the laboratory in over ten years. For a few moments he felt a prickling sensation on the back of his neck: a cold draught doubtless invading the space via small cracks in the windows. More than this, though, there seemed to be a presence in the room with him. He looked around but saw that he was alone.

Dennistoun was not a chemist; the array of bottles and test tubes meant nothing to him. It was enough just to drink in the strange atmosphere of the space. The silence was interrupted by a low buzzing sound. It lasted half a minute then stopped. The academic approached the table and saw a large, sealed earthenware jar. He struggled to open the jar, but after a mighty effort he pried to loose. A sweet-smelling fragrance caressed his nostrils. There was a liquid inside. Just then the buzzing started over. He looked around to locate the source of the noise. Then it stopped once more.

His heart began to beat more rapidly as he dipped a finger gently into the jar. The substance inside was a liquid of thick viscosity. Just as he did this he felt a sharp pain in his other hand. He cried out. Examining his finger he saw a mark like a sting. It was burning his hand just behind his knuckle. He touched it with the finger that moments earlier had touched the liquid in the jar. Within seconds the pain subsided and when Dennistoun examined his finger again, the angry sting had all but disappeared. This was one of the most astonishing experiences of his life. Barely able to breathe, he dipped his finger once more into the liquid and then sampled it with his tongue.

The taste and texture was like honey, but with base notes of something slightly sour. Altogether it was not unpleasant. He tasted a little more of the substance and then replaced the top on the jar. At the far end of the workshop was a door. He presumed this would lead to the gardens. He walked towards the door. Unlocking it, he opened to find that he was, indeed, able to access the gardens.

Yet, he hesitated.

All at once a coldness descended on him. Now he understood the reservations of that good man, Mr Padgett. The scene which greeted him was one of utter desolation. Stretching far into the distance were dozens and dozens of beehives. The garden was as silent as a church. The deep stillness was disturbed only by the flakes of snow fluttering in the air, landing on his face and immediately forming teardrops on his cheek.

He walked forward slowly, unsure if he really wanted to see more of this grim sight. The first beehive was greying with age. There were cobwebs surrounding it. As soon as he touched it the hive collapsed into dust.

He drew back immediately, fearful of having unleashed any remaining inhabitants. But they were long dead. Dennistoun began to count the hives. They were laid out in neat rows and columns. After a minute he estimated there were around one hundred and twenty. Unquestionably all were dead; drained of all life. A feeling of great sorrow arose within him, and he stumbled away from the mass graveyard back into the workshop. Padgett had been right. The visit was a mistake. A mortal coldness assailed him. All at once he wondered if the Colonel, far from being a visionary scientist, was altogether something more malignant.

Something compelled him to lift the jar containing the liquid from the table and he ran out the front door without looking back. Arriving at his pony and trap, he placed the jar on the back and hoisted himself up. A gentle nudge with his stick caused the horse to jump forward. It was as if it sensed the sadness of the God-forsaken home of Colonel Ravel.

The evening saw Dennistoun back at his desk reading the through the diary. His chief interest was understanding more about the strangely sweet substance he'd taken from the makeshift laboratory belonging to the extraordinary colonel. Ravel proved meticulous in his recording of the experiments undertaken although the quality of the notes began to show the clear signs of deterioration alluded to earlier. However, by this stage he had identified the key ingredients in the substance.

It seemed Ravel had been harvesting large amounts of Royal Jelly from the dozens of beehives located on his grounds. Royal Jelly, it should be noted, is the special food provided to the Queen Bee and the larvae to assist in their development. As far as Dennistoun could ascertain from reading both the journal and the Grimoire, Ravel put it through a chemical process that changed its character. A clue to this character came in a passage from the second journal.

I believe that this knowledge gives proof to the idea that the soul, far from being under the control of spirits, is subject to the same physical and chemical reactions as any organ in the human body.

A little later Ravel wrote in a hand that was no longer neat:

My studies advance far but at what cost?

Dennistoun gazed at this and, for the first time, felt a fear which he knew to be an emotional not rational response to what he was reading. The later pages of the journal were full of blotches of black ink as well as uncoloured splashes where something else had been spilled. It was clear that he had to return to the college and hand his find over to men with expertise in chemistry so that they could make sense of the liquid, or should that be elixir? Such was his immersion on the document that he only realised that the low humming sound had returned. Just as he was about to complain to the innkeeper, it disappeared.

Before turning in for the night, Dennistoun opened up the jar and dipped his finger inside. The liquid remained cool to the touch. He sampled it and was once more struck by the perfect balance between its sweetness and the sour notes. He tried a little more before replacing the lid and settling down for the night. He would leave on the morrow and return to Cambridge.

It was a much-troubled sleep.

Very early next morning he embarked on his journey back to the university. More than once he returned to the mysterious jar and found the temptation to taste its contents too much to resist. By the end of the day the desire to try the intoxicating liquid once more was overwhelming. He realised that something in its composition was addictive in nature. The sooner he was able to hand it over to his friends in the chemistry department the better.

He arrived back at his lodgings around midnight. Oddly, he was not as tired as a full day's travel should have left him. Instead, his mind and body felt alive with sleep the last thing on his mind. He retired to his room with the books and the jar. Lighting a candle he settled down at his desk and opened the diary. The lure of the jar proved too great, however. As he approached it he heard a low hum. This was similar in character to what he'd heard in the innkeeper's room.

In the familiar surroundings of his own lodging he decided to initiate a search to locate the source of this sound. His rooms were not large. They consisted of a study, a bedroom, and a bathroom; his study was taken up most with bookshelves filled to the ceiling with books; there was a bureau desk and two leather Chesterfield armchairs. His search of the study revealed nothing, yet the hum remained. His bedroom appeared to be free of this sound. From this he drew the obvious conclusion that the sound must be coming from outside.

He returned to his study and sat down at his desk. It was the final page in the diary dated 27th August 1866.

I cannot make enough to feed my hunger. My life is forfeit.

The journal ended at this point. Dennistoun had read this passage many times. Unthinkingly, as he stared at the final line, he opened the jar and dipped not just a finger but squeezed his whole hand inside. The sticky liquid dripped off his hand onto the table and a little onto the journal. Dennistoun in an uncharacteristic bout of anger swore out loud before consuming the liquid on his fingers and then scooping what he could from the table and journal before putting it in his mouth. All the while the humming was growing louder.

Where was the sound coming from?

He looked around the room frantically. It was becoming more than a nuisance - it was driving him out of his wits. He picked up the jar and guzzled some more of the liquid. His head was spinning now with the loud buzzing sound, the increased alertness of his mind and the energy surging through his limbs. He wiped his mouth with his sleeve. This surprised him. He had not performed such an action since his childhood. Spinning around to the Grimoire, he opened it up to the page he believed related to the experiment conducted by Ravel. On one page was a description of the process that must have been undertaken. On the facing page was a peculiar and nightmarish engraving showing all manner of hellish grotesques being eaten by large malevolent bees.

Dennistoun stared at the enormous bee. For a moment he could not believe what he was seeing because it seemed to move. He looked away and then back to the page. It *was* moving. Before his very eyes it was coming to life. A horrible black Queen Bee began to move on the page. The sound was no longer a low hum, but a buzzing that seemed to cut through the air and Dennistoun's body to his very core. He tried to scream. He did scream, but the sound was drowned out by the deafening roar of buzzing.

*

Dennistoun's body was found the next afternoon when a number of the teaching staff noted that the professor had not yet appeared from his room despite evidently returning the night before. His remains were found by the old porter, Titus Wilkins.

Porter Wilkins had been with the college, man and boy, some two score years. In this time, he'd seen many an uncommon sight. Nothing prepared him for what he saw when he entered the room of Dennistoun. The professor was lying on the ground. There was no question he was dead. It was the manner of his passing that shocked. His body seemed to have been drained of all its blood, bones, and organs. He was as flat as a tabletop. His skin was pockmarked by horrible stings.

Wilkins clutched his breast and fought desperately the urge to be ill.

'O Lord, what is this sight?'

At the window, a fly or some insect was buzzing trying to escape. Glancing in its direction, Wilkins saw immediately that it was like a bee only larger and black as sin. Wanting anything to divert his attention from the horrible remains of the professor, Wilkins tried to swat the engorged horror but missed several times. Finally he opened the window.

The large black insect escaped into the snow, the chill and the joy of Christmas time.

The End

5

Agatha set the story down. Much to her irritation, the story had impressed her although some of the grammar and punctuation was questionable. Sausage glanced over at the manuscript with her eyebrows raised hopefully. Agatha handed it over to her without comment.

'I don't like the look of that snow,' said Eustace whose eyes had been fixed on the passing fields.

Agatha turned to gaze outside the window. It was certainly heavy and coating the countryside in a blanket of white, but this was not what Agatha wanted to talk about. She wanted to discuss the story. Unfortunately, she did not want to be the one to raise the topic. It was vexing not to be asked her opinion of it. Naturally, she would give faint praise. Not to be asked was beyond the pale. Didn't the man care what she thought? Her fingers began to drum on the windowsill.

'Oh we still have a good hour to go, Lady Agatha,' said Eustace pulling out a pocket watch. 'I believe we will be stopping soon for a few minutes.'

The few minutes before the first stop was a private sort of hell for Agatha who found herself stuck between Sausage saying, 'I say', every so often while Eustace resolutely refused to solicit so much as a syllable of opinion from Agatha on the story. What made this worse was the feeling that Eustace gave every appearance of being enjoying her discomfort. She contented with stroking the sleeping canine whose head was on her lap.

Sausage handed the story back to Eustace just as the train pulled into the station at Bucknell, only fifty minutes late.

'Jolly good story. You're rather talented,' gushed Sausage which only increased Agatha's annoyance. Eustace smiled but appeared to wave away any praise.

'Perhaps we should avail ourselves of the chance to stretch our legs,' suggested Eustace.

'Good idea,' agreed Sausage. Eustace opened the carriage door and climbed down onto the platform first before helping the two ladies out.

'I must go and see Fish,' said Eustace looking around. 'I think I see your young lady approaching.'

Polly was indeed rushing down the platform, hand planted firmly on her head to keep her hat in place. Eustace departed with a tip of his hat and a wave.

'Hello Polly,' said Agatha. 'I trust everything is to your satisfaction?'

'Oh yes your ladyship. Is there anything you need?'

Neither of the two ladies required anything other than a short walk with Talleyrand up and down the platform to encourage some circulation. In truth, the carriage had become increasingly cold as the journey progressed and a certain seizure of their muscles was threatening to spoil an otherwise enjoyable journey. Not that Agatha would admit this.

'I must say, Lord Eustace is rather charming,' observed Sausage.

Agatha glanced at Sausage, but felt no need to reply as, knowing her friend, this was merely a prelude to a number of other thoughts, some of which were likely to be related to the original proposition while many were not.

'The story was bang up to the elephant, wasn't it? Gory and disturbing, I thought. Just what one wants in a Christmas story really. I do hope the snow lets up; I don't fancy being stuck in a castle for Christmas. I promised Gilbert we would have a family Christmas. He wants goose though. I'm not so keen on goose.'

Agatha listened patiently to this and more before Sausage rounded off her treatise back on topic.

'I hope he shows us more of his work.'

'Indeed,' said Agatha, but her attention had momentarily been taken by the approach of one of the men she'd seen earlier dressed in raincoats who she took to be policemen. This was confirmed a few moments later.

'Madam,' said the man in the raincoat, touching his bowler hat. He was quite tall, although everyone was tall from Agatha's perspective. He had a bushy moustache and a very serious demeanour. 'I couldn't help but notice that you are travelling with the gentleman over there.'

He pointed directly at Eustace who was in conference on the platform with his man, Fish.

'Yes. He helped recover my bag earlier. Some ruffians stole it. Why do you ask?'

'May I ask madam how well you know the gentleman?'

Now if there was something more perfectly designed to spark consternation in Agatha it was having a question of hers being answered by a question. The line of her mouth firmed up like an overcooked cake. Sausage recognised the signs and held her breath. Thankfully, Agatha's suspicion that she was dealing with an officer of the law softened her response. This is to say she did not explode. Instead, she adopted a tone that bordered on insistent without quite crossing over into peremptory.

'You may ask, sir, but first, may I ask who is asking and why?'

If the detective was either surprised or dismayed by the question he disguised it well. He bowed before replying, 'I am Detective Inspector Banks, madam. The reason why I am speaking to you now is that the valet of the gentleman you are travelling with was seen by my detective constable handing money over to the ruffian you mentioned before the incident took place.'

Sausage was shocked by this revelation but did not doubt the veracity of the messenger despite the extraordinary nature of the revelation. She turned to Agatha, expecting an eruption of Vesuvian magnitude. What Agatha lacked in ambiguity she more than compensated for in volatility. However, as had happened so often before, Agatha astonished her.

She burst out laughing.

Both Sausage and the policeman stared at her unable to believe what they were seeing. The laughing wouldn't stop though. It was actually a delightful sound which made Sausage wish her friend would do it more often. When things had subsided, Agatha smiled at the policeman and offered her hand. The dumbfounded man shook it without thinking.

'Thank you Detective Inspector Banks. I think I understand what's happened. There's nothing to worry about.'

Banks bowed and muttered something about being happy to assist. Sausage, however, was far from happy about the situation and as soon as the inspector was out of earshot she rounded on Agatha.

'What on earth are you saying Agatha? Lord Eustace has indulged in a reprehensible practical joke. I for one have a good mind to...'

'Leave it Sausage. It's really rather sweet if you think about it.'

Sausage jaw dropped several inches as it was wont to do when she was flabbergasted, invariably by Agatha.

'Don't you see Sausage? Eustace merely staged this charade as a means of engineering an introduction to us for the journey up to Pru's.'

'But...'

'But what?' said Agatha. 'It doesn't matter that we would have been introduced anyway at the house. I think he just wanted company on the way up.'

'Well really.'

Agatha started to giggle again, clearly tickled by the ridiculousness of the situation.

'We should return to the carriage,' observed Agatha. Other passengers were climbing back in, and Eustace was on his way back. Agatha studied him surreptitiously from beneath her hat.

'I wonder Lord Eustace. I wonder.'

'What was that dear?' asked Sausage.

Agatha turned to her friend; her face was more serious.

'Not a word of what has transpired,' said Agatha which brought a gasp from Sausage followed by a face that was suspiciously sulky. This was very much in the character of her wonderful friend, reflected Agatha. Sausage was a sportswoman to her fingertips: hockey, equestrian sports as well as being a rather effective middle order batsman and a good shot. She believed in rules and the governing principles of fair play. Anyone who disregarded such sacred notions was at best a bit of a cad or worse, a bounder. Agatha's brother, Lancelot and her brother, Rory, were exceptions to this general rule as they had the ability to be both, often at the same time.

Sausage stomped off to the carriage, ignoring Eustace's outstretched hand of assistance. Agatha, instead, took it as it was quite a step up to the train. Eustace then helped Talleyrand hop on board before joining them.

'One has to admire a rail company who instinctively try their hardest to stop passengers boarding,' said Agatha looking at the gap between the platform at the train.

Very soon the train was off again throwing everyone forward. The beauty of the snow-lit night captured everyone's attention. They gazed out into the snow-carpeted fields. The snow had stopped, but the frostiness in the carriage was not just emanating from Sausage. It was genuinely cold now. Arrival at Pru's house and the prospect of a warm fire could not come soon enough for all.

Conversation was more muted on the second and final stage of the journey. This was partially triggered by the evident deterioration in Sausage's mood. If Eustace had any inkling of what had transpired he kept it well disguised behind eyes that radiated amusement. Agatha used the time to catch up on a new edition of Spring-Heeled Jack while Sausage stared mutely out of the window.

The snow was falling thickly again. A frown creased Eustace's face for the first time. This was noted by Agatha, and she inquired as to why he was worried.

'I wasn't expecting such heavy going,' admitted Eustace enigmatically.

'Do you think we will make it all the way to Greater Recton?' asked Agatha, a little concerned. It was dreadfully cold in the carriage. The prospect of any extension to their journey was unwelcome. Eustace took out his pocket watch to help aid some calculations around how much further they had to travel. If the look of unease was any guide, surmised Agatha, they still had a fair distance to travel.

Eustace cupped his hand to the window and peered out into the drifts of snow. When he leaned back from the window, his eyes met Agatha's. Nothing was said or needed to be. She read his face while he understood that Agatha had immediately grasped their situation. A few minutes later, Eustace removed from his pocket a railway timetable. He leafed through it until he found the page he needed.

'What is your assessment, Lord Eustace?' asked Agatha.

Eustace sighed. He appeared genuinely caught between revealing his fear over their ability to progress or disguise it, as most men tend to do, behind humour. He chose the former course suspecting, rightly, that Agatha would not appreciate any disingenuous response.

'Lady Agatha, Lady Jocelyn, sorry Sausage, I think we should prepare ourselves for any eventuality.'

'Meaning?' asked Agatha.

'That we may not reach Greater Recton.'

This caused Sausage to gasp. She did this as a matter of course and Agatha usually ignored it. Eustace, however, was not familiar with the more dramatic tendencies of the former captain of 'the Invincibles' and sought immediately to reassure.

'Don't worry Sausage. There are a number of places that we can stop en route. It may require an unscheduled overnight stay along the way. Then we can make our way to the house in the morning when things, hopefully, improve.'

This appeared to have the dual effect of reassuring Sausage while also thawing her tacit frostiness towards Eustace.

'What do you think will happen?' asked Sausage.

'I suspect we may have to stop at Ledburn. We might reach Little Recton at a push but,' said Eustace glancing out the window, 'this may not be wise. Little Recton, if my memory serves, is a tiny village whereas Ledburn at least offers the chance of warm accommodation.'

Agatha appreciated the candour and nodded to Eustace. His assessment was not far from her own. She studied Eustace's face once more as he stared out the window. Despite his manner and the rather silly charade with the thieves, he was clearly more thoughtful than he professed. He turned suddenly and, much to Agatha's frustration, caught her looking at him.

'One thought does strike me,' said Eustace. He appeared not to notice Agatha's attention. 'If we did reach Little Recton then we would not be all that far from the house. I suspect Greater Recton is no closer, but merely enjoys better roads and we can avoid any marshes. Wouldn't do to get caught in one of those.' He glanced down at Talleyrand and realised that travelling through the snow with the hound would be difficult.

After this, silence fell on the carriage as they passed pastures turned white by the flurries. The train grumbled and trembled through the worsening weather. Lights sailed by suggesting they had passed through Ledburn. Agatha felt some concern at this, but noted that Eustace, while pensive, seemed to accept the decision. She suspected that Eustace was a gambler. As ever, Agatha's assessment was very close to the mark.

The landscape was like a vast apron of white fields enclosed within black hedgerows. Suddenly everything went black as the train rumbled through a tunnel. As they exited the tunnel the train whistled, but then for all the world they heard what sounded like a scream. Perhaps one of the passengers had been frightened by the sudden darkness of the tunnel. However, the one perturbing thought was that the sound they'd heard was male. Agatha exchanged looks with Eustace. He'd heard it too; his brow furrowed.

'What on earth was that?' said Eustace, looking out the window.

'Did I miss something?' asked Sausage.

'A scream,' suggested Agatha.

The rhythm of the train slackened which suggested they were approaching a station. Eustace took out his watch before consulting his timetable.

'I think ladies that our journey may soon be coming to an end.'

Agatha frowned but believed him.

'We are either slowing down because of the snow or the driver has decided to make an unscheduled stop at Little Recton.'

The scene outside suggested either was a possibility. The train was certainly giving every impression that it was rolling to a halt. Outside presented the unpleasant prospect of freezing in a white wilderness. There was no evidence of life. Tall black trees flashed by like malevolent shadows. A minute later one or two lights appeared in the windows of a few scattered houses. The train rolled to a halt at a small station. The sign read Little Recton.

They remained in the carriage for a minute and then they heard the voice of the conductor ordering everyone off the train.

'Congratulations, Lord Eustace. It seems you are right.'

'Sadly, yes.' Eustace's natural effervescence had diminished a notch of two. He looked badly in need of a restorative of the non-medicinal kind. Agatha, too.

They disembarked from the train and were approached by the conductor. Behind them, steam belched from the sides of the train.

'I'm sorry, but we cannot continue. If you have any luggage, it must be removed.'

There seemed little point in asking why they were stopping. The evidence was all too plain. Up ahead, the snow was piling high over the sleepers, lightening the darkness with a purplish glow.

'Ahh here's Fish,' said Eustace. The poor man was carrying more bags than a man of his singularly indolent nature was ever meant to carry.

'That's decent of him,' noted Agatha, who realised he was helping Polly, who was walking alongside him.

Just behind, Agatha noted that aside from the policemen, their prisoner and another man, they were the only passengers left on the train. It was then she noticed that either one of the policemen had changed his overcoat or he had left the train at the previous stop and been replaced by the new man. Any further thoughts on the subject were halted when she saw Eustace speaking animatedly with the conductor and the driver. A minute later he returned to the group and announced, 'They are leaving us here and making a run back to London or, at least, as close as they can make it. They've offered to take us back. Alternatively, we can stay inside the station tonight. It might be possible to try and reach the house from here. I estimate it's a mile or so, but it would be tough going.'

The conductor went towards the policemen to update them. Agatha overheard the new man saying that they would stay here for the night. This presented an unusual and far from tantalising prospect of spending a night at a tiny train station with a criminal, albeit one who was in handcuffs.

'What do you think ladies?'

Sausage, game as ever, was all for making their way to the house. Agatha, while not worried about the conditions, was more concerned about losing their way through the woods that blocked their path to the great house and they were in the middle of the Fens. The prospect of being lost in the marshes was very real. Eustace seemed relaxed on this point. He'd visited the house many times and walked through the woods, often with their host. They marked a boundary to both the estate and the marshes. Finally, the decision was made that they would risk finding their way to Pru's.

The conductor nodded to the small group on the platform and then relayed the decision to the train driver. This was greeted with a have-it-your-own-way shrug. Before long, the train began to reverse out of the station to make the short trip back to Ledburn where it could be turned around to ensure faster progress.

Fish and Polly were now standing with the group. This was Agatha's first chance to observe Eustace's valet. He was only a little taller than she and Agatha was no Amazonian. He was well made with a genial countenance. Agatha judged him to be nearing forty. He was certainly older than Eustace who she guessed to be around thirty.

'Well, to the house then?' said Agatha decisively.

'To the house,' agreed Sausage.

Eustace nodded, but Fish was certainly able to contain his glee at the prospect of wading through snow laden with bags. Eustace, seeing it was a task that would have caused Hercules to throw in the towel, stepped in to take a couple of bags thus lightening the load for Fish.

'Well, shall we be off then?' asked Eustace more brightly than he was feeling.

'I wouldn't if I were you,' said a voice from behind the group. Talleyrand began to growl. There are more threatening things in life than a grumpy Basset hound. Much to his annoyance, he was ignored. Instead, everyone turned around to find the policeman, his prisoner and the other man standing close by.

The new man was quite young looking, tall and clean shaven. None of these features mattered so much as the revolver he was holding. It was pointing directly at Eustace.

6

'What on earth do you think you are doing?' expostulated Agatha. On the face of it, the question was somewhat redundant as it was fairly evident what the man was doing. Agatha understood this but felt that some explanation was required on how they had arrived at this uncommon situation. Sometimes she used a peremptory tone to disguise her tears, fears and everything else besides but, just at this moment, she was genuinely enraged.

Inspector Banks stepped in at this point to provide a brief explanation.

'This was my prisoner. It now appears, I am his. I'm afraid we shall have to do as he says.'

The prisoner grinned malevolently.

'That scream?' asked Eustace.

'Was my police constable,' said Banks, his voice heavy with sadness. He was killed by these men.'

The prisoner spoke up at this point as he registered the shock on the faces of their new captives. He didn't look too chipper himself about what the inspector had said.

'Nonsense, we didn't kill him. He'll have a few bruises. Nothing more. We threw him off the train.'

'You might have killed him,' snarled the policeman in response.

'The snow will have softened his landing. Now, I don't know about you, but it's rather cold. We should retire inside and light up a fire.'

The prisoner, despite his long thin face and sly eyes was quite well spoken. His blue eyes seemed to twinkle. He, too, had a gun. Flicking it in the direction of the small station building, the group walked towards a wall that had been blackened by age or perhaps it was a character of the bricks used in its construction or even a fire.

Under normal circumstances, Agatha was of a character to be affronted by anyone ordering her around, particularly at the point of a gun. This was perhaps a unique case when the suggestion chimed with her wishes. The group headed towards a door. Eustace was the first to arrive. He tried it.

It was locked.

'It's locked,' said Eustace turning to the man with the gun.

'I can see that, you useless fool,' replied the former prisoner. 'Let me try.' The prisoner was almost about to hand the gun to Sausage when he remembered that this might compromise their advantage. He gave the gun, instead, to his confederate and began to shake the door. This attempt was a dismal failure.

'Told you,' said Eustace helpfully.

Agatha glanced at Eustace. He was sailing a little close to the wind with this comment. The response from the former prisoner was a scowl as he went about the task with renewed vigour, or perhaps it was driven by the irritation caused by Eustace. Agatha could see how this might be the case. The younger man who was more powerfully built had a try.

The door still refused to shift.

'Damn and blast,' said the younger man, wiping his brow. His accent was Scottish.

'Sir, there are ladies present,' said Eustace in a voice that suggested amusement rather than indignation at the breach of good manners. Thankfully, it was ignored as the man took the gun from his comrade. He pointed the gun at the lock then a thought struck him.

'Stand back.'

The group needed no second invitation to take him up on this sensible suggestion. He was on the point of firing when a voice shouted from further down the platform.

'Oi! What are you doing?'

The owner of the voice was an old signalman holding a lantern. He marched down the platform in the manner of a man about to deliver a piece of his mind and that piece was outrage.

'Trying to open the door,' said the man with the gun. Agatha wondered if this comment sounded as pathetic to the man as it did to her.

'You can't do that,' said the old signalman. He seemed oblivious to the fact that a man holding a gun was probably able, if not necessarily entitled, to do as he wished.

There was silence as everyone glanced from the gun to the signalman and back again. Then the man with the gun felt the need to state the obvious.

'Yes I can. Open the door.'

The old man grumbled something under his breath and moved with a limp towards the door. He extracted some keys from his pocket and took an age to choose the correct one. This was met with much eye rolling, from Agatha. For a moment she considered taking the gun from the man and threatening the old signalman herself.

Finally, the door screeched open. Agatha thought about making a pointed observation about the upkeep of the station however, she decided this was not the time. Inside proved only slightly less inhospitable than being out in the snow-flaked elements.

'Start a fire,' ordered the gunman.

'All right, all right. Keep yer hair on,' grumbled the old signalman.

It took another few minutes, but finally some warmth and light began to infiltrate the dark interior of the station waiting room. The signalman found another couple of lamps and lit them. The waiting room was quite large and contained seats for everyone and a large table. There was a door marked 'Stationmaster' opposite the door through which they'd entered. The two men, both armed, stood in front of the office door while everyone else sat down facing them.

'I don't believe we've been introduced,' said Agatha with brisk authority. In situations such as this, Agatha always felt it best to establish as early as possible the pecking order even when you are standing at the wrong end of a pointed revolver. The gunman had the grace to smile at this. Eustace, too, seemed to beam in the candlelight.

'You are quite right. My name is...'

'Kurr. You're William Kurr aren't you?' said Eustace suddenly. It was like a clap of thunder in the room. 'I saw you at a race meeting once.'

Kurr nodded and a smile appeared on his face. He appeared to be in his thirties, clean shaven with dark hair.

'Kurr?' said Agatha in shock. 'You're the man involved in the trial of the detectives, Druscovich and Palmer.'

Kurr laughed at this before replying, 'There were a few more than that....' He paused at the end and raised his eyebrows. This was Agatha's cue to introduce herself.

'My name is Lady Agatha Aston.'

'I'm Sausage,' chipped in Sausage.

'That's Lady Jocelyn Gossage,' continued Agatha without missing a beat.

All eyes then turned to Eustace who had been busy examining the room and was thus unaware that it was his turn. Agatha cleared her throat. Eustace remained unaware still. Finally, he turned around to find himself the centre of attention.

'My turn is it? Eustace Frost at your service.' Although his tone was neutral it appeared to be mocking, due to the querulous look on his face. Agatha wondered if he ever took anything seriously or whether this was merely an accident of birth.

Just as Agatha was on the point of reasserting her authority, Kurr broke in first. Interestingly, even with the criminal element, rules of social hierarchy were maintained. The names of the servants and the signalman were neither requested nor offered.

'This is my associate, Sebastian. Good. Now that we all know one another, doubtless you will want to know what will happen now.'

The tilt of Agatha's head and the elevation of one eyebrow told Kurr that not only was this a statement of the obvious, but he would be best employed in getting on with whatever he had to say. Kurr received the message.

'I, despite my friend Banks' assertion, am not a murderer. I have no doubt your constable is, even as we speak, sitting comfortably in some house with a warm mug of tea. We have no intention of harming any of you. I must confess, I'm still undecided if this weather is a help or a hindrance so we must make virtue of necessity. I have a number of friends who planned to liberate me at our destination. Alas, as you can see, we have not been able to reach Greater Recton due this somewhat inclement weather. Kurr turned to Sebastian at this point.

'How far do you think we have to go if we cut across country?'

'It's a couple of miles at least, Mr Kurr.'

'I'm not sure we've any choice. We can't stay here. It might take an hour or more, but then we'll have horses and the rest of the night to reach the coast.'

'In this weather?' pressed Sebastian, clearly unhappy at the prospect of braving the extreme cold.

'True, but I think we can tip the odds in our favour. My coat is very warm. Yours is a little thin. Perhaps the good Inspector Banks can donate his coat to our cause. Remove his handcuffs and take his coat. I'll keep you covered,' said Kurr. The last comment was made for the benefit of Banks lest he undertake any heroic attempt at escape.

For the next few minutes there was silence in the waiting room as the two gunmen prepared to leave. The final act was to handcuff Banks. Kurr held up the key to the handcuffs and made a show of putting it in his pocket. Then he and Sebastian went to the door.

'I wouldn't advise trying to follow us,' said Kurr.

Eustace was buggered if he'd any intention of following him but decided against saying this. Agatha shared the sentiment if not Eustace's unspoken nomenclature. Moments later the two men were through the door and making good their escape.

There was shocked silence in the room. It lasted only moments. Banks was on his feet immediately and straight over to the window. Then he spun around and looked at the signalman.

'Have you a hacksaw?'

'No,' said the old man with a shrug.

'Have you anything that can cut these handcuffs?'

The signalman did not bother replying. A shake of the head was sufficient.

'Blast it. I can't let them go free. I must catch them.'

Eustace stood up and went to the window. Snow was falling with an almost Biblical ferocity.

'Oh I wouldn't worry. They'll be back soon enough,' said Eustace in the manner of a man who was chatting amiably about the weather. Which he was. Agatha and Sausage joined him by the window. It was a fair assessment of the situation. No one could walk very far in such conditions, even armed with Agatha's umbrella.

'I have an idea,' said Agatha. All eyes turned to her. 'I think you're right. They'll be back and we should be ready for them. Inspector Banks, you stay by the window and act as look out. When you see them, step back and give us a warning. Mr Fish, Polly, start talking in loud voices. An argument perhaps. Lord Eustace. You stay by the door. They will not be expecting anyone to attack. Disarm the first man and shut the door. Are you ready to do this?'

Eustace indicated he would by bowing.

'I say, Agatha, are you sure. It sounds risky,' said Sausage. Now there was no one less likely to question Agatha than her dear friend. It was a reminder to Agatha that what they were planning had a degree of risk. However, one look at Eustace confirmed that he was up to the task. He smiled to Agatha and shrugged. It was better than nothing, she supposed.

'I think it's worth a try,' said Banks. He exchanged glances with Eustace. The two men nodded. This settled matters. Now the only thing left to do was wait. Silence fell on the waiting room like a clap of thunder. To pass the time they watched shadows dance on the wall caused by the fire. Banks stood by the window as instructed while Eustace waited at the door holding the poker used in the fire.

A few minutes later, Banks spun round and whispered, 'They're coming.'

Agatha and Sausage immediately extinguished the lights. Fish and Polly began to speak loudly. Talleyrand, overcome by the excitement of it all, fell asleep.

'How long have you been in Lady Agatha's service?'

'Six months Mr Fish,' replied Polly. 'And how long have you been in Lord Eustace's service Mr Fish?'

Another few seconds of this would feel like years, thought Agatha moving to the corner of the room. She tried hard to listen to the sound of footsteps crunching through the snow.

'...before that I was with a Miss Harper,' said Polly who was fast running out of ideas on what to say next.

'How did you find her, Miss Polly?'

Hurry up, urged Agatha. I can't take more of this conversation.

'She liked to sleep very late, although there was one time...'

'Yes?'

'She rose early...'

The door flew open. Talleyrand, who thus far had been snoozing, suddenly barked. A man walked in holding a gun. There was a shout, and the gun flew to the floor. Sausage dived on it instantly. Agatha never felt prouder of her friend's courage than at that moment.

'Very good,' said a voice from the other side of the room.

Everyone turned and saw Kurr emerging from the stationmaster's office. Anticipating an ambush, he'd obviously climbed in through a window at the back without anyone realising. He stepped forward into the room that was lit only by firelight, his revolver pointing at Sausage who was rising to her feet. The other revolver remained on the ground.

'I had a feeling that you might try something,' said Kurr in a self-satisfied voice. He walked forward towards Eustace, who was holding a poker. 'Step away from the door Lord Eustace.'

Eustace lowered the poker and stepped back from the door as requested. There was mute astonishment in the room at the sudden turn of events. Except Talleyrand, who growled at the gunman. He was ignored which was always guaranteed to upset the rather vain Basset hound. Instead, keeping his eyes fixed on Banks, Kurr motioned towards the gun.

'Pick up the gun, Sebastian.'

7

'I wouldn't do that,' said Agatha. Her voice came from behind Kurr like a scream in coalmine. All of a sudden, the gunman became aware of a sharp object sticking into the base of his spine. All heads turned towards Agatha who was standing just behind Kurr. There was a collective intake of breath.

'I shan't miss from here Mr Kurr, I assure you,' added Agatha threateningly. Her voice was steady, determined with just the usual soupçon of irritation.

Kurr's gun clattered to the floor before Agatha had finished her sentence. Sausage immediately grabbed both guns and stepped back from the two criminals. Kurr's hands shot up but could not help noticing the look of amazement on his confederate's face. He turned around. Agatha was armed only with her umbrella, pointing rifle-fashion towards him.

'Good Lord,' said Kurr, stupefied.

Eustace couldn't have agreed more but was too awestruck to say anything. He watched as Banks woke up to what had happened. He was over quickly to Kurr to dispossess him of the handcuff key. Within a few minutes the two gunman were handcuffed to one another sitting near the fire in a sulking silence.

'What shall we do?' asked Sausage. She was a girl who liked a plan. Preferably someone else's. Someone like Agatha.

Agatha glanced towards Eustace who was standing by the window now with Inspector Banks. They were talking in low voices. Then Eustace turned around and shook his head. It was too risky to attempt to make it to the house. They would have to spend the night in the station waiting room before making their way to the house in the morning.

The plan was swiftly communicated to the rest of the group and the men agreed a schedule for watching the two prisoners. Banks would take first watch until midnight. Fish was to take over until three in the morning to be replaced by Eustace. Naturally, Agatha and Sausage both offered their services, but they were politely declined. Agatha bristled at the inevitable refusal but was honest enough to admit to herself some relief. The night would be challenging enough without adding guard duties to their already uncomfortable sleeping arrangements.

*

A few hours later, the sun rose and so did Agatha. She found everyone asleep, including Eustace who was meant to be on guard. His posture was a reminder of when she had first seen him. Head tilted back, his mouth was open, and he was out for the count. At least he wasn't snoring.

'Useless,' said Agatha under her breath. She stopped for a moment as it occurred to her how like this word was to his name. She repeated it. 'Useless.' She began to laugh. At first it was a giggle, but soon the ludicrousness of their situation caused her merriment to increase along with the volume of her laugh.

Eustace awoke to find Agatha clutching her stomach such was her mirth. It required little in the way of intuition to comprehend why she was so amused. He sat up and glanced sharply in the direction of the prisoners he'd been guarding.

Thankfully, they were both still there, sleeping like children. Agatha stopped laughing and looked wryly at Eustace.

'Don't worry. You're secret's safe with me.'

'All's well that ends well, I suppose,' said Eustace. He glanced at the snoozing Basset hound and added, 'Some help you were.'

'Indeed,' agreed Agatha, wandering over to the window to gaze through the icy film on the pane to the wintry scene. She felt a chill once more gazing out at the whiteness. Frost glittered on the snow, but there was no sign of life outside. A noise behind her suggested that Sausage was re-joining the world. Agatha turned around and saw that this was indeed the case. So, too, was Banks. The rest of the small group were still sleeping. The signalman had disappeared sometime during the night. Probably had his own house to go to. A warm fire, too. A bed.

Eustace rose to his feet and joined Agatha by the window, He took out his pocket watch. It would soon be eight in the morning. They had slept quite a lot longer than seemed possible, given the cold, their hunger and their rough accommodation. Eustace wondered idly how long it would be before his travelling companion's boredom threshold was breached and she began to rouse everyone from their slumber. He estimated no more than ten minutes.

Three minutes later...

'Everybody up,' exclaimed Agatha, clapping her hands. She kept this up for fully one minute. Relentless, thought Eustace. What a woman! The room stirred, reluctantly at first; rebelliously in one case, but Fish soon recovered his usual beleaguered poise. The detective got to his feet and made straight for the window.

'Do you think you can lead us to Campbell House, Lord Eustace?'

'Oh yes,' said Eustace airily which immediately made Agatha sceptical. 'We'll be there in two ticks.' He noted the look on Agatha's face as he said this and revised this assessment. 'Well, no more than an hour.' He then compounded the level of disapproval in Agatha's eyes by saying, 'Are you ladies ready..?'

'Come on Sausage,' interrupted Agatha, grabbing her Gladstone bag and moving straight for the door. 'I need a cup of tea. We'll see you up at the house.'

The two ladies marched out the door leaving the rest of the group staring on in a mixture of admiration and fear.

'That would be a yes then,' said Eustace, glancing out the window, noting with satisfaction that Agatha was going the wrong way, albeit with a very brisk determination. Inspector Banks looked at Agatha before turning to Eustace.

'Is Lady Agatha going the right way...?

'No, it's the other direction.'

'Shouldn't we inform her?'

Eustace thought for a moment, his face brimming with mischief.

'I think we'll let them reach the other side of the field before we say anything.'

*

As Eustace had predicted, their journey took around an hour. Although the distance was not great, wading through snow proved a challenge. So too did Agatha's ill humour. She was under no illusions that Eustace had deliberately misled her by not immediately pointing out the error in her directions and she spent the best of the next hour making him regret such schoolboy humour.

Much of their journey was conducted in an antagonistic silence that thickened the air. This was only amplified by the eerie quiet of the wood they walked through on their way to Campbell Hall. Eustace walked with Inspector Banks, having taken charge of the second pistol, while Agatha and Sausage walked behind as no one trusted their sense of direction.

This was especially galling for Agatha who prided herself on such things and added to the heavy atmosphere of the party. However, she realised also that they were in the Fenlands. The last thing they needed was to end up in a marsh. Whatever her feelings were towards Eustace and hostile barely covered it, she sensed that he knew where he was going.

Both Kurr and Sebastian looked beaten. This was not helped by the fact that they were tasked with sharing the carrying of Talleyrand between them at certain points in the journey. Neither man seemed much like a hardened criminal. In fact, the rather genial Kurr's career in crime had been noteworthy by its utter absence of violence. He was a fraudster. A con man.

Over the last few years, until his arrest, he, along with his accomplice, Harry Benson, had engineered a fraud involving horse racing that had seen them part the rich, the greedy and the stupid from their hard-earned or inherited riches by means of a betting scam.

They created a weekly sports newspaper in France which promised great horse racing tips from a betting man known as Mr. Montgomery. The scam worked by asking people in France to place bets on his behalf under their name as his was so well-known in the racing world. Anything he bet on automatically caused a drop in odds.

Investors would receive a fake cheque from Montgomery drawn from an imaginary "Bank of London." The marks would deposit it and send Montgomery legitimate cheques to the bookmaker making sure to place their bet on Montgomery's tip. If the horse won, the bookmaker would send their winnings via an imaginary cheque back to the mark. The scam would be revealed when they went to cash the cheque. Investigations into the scam revealed that some of Scotland Yard's detectives were on the payroll of the two men. Their capture, along with the revelations about the detectives, made headlines. Kurr was no killer, but this did not make him any less dangerous in the eyes of Banks and Eustace. They made sure that the two men marched a few yards ahead of the main group.

It was ghostly and silent as they walked along a rough track until they reached a clearing where ahead lay the great mansion house. Emerging from the forest they had their first view of Campbell Hall. While not quite of the first, or indeed, second rank of English country houses, just at that moment as they stood at the forest clearing, tired and cold, no house looked finer or more welcome. It was a mansion from a gothic novel; stone spires stabbed the wintry sky. Thankfully, there were chimneys there too. This meant the rooms had fires. This was welcome. The field in front of them was a boundary to the marshland which meant it was relatively safe underfoot if no more pleasant. By now, the wet had leached into their footwear causing all of them to squelch as they walked.

Then it began to snow again.

At least Agatha had an umbrella, which she immediately offered to Sausage. The rest had to suffer the stinging cold of the flakes blowing randomly into their faces like inebriated insects. They struggled silently towards the destination. As they approached the great mansion house, the door opened to reveal a young woman.

'Good Lord,' was the first greeting they heard. This came from a maid who was carrying a broom. The broom clattered to the floor as the frightened servant ran inside shouting

'There's someone at the door.'

'I think some more training required for that one.'

Oddly, it was Kurr who had made this observation and Agatha, for one, agreed wholeheartedly. She strode forward to the door and gave it a sound rap with the base of her umbrella. Within seconds it appeared all hell had been let loose within the household. A butler appeared from somewhere and jogged towards the door. He was a man of generous dimensions and a genial smile. He looked exactly like the character Padgett from the story of Eustace's she'd read on the train.

It took a moment and then Agatha recognised him as Mr Jolly, Pru's butler from since when she'd been a child. A little like Flack, her own butler, he had obviously followed the young woman to her new residence.

Seconds later a man and woman appeared who were most definitely not staff. They looked askance at the apparition of Agatha and a party of tramps standing in the doorway. Standing beside them was an older woman who looked at the new arrivals with more than a hint of disapproval.

Moments later, they heard the sound of barking. A large, rather hairy German Shepherd appeared. He fixed malevolent eyes on Talleyrand causing the Basset to disappear rather swiftly behind Eustace.

'Agatha?' said the young woman standing in a hallway with stone walls, torches burning in the brackets on the wall and an undecorated Christmas tree. The Gothic feel was not confined to the spires outside.

'Pru,' replied Agatha thus confirming who it was in the questioner's mind.

'What on earth?' asked the man. This question came within a beat of being repeated when the two handcuffed prisoners entered with Eustace and Inspector Banks pointing guns at them.

*

A quarter of an hour later, the prisoners were incarcerated in a dungeon or something approaching this, the servants sent downstairs and the guests from the train, aside from Inspector Banks, were in the drawing room, stockings and socks hanging up to dry. Cups of tea were consumed thus restoring some badly needed sanity to Campbell Hall.

Eustace recounted the story of how they had re-captured the criminals giving Agatha the spotlight in a manner that was almost, but not quite, too much even for her vanity. All were agreed that she had proved resourceful and brave, as had Sausage who'd actually been the first to retrieve the weapons. Agatha waved away the praise with a practiced, if unconvincing, air of nonchalance. She had never quite mastered humility and had given up trying at an early age.

The late arrival of the group plus the added bonus of their extraordinary adventure proved a very satisfying start to the weekend. The group were all young, noted Agatha, with no parents or aunts to interfere with or, in Daphne's case, instigate, the activities that young people are wont to engage in.

Pru Parrish clapped her hands at the end of Eustace's very funny and often self-deprecating recount of the night. He even admitted to falling asleep whilst on guard duty which brought laughter from everyone except Agatha, who merely raised an eyebrow in disapproval. Despite this, she felt a warm glow at being among mostly good friends. In particular, she and Sausage were delighted to be with Pru, another member of 'the Invincibles' hockey team that had been unbeaten between the years 1863 - 1867.

Pru, was a year older than Agatha. Tall, elegant and very handsome, she had been chased by a dozen suitors, but had surprised no one by marrying John Parrish, or "Beefy" as he was known. He was even taller than she, dashingly fair-haired, broad-shouldered and had once been a member of the household cavalry until he had come into a title. It was love at first sight on both sides and certainly enough of a match to give Aunt Daphne more grist to hurl into the mill when she saw Agatha immediately after the marriage.

Pru glanced down at Talleyrand who was busy exploring the room. 'Shall I let him join the dogs.' Agatha's head shot up and she looked alarmed.

'I wouldn't. He rather let himself down at Nobby's house.'

'Ahh,' smiled Pru bending down to stroke him. 'He has a romantic nature. Does he?'

'Well that's one way of putting it Pru. He's French.'

Agatha considered this sufficient explanation and Pru certainly understood the implication. Somewhere in the house, the sound of barking could be heard. Talleyrand disappeared behind a chair.

'That's Bismarck. He's rather excitable,' explained Pru. 'Anyway, I must say it's a relief you've been able to come. I'm afraid Emma and Joanna have sent their apologies,' said Pru with a sigh. 'They're such fun.'

Agatha tried not to cheer. The prospect of a weekend with the twin sisters had not been so welcome to her as Pru or Sausage. Not that Pru needed to apologise to anyone when it came to practical jokes. She knew where to draw the line in a way that the Potts' sisters never did.

'What about Ernest and Tommy, sorry Mr Pilbream?' asked Sausage.

'Ernest can't come either, but both Tommy and Frederick are on their way. They're due this morning, but I daresay they'll have had the same problems as you,' said John.

'I hope not,' said Agatha tartly. It took a moment for Parrish to realise she was referring to the additional guests in the makeshift prison. He was a good sort, but not the fastest horse in the race. The others broke out into good-natured laughing, including Parrish.

'Ah, yes. I see what you mean,' he said, his face reddening slightly.

'I'm not sure I've met Frederick,' said Eustace.

'He's my cousin. He was at the wedding, you know.'

'So were three hundred other people, Beefy,' pointed out Eustace. He said this kindly, and the group chuckled with Eustace.

'Ah yes. I see what you mean,' replied Parrish. He said this a lot. Pru looked at him lovingly. He was *very* dashing, thought Agatha, but she sometimes wondered if her friend ever became frustrated by his genial stupidity. As she thought this, John stood up to his full six-foot three height and brushed some lint from a very flat stomach.

Perhaps not, reflected Agatha wistfully.

*

Around ten, a carriage was sent to the station at Greater Recton but returned within minutes. There was no way to the station except on foot. At least the snow had stopped, observed Sausage, hopeful as ever. This gave some grounds for optimism that a train would be able to make it through at close to the appointed hour of eleven. A couple of footmen were sent to the station which was a mile away to help carry any belongings from the remaining guests.

Agatha and the other guests were shown to their rooms. Polly was already there arranging Agatha's clothes in the wardrobe. She greeted Agatha with a curtsey more out of habit than any desire of Agatha. She helped Talleyrand onto the bed before turning to Agatha for her instructions.

'Have you packed Lady Jocelyn's clothes away?'

'Yes all done, your ladyship.'

'I hope you've had a chance to have a cup of tea.'

'Oh yes, thank you.'

'How are the staff?'

'Oh, the cook, Mrs Reid is very nice and the butler, Mr Jolly is very jolly if I may say. The housekeeper, Mrs Gallagher, on the other hand...'

'Is quite severe?' suggested Agatha.

'Yes, how did you guess?' asked a surprised Polly.

'The pursed lips were a clue,' replied Agatha enigmatically.

Polly decided not to say anything more about the staff. There were two footmen, the Gooch brothers, who were rather good-looking. The prospects for the weekend had certainly picked up. For a few seconds nothing was said then Polly was dismissed with a smile and a nod. She departed downstairs immediately to join the two young men that had caught her eye.

The room was simply furnished and benefitted enormously from a small but effective fireplace. How often had she gone to old mansions and suffered from the cold? At least this house had all the modern conveniences. The night had taken its toll on her, so she lay down on the bed to rest, alone. She wondered about the new arrivals. It sounded as if this chap Pilbream was someone Sausage was particularly interested in. She hoped so. Her friend's happiness meant everything to her. This could only be realised through finding someone she could love and would love her.

Why didn't she feel the same as her friend? What was holding her back? Perhaps she was merely in denial. Denial and permission are two sides of the same coin. Neither would admit to the other's existence, but one would have to die in the end. If permission were to die then it would be joined by its two friends, trust and hope. In her heart, Agatha knew that this could not happen. She knew that Aunt Daphne was right. One day she would have to place her trust in the hands of another. Each passing day brought that moment closer, but it had to be on her terms. It had to be a genuine joining together of two spirits, two intellects: not submission to a treasonous heart. Sleep washed over her followed by dreams of murder, deception, and love. It all seemed so real.

Soon it would be.

8

Agatha awoke to the sound of urgent knocking on the door from Polly. This was a great pity as Agatha had been on the point of announcing that Lord Shotton was the murderer. Or was she the murderer? It all seemed so frightfully confused now. The knocking continued and Agatha finally conceded that her eyes must open, a response must be made, and reality faced once more in all its grim hope.

'Yes, yes, Polly come in,' said Agatha balefully. Polly entered with a face flushed by something more than the navigation of a steep set of stairs. She paused and gazed at the snoring Basset on the bed. Then Agatha raised her eyebrows questioningly.

'The other guests are here,' said Polly.

Agatha was unsure as to why this merited such excitement. She smiled and rose unsteadily from the bed. The clock on the mantlepiece over the fire indicated she had been sleeping nearly an hour. It was almost twelve. Outside in the corridor she could hear male voices. Why did they have to talk so loudly? Was quiet conversation beyond the species? On the evidence below, hail, and hearty was going to be the main dish on the menu over the weekend. Agatha could hardly wait.

'Yes, so I gather,' answered Agatha sourly. 'Is Lady Jocelyn up and about?'

Polly smiled before replying, 'I think she's up now.' Agatha sent Polly to check on her friend while she dressed. Agatha was not one for being dressed by a maid; she was a modern woman to whom such practices were a relic from the Regency period. Strolling over to the window, she saw snow falling heavily once more.

Sausage's excited voice broke her reverie, so she went out to join her. There was no question, Sausage did look rather animated and, if Agatha was not mistaken, something she rarely conceded, the flush on her cheeks was caused by more than a touch of rouge. There was also a sparkle in her friend's eyes that suggested the light of love had been lit with the aid of dynamite. Intrigued, Agatha followed her friend to the stairs that led to the main hall. In fact, she struggled to keep up as Sausage moved at a pace not witnessed since she'd left defenders for dead on the hockey field a decade before.

At the top of the stairs, the two ladies could see a group of men, backs turned, chatting to Pru and John. Just as Sausage was about to tear down the stairs, Agatha put a restraining hand on her arm. She strongly suspected this would not be the last time she had to do this.

'Wait,' counselled Agatha.

Sausage nodded without quite knowing why. This was not a problem as Agatha's reasons were often opaque, but she trusted her friend implicitly. They stood for a few moments and then Pru spotted them. A ghost of a smile appeared on her lips. She nodded to Agatha. A moment later she drew the attention of the young gentlemen to the ladies.

Agatha gave Sausage a slight shove so that they could commence their 'entrance' under the full gaze of the men. The gentlemen turned around. The first gentleman to catch her eye certainly provided an interesting prospect for the weekend. As tall as John Parrish, every bit as well made as John Parrish only with dark, curly hair and ice blue eyes; danger was written all over him. Agatha took a deep breath, stared at a spot around two feet over everyone's heads. She opted against smiling. No point in making it too obvious that that they were making an entrance.

The group greeted the ladies with the usual compliments that Agatha had long since stopped listening to. Then it occurred to her that Sausage had stopped and was staring at a young man of strikingly similar characteristics. He was just under six feet tall, very slim with dark unruly hair and a set of teeth that might once have belonged to a Derby winner. Like Sausage he tended to shift from one foot to another in a side-to-side motion that suggested a winger on a hockey field.

'I say,' said Sausage.

'I say,' said the young man, beaming. With the preliminary 'I says' out of the way they resorted to staring at one another in a rather moon-eyed fashion. Eventually, Agatha held her hand out to him.

'Are you Mr Pilbream by any chance?'

'Lady Agatha,' said the young man, tearing his eyes away from Sausage. 'This is a pleasure. Please call me Tommy, all my friends do.'

Agatha nodded then turned to the other member of the party. Pru stepped forward at this point with a knowing smile.

'Agatha, may I present, a cousin of John's, Mr Frederick de Courcy.'

Agatha nodded to the god-like young man.

'All my friends call me Freddie,' said the young god. His voice that of a gentleman, but not quite of a noble.

'I hope I will one day be counted among them, Mr de Courcy,' said Agatha, immediately establishing her shrewish credentials in his eyes. He smiled at this, revealing very even, very white teeth. He was certainly an Adonis, thought Agatha and by the smugness of his smile, he knows it too.

'Well, the good news is that you've arrived just in time for lunch,' said John Parrish. 'Jolly can take you to your rooms. Lunch will be served at one.'

The three men departed while Agatha joined Pru and Sausage in the drawing room. Agatha suspected that the subject of the conversation would be one close to her Aunt Daphne's heart. It was with this in mind that she initiated matters as soon as the door shut behind them.

'He's rather good-looking isn't he, Mr de Courcy,' announced Agatha. She did this to spike Pru's guns which she suspected were already being trained on her.

'Is he?' asked Sausage. It seemed her eyes had truly been turned by the other young man.

Pru was no fool and had observed how smitten Sausage was by the other young man. 'Well,' said Pru, kindly, 'You did seem rather taken by Tommy.'

'Was I?' said Sausage ingenuously.

Her two friends stared at Sausage who looked nervously from one to the other without saying anything. At this point Agatha upped the ante by raising one eyebrow. This was the equivalent of a scream and was interpreted as such by Sausage.

'He's a pal,' offered Sausage lamely before adding hopefully, 'You know.'

'Pal?' said the two ladies in a response that was as remarkable for its unified timing as it was in its outright derision.

Sausage was not a young woman skilled in the dark arts of deception. Honesty was not so much a principle that she lived her life by as an unavoidable consequence of her biological makeup. No one coloured quite so quickly as Sausage when she was caught in the no man's land that existed between a desire to mislead and truth.

'There's nothing going on between us, if that's what you're suggesting,' said Sausage, wisely adopting the course of truth, but not full disclosure. She was confronted by not one but two sets of raised eyebrows.

Silence followed.

Then her two friends burst out laughing which, if anything made Sausage colour even more. Finally the dam broke and, with a worried expression, admitted, 'I do quite like him. Do you think he likes me?'

The laughter stopped immediately. For a few more seconds silence fell on the room. Then her two friends burst out laughing again. This time, however, Agatha put her hand on Sausage's arm. Her expression was one of genuine affection for her friend. Finally she said, 'He likes you my dear.'

'Do you really think so?' asked Sausage. Years spent in romance's wilderness had done little to help her confidence. She had never had the chance to rebuff admirers in the way her two friends had. This was a blessed relief as she could never imagine wanting to inflict heartbreak on anyone. Not that she'd had the chance. Until now. And she certainly had no intention of doing so on this occasion.

'Yes, we really do, Sausage,' said Pru, with a smile. Sausage looked into the eyes of her two friends and saw the only two things she needed to see at that moment: truth and love.

'I say.'

Having established Sausage's credentials as a scarlet woman, which delighted her no end, conversation turned to the arrival of Mr Frederick de Courcy. Pru had noted Agatha's reaction to him and naturally an interrogation would follow. Agatha, knowing this, was already preparing her responses.

'Yes, Mr de Courcy is good-looking,' said Pru answering Agatha's original question. 'He seemed to have stepped off the pages of a romantic novel.'

Agatha laughed at this and recognised an invitation when she heard one. The invitation was not to agree to the proposition, but do something else which she was renowned for, much to Aunt Daphne's annoyance. Agatha began to talk in a breathless voice.

'There was no denying Mr de Courcy' charms. His dark, gypsy-like hair fell in an unruly manner. He'd spent too much time in ladies' bedchambers and not enough with his barber...'

Pru and Sausage were both helpless with laughter as Agatha continued her one-woman assault on romantic literature.

'Women never tired of staring into the inky blackness of his eyes...' said Agatha dramatically.

'They're blue,' pointed out Pru between laughter and gulping in air.

'His inky blue eyes showed all too clearly the signs of his recent drinking and...' Agatha paused for dramatic effect before slapping the palm of one hand in another, barking in a voice of scandalised piety, 'wenching.'

Pru fell of her chair at this point. This is how the gentlemen found them when they entered the room, led by John Parrish. A look of concern crossed his face.

'My dear, are you unwell?'

The peeling laughter was an answer to this question if not a very satisfactory one. Parrish rolled his eyes but was relieved to see that both Tommy and de Courcy were amused by the evident merriment in the room. Pru recovered her composure and her position on the seat rather than the ground.

'Agatha is incorrigible,' warned Pru looking pointedly at de Courcy. Then she noted that Eustace was not with them. 'Where is Eustace?'

'Oh, he's with Inspector Banks and the prisoners,' replied Parrish. 'You know what Eustace is like.'

Agatha did not although she also would like to have been with the detective and the men she'd helped capture. Their story seemed much more interesting than the likely limits to conversation that would be imposed by the arrival of the men. Conversation between women was always of a wholly different character to that between men and women. Agatha found the latter constraining. Men often took centre stage and directed the conversation between excessive flattery on the one hand and barely concealed conceit on the other. She would have much preferred to have time to catch up with an old and dear friend. Perhaps after lunch.

A gong sounded in the corridor, and everyone rose before there was time to watch the male stags verbally rutting with one another to establish some sort of ridiculous precedence in their own minds if not exactly in those for whom the display was intended. The three ladies were each escorted by one of the men into the dining room. Agatha found herself being led by de Courcy.

'May I,' asked de Courcy, a smile shimmering on his lips.

Agatha decided that the inky blue eyes deserved at least some attention. They walked through to the large dining room of Campbell Hall. The view over the Fens was spectacular, although it also represented a reminder of the dangers of walking too far away from the forest. Equestrian scenes adorned the walls of variable quality which ranged between inept to preposterous, in Agatha's estimation. Many of the artists had clearly never seen a horse before: they seemed more like giraffes than the beautiful animals that Agatha so adored.

A quick scan of the table suggested that eight places had been laid. Agatha's arithmetic would have given Newton a run for his money, and she quickly glanced at Pru. Eustace appeared at this point and introductions were made. Eustace appeared to know everyone except de Courcy. John Parrish took Eustace over to de Courcy who was sitting beside Agatha.

'Have you met my great friend, de Courcy?'

Eustace and de Courcy shook hands, but there was a notable coolness between the men. Eustace immediately took his place on the other side of Agatha. The battle lines had been drawn it seemed. Agatha steeled herself for a siege from both sides.

Except Eustace then chose to ignore Agatha throughout the light lunch and spoke only with Pru and Parrish. He appeared to know them rather well if their laughter was anything to go by. Sausage had angled for and achieved a seat beside Thomas. They became engrossed in conversation to the exclusion of the rest of the table. Such was the level of affection for them that any contravention of social etiquette was happily overlooked by all. This left Agatha with no option but to engage in conversation with de Courcy.

'How do you know Pru and John?' asked Agatha, trying her best to show interest.

'We're cousins but we were also at school together,' said de Courcy. 'Neither of us had a title, at least John didn't then, anyway we've always been good friends. My father is in business. I shall join him. Shipping.'

'Like Mr March?' asked Agatha, suddenly very interested. Pru's father was called March and also in shipping.

'Indeed,' smiled de Courcy. Agatha was once more struck by both the evenness and the whiteness of his teeth. There was an attractive crinkle at the sides of his eyes. The man was unquestionably attractive with self-confidence radiating from every pore and just enough arrogance to make him interesting but not repellent. 'Yes my father and he are both in shipping albeit in different areas. They are good friends.'

'Did you know Pru?'

'I did, yes. She's an old friend too. In fact, I believe I can claim some credit in introducing her to Beefy.'

This was, of course, where Agatha had been heading. The man before her was charming, good looking and clearly a gentleman. In fact the only person who could rival him for looks was the man that Pru had married. Yet, Agatha wondered why she'd chosen John Parrish over de Courcy.

'If you are wondering why she and I...?'

'I was,' admitted Agatha, eyes narrowed in shrewd appraisal.

The smile on de Courcy's face grew wider and he appeared to redden slightly.

'I must admit that in my younger days I was a little immature,' said de Courcy in response.

'I think I understand. Do you have no regrets about missing out on Pru? I can see why many men would fall in love with her.'

'Many did,' laughed de Courcy.

'I remember all too well,' replied Agatha, also laughing.

'Beefy had more sense than I did. I'm very happy for them both and I can assure you, Lady Agatha, there are no regrets on my part.'

This seemed a genuine response to Agatha and the subject was dropped with tacit consent. Much to her surprise, she found de Courcy much less arrogant than she'd thought he would be. The lunch passed off without unnecessary flattery from him or undue modesty from Agatha. In fact, it went rather quickly, for, all too soon, Parrish was suggesting the men retire and leave the ladies to chat. No doubt the men think they can talk about business and the issues of the day, thought Agatha sourly, while the ladies discussed puppies, hats and crochet. Thankfully, Pru suggested a walk. It had stopped snowing, the sun was out and while it was far from warm, a stout pair of shoes and a warm coat would more than suffice.

The guests exited the dining room and spent a few minutes watching the servants, including Polly, helping put Christmas decorations on the tree before parting. She seemed to be enjoying the attention of two young footmen if Agatha wasn't mistaken. Perhaps a word would be appropriate to Pru to ensure that nothing untoward happened. However, was she being fair? Why shouldn't Polly enjoy being noticed? Before she had time to settle the manner in her own mind she realised there was no time to reflect on such matters. The ladies went to change for the expedition while the gentlemen went to the billiards room.

A few minutes later, Agatha, Sausage and Pru, suitably attired, went to the library which opened out to the lawn at the back. It was a large room with books virtually floor to ceiling. Agatha had every intention of returning after the walk to peruse the collection. Pru grinned at her friend and said, 'I'll take you on a tour later.'

The three friends walked out through the French doors, onto the patio. This led down to a small lawn which was enclosed by a hedge with a wrought-iron gate. They followed Pru's footsteps and crunched through the snow which was shin deep in some places. The ground underfoot slowly transformed from snow to ice to mud.

'A bit like good King Wenceslas,' observed Sausage to her friends' amusement as they walked in a line.

Pru held the gate open for her friends and waited for them to pass. Sausage was the first through. She stopped dead in her tracks causing Agatha to bump into her.

'I say,' said Sausage, her eyes wide with something approaching fear.

Agatha moved around her and noted the look on her face. Then she turned to look at the sight that had so disturbed Sausage.

'Good Lord,' said Agatha.

9

'You have a lot of beehives,' said Agatha.

The group had stepped through the gate and stared at the wide, white expanse before them. A hundred yards further up ahead were some trees and a tall, well-maintained hedge marking the boundary of the lawn. In the centre was a fountain with a pathway leading up to and then encircling it. The pathway had obviously been cleared by the staff earlier as everything either side was covered with a thick white pillow of snow. Immediately in front of them, stood around ten beehives.

Pru turned and stared at her two friends who were obviously in shock. She was evidently concerned although Agatha had noted a shadow on her friend's face earlier.

'Is everything all right? You look like you've seen a ghost.'

'I wasn't expecting beehives,' continued Agatha. Sausage had been struck dumb by the sight. Both felt an unsettling chill descend on them which Pru sensed. She raised her eyebrows in the hope that it may prompt an explanation to the sudden bout of anxiety that had assailed both her friends.

'Do you have a problem with bees?' asked Pru. 'They're quite safe. Probably snoozing.'

Agatha and Sausage glanced sceptically at Pru who promptly began to chuckle. Few things were guaranteed to raise Agatha's temperature gauge more than the feeling that she looked foolish. Rather than stay facing the rather ominous sight of the beehives she nodded her head in a direction that might well have been Japan for all she cared. She just wanted to get well away from the frankly terrifying vision of the bee colonies.

Sausage, for once, was quick on the uptake and immediately began to walk, followed swiftly by Agatha then Pru. As she walked, Agatha made a mental note to castigate Eustace when she returned to the house. She had no doubt that he had somehow engineered this although how, was a matter that was up for debate. She recalled the butler Jolly and his evident likeness to the character Padgett from the story.

Once they were well away from the beehives, Pru inquired, 'Now, would you mind telling me what is going on?'

Agatha told her.

Pru's laughter split the silence, followed soon by that of Agatha and then Sausage. When she had recovered the power of speech, Pru said, 'Am I to assume we shall have to return by a different route when we've finished our tour?'

Sausage answered for Agatha and herself, 'Rather.'

They started skirting the edge of the hedge around where the beehives were located when they saw Thomas Pilbream taking a little bit of air.

'Isn't that Tommy?' asked Pru, knowing full well that it was. She glanced meaningfully towards Agatha, who needed no second invitation.

'Yes, Pru, I believe it is. I'm sure he'd love some company. Don't you think Sausage?'

'Oh. Do you?' asked Sausage guilelessly.

Agatha's 'yes' in response to this was a tad firmer than she'd intended but thankfully Sausage was more than happy to accede. She bounded, there's no other way of describing her gait, like a young gazelle seeking its mummy after being cruelly dumped by a stag.

'I say, Tommy,' shouted Sausage, waving.

A delighted smile crossed her quarry's face, and he waved back. Agatha's feelings at that moment were decidedly more mixed. On the one hand she was delighted that her friend may at long last have found love. On the other, she acted in a manner that Aunt Daphne would have heartily approved of. This was not what worried her, though. More perturbing was that she had *enjoyed* her role in facilitating the reunion.

'Poor Sausage,' said Pru. 'I do so hope Tommy is the right one for her."

They stopped and looked at their two friends smiling at one another, each swaying a little from side to side. Agatha turned and looked archly at Pru.

'Are you a betting woman?'

Pru grinned and they turned away to return to the house. She took Agatha's arm. For a few moments there was silence then Agatha spoke.

'Is something on your mind Pru? Your invitation was welcome and overdue, I might add. But I sensed something in what you wrote.'

They continued while Agatha waited for her friend to respond. Pru took a deep breath.

'You're right Agatha. Something is worrying John. I didn't take any heed of it, it's an old wives' tale, but John...' Pru paused at that moment, before continuing, 'Well, John takes things a lot more seriously than I.'

Agatha knew this to be true. Pru had been a notorious practical joker at school thanks to having older brothers who supplied her with all manner of trick items that made her teachers' lives a misery.

'What's wrong?'

Once more, Pru paused. This time she was evidently fighting not anxiety, but embarrassment. Perhaps both, thought Agatha. Anxiety and embarrassment often live alongside one another like bad neighbours.

'There's a legend about the Campbell family who originally built the house. I think it was the third person to inherit the title was the first not to be a Campbell. There was no male issue from the previous title holder. This caused a ruckus after the old boy died, about who should become the next Lord Recton. Anyway, they found some young man, a distant relative and he duly took the title.'

Agatha listened intently. They had stopped outside the house. Vapour surrounded them from their breathing.

'Within six months he was dead,' announced Pru unexpectedly.

'Good Lord,' exclaimed Agatha. 'What happened?'

'They say he died of fright.'

Agatha's eyes widened and then she did the most Agatha thing that Pru would have imagined. She burst out laughing.

'Did the old boy come back and haunt him?' asked Agatha when her hilarity had subsided.

'Well, yes,' said Pru, slightly put out to have the denouement filched by her smart friend.

Agatha sensing that, not for the first time in her life, she may have been a little too dismissive said, 'But why would they think such a thing?'

'The ghostly light.'

Agatha had to fight to stop herself laughing once more. However, she reserved the right to remain sceptical. She achieved this through her favourite ploy of arching one eyebrow. Friends knew what this meant.

'I know it sounds ridiculous, but you must come and see something with me.'

The two ladies returned via the entrance they'd exited from not half an hour earlier and went through the drawing room into a corridor that lead to the games room. There was quite a lot of raucous laugher coming from the room, which suggested that the conviviality had continued apace following lunch.

The corridor was wood panelled with small paintings on each side leading to the end where a portrait of a beautiful young woman hung.'

'She was the widow of David Telford, the young man I was telling you about.'

'What became of her?'

'She married the man who inherited after his death.'

'She came with the castle, did she?' observed Agatha drily.

Even Pru, who was obviously a little uneasy, had to laugh at her friend's typically gallows humour. They were standing in front of a rather odd painting that Agatha's friend, James Whistler, would have described as a nocturne. It showed Campbell Hall at night. The only illumination in the picture was a strange light that seemed a little too low in the sky to be the moon. The work was unsigned, but there was a small, engraved plate with the name of the artist and the painting. The artist was called Renato Lima. Agatha squinted to see the name of the painting which was written in a cursive font so beloved by schoolchildren in the country. She raised her eyebrows when she had finally deciphered it. It read: *The Ghost Light*. The frame and the plate both looked new.

Pru led her towards the games room after Agatha had studied the picture for a few moments. She opened the door and peered in. John Parrish and de Courcy were playing a game of billiards. A half empty bottle of brandy was perched dangerously on the side of the table.

'I see everyone is well,' said Pru archly, but not harshly. 'Where is Eustace?'

'He went down to see the detective chappy again. You know what Eustace is like,' said Parrish with a shrug.

Pru plainly did and chuckled. Meanwhile, de Courcy looked as if he were about to belch so the two ladies politely withdrew to allow the men the freedom to express themselves more freely when not constrained by the sensitive natures of women folk.

'Shall we go down to the dungeon?' asked Pru.

'Lead on Macduff.'

They descended a narrow staircase that led to the servant's quarters which was the first floor on one side of the hill, but a lower ground floor when viewed from the front entrance of the castle. There was one more flight of stairs that did indeed lead to a dungeon of sorts. It imprisoned many wine bottles and might also have been described as a cellar. There was a small storage room which adjoined the cellar. It had been converted into a makeshift accommodation for the two men while arrangements were made to ensure they completed the next stage of their journey. To prison.

The door leading to the cellar was locked, but soon opened after Pru gave it a jolly good rap. It took another minute before the door squeaked open. The two ladies were greeted by Eustace and Inspector Banks, both of whom gave every appearance of having sampled some of the contents of the cellar if the open wine bottle was any guide. Banks reddened as he noted the direction of travel of Agatha's eyes. Eustace was unrepentant, however.

'Don't worry Lady Agatha, our prisoners are safely locked away.'

'I don't doubt we can rest easily in our beds at night with two such diligent gaolers,' noted Agatha, drily.

The tone appeared to amuse Eustace, but he felt under no obligation to respond. This vexed Agatha who was itching to rile the man. She chose another tack.

'You seem to be spending an inordinate amount of time, Lord Eustace, supporting Inspector Banks' efforts. I must congratulate you on your sense of civic duty.'

Oddly, a shadow appeared on Eustace's face, but not one, judged Agatha, that suggested anger. Even the policeman seemed perturbed but remained tight-lipped. They exchanged glances without responding. Few things were guaranteed to pique the curiosity of Agatha more than the sense that something was being held back from her. She went on the attack.

'Are we interrupting something? I have a feeling that you men are keeping something back. Our prisoners haven't escaped, have they?'

'Oh no, Lady Agatha,' replied Eustace, but his look of discomfort was all too plain.

By now Agatha was on the point of strangling Eustace. He was obviously hiding something, and she was desperate to know what it was. She turned to Pru and with a voice that was an octave shy of being shrill. She said, 'Well, the gentlemen plainly do not want us here and have important business that they wish to discuss away from the fragile sensibilities of we weak females.'

The acid dripping from her voice might have burned through stone. Of course, she instantly regretted this acerbity as she saw a hurt expression on Eustace. At least she knew he could be reached, but perhaps a gentler way of doing so would have been preferable. The two ladies began to withdraw from the cellar.

'I'm sorry if it appears we are holding back Lady Agatha,' said Eustace as she turned to leave. 'It's just that I had a police matter to discuss with the inspector. I did not want to trouble you with something that is possibly a figment of an overactive imagination.'

Agatha and Pru turned back to the two men. This was an olive branch and Agatha was not the sort of person to ignore it.

'I do not claim to be a member of the police force Lord Eustace, but I have recently provided some help on a case which you may be familiar with.'

Inspector Banks looked surprised at this. He asked her, 'Which case was this?'

'I helped Mr Whicher and our mutual friend James Simpson capture Black-Eyed Nick. I imagine you're familiar with the case.'

This resulted in a number of 'Good Lords' from both mean and a 'fancy that' from Eustace which was gilding the lily slightly in Agatha's book when he knew fine well. Banks was clearly aware of the case although ignorant of her role in its successful resolution. Eustace winked at Agatha to suggest that he'd engineered it all along. If Agatha was receptive to olive branches, she was even quicker to strike when the proverbial iron was at its hottest. She briefly mentioned her role in the affair, impressing the detective with her friendship with the legendary Whicher and the chief of detectives, Dolly Williamson. The happy result of this disclosure was an immediate willingness for her to be included in the confidence of the policeman.

'I must preface what I say,' began Eustace, 'by saying that this may just be a fancy of mine with no basis in reality.'

Agatha nodded in a manner that suggested she understood this and would you please make your way at great haste to the point.

'You are aware of my hobby in relation to a publication which relates tales that have a popular following with the public?'

'You write for penny bloods?' exclaimed Pru in delighted shock. She began to chuckle. 'Why Eustace, you are a man of many accomplishments?'

'All too modest, Pru,' replied Eustace, modestly. 'A few months ago I published one of my stories, '*The Murder Most Foul of William Pigg*.'

'I read that,' interrupted Agatha. She'd enjoyed it too although she was not prepared to admit this.

'Have you read my other tale, '*The Death of a Daemon*'

'I have,' said Agatha, finding herself dangerously impressed with the writing skills of the man before her.

'Well, Lady Agatha, the matter to which I wanted to speak to the good inspector relates to these two tales. Did you perchance see the newspaper headlines on the way to the station yesterday afternoon?'

'Yes,' replied Agatha. 'The murder of the man accused of murdering two women.' Agatha paused for a moment and then her eyes widened. 'When was your story published?'

'Four months ago.'

Agatha paused for a moment to recollect the story. It was a story of revenge that bore an uncanny resemblance to the recent murder of Titus Mourdock, a known criminal accused of murder. The other story about the murder of a man named William Pigg also reminded her of another recent murder, a banker named Augustus Fitch.

'When did you publish your story about William Pigg?'

'Three months ago.'

Agatha did not have make much of an effort to recall the details of the two crimes. She and Betty had corresponded on both at great length. She missed her friend. Betty would have put together a scrapbook of newspaper cuttings related to the crimes. They would pour over the details of the gruesome events with a relish that was decidedly unladylike. No longer though. Such analysis was confined to their weekly letters to one another. It wasn't the same.

'Are you suggesting that the murders of Augustus Fitch and Titus Mourdock are somehow related to the stories that you published, Lord Eustace?'

'I can scarcely bring myself to admit as much but, yes, Lady Agatha; I have entertained the possibility and discussed it with Inspector Banks.'

The two women turned to Inspector Banks. It appeared that the detective was treating the matter with all due seriousness. This surprised Agatha, but then she realised that Eustace had just published a third story: the one she'd read on the train.

A chill descended on her as she thought once more about the ghostly beehives on the snowy lawn. She tried to shrug the thought from her mind, but it was lodged there now. From somewhere in the cellar she heard a humming sound. They all looked around however they could not locate the source. But Agatha knew what it was she'd heard.

It was a bee.

10

Agatha and Pru made their way out of the cellar with a haste that confused the two men. On the way out, in fact at the door, Agatha offered to give the case her consideration. Eustace's acceptance of the offer was met by an empty doorway and the sound of the two womens' footsteps running up the stairs. When they reached the top of the stairs, Agatha turned to Pru.

'An interesting case.'

'Yes,' agreed Pru. 'Am I to take it you heard the buzzing?'

Agatha nodded and then the two ladies burst out into giggles. When she'd first heard it, a suspicion had lurked in Agatha, that it was Eustace. But unless his talents as a ventriloquist matched his not inconsiderable ability with the pen, then it seemed improbable. Yet the idea of a bee in the cellar in the middle of winter was incredible. The two ladies were in accord that tea was in order. Its presence denoted by the teapot hidden under a flowered tea cosy, the mere act of pouring it, of tasting it in combination with a teacake, represented a lifeline to normality. After the shocks of the last hour, both needed its reassuring balm to confirm that they were not going out of their wits.

They retired to the drawing room where tea and teacakes were ordered and delivered with a genial absence of dignity by Jolly the butler which made Agatha relax even more. Pru poured the tea, and they gazed out of the window to the glistening whiteness. The snow had stopped falling and the view was undisturbed except by the sight of Sausage who appeared suddenly, gambolling towards them with tears in her eyes.

'Oh, I wonder what's upset Sausage,' said Pru.

Agatha had no doubt what had upset her dear friend. She felt a wave of anger gush through her in the manner of the oilwells she'd recently read about in Pico Canyon. Both ladies set their teacups down to wait for their friend to open, or burst through, the French doors. At her current rate of knots it was a close-run thing as to which it would be.

Thankfully, Sausage slowed down as she approached the doors thus ensuring a less dramatic entrance. She collapsed on the sofa beside Pru and promptly began to cry unconsolably. The sympathetic shoulders needed at that moment were duly supplied, comforting words dispensed, and tea imbibed. Finally, Sausage was in a position to share what had caused such un-Sausage-like upset.

'Tommy and I met at Betty's wedding. It was your Aunt Daphne who introduced us, Agatha. She's so sweet,' said Sausage, dabbing her eyes.

Mischievous wench, thought Agatha, but not without amusement. Aunt Daphne, having pretended to give Agatha up as a bad job, had decided that marrying her friends off would leave her so isolated that she would have to consider joining that particular club or risk the loneliness and social ignominy of spinsterhood. When she thought about it, its genius was all too apparent. Agatha was inclined to think better of her aunt for such outright deviousness.

'Well, we rather hit it off I think. He's jolly nice. We corresponded a few times,' added Sausage before taking more tea and wiping her nose. 'Then we met up at a few events in London. Anyway, I rather took the idea that he liked me.'

Sausage coloured at this point which led Agatha to conclude that this affection had moved beyond mere words.

'I thought we were soon going to reach an understanding if you know what I mean.'

Both ladies did. Such was their nature that both smiled and joined their friend in shedding tears at the same time.

'Anyway, we were just out in the garden a few minutes ago and, well, he tells me he loves me.'

Now Sausage was not one of those ladies who cry when they are happy and cry when they are sad which is often to the confusion and consternation of men who prefer their emotions to be easily verifiable. No, Sausage smiled or laughed gaily when she was happy and cried when she was sad. What she lacked in complexity she more than made up for in a winningly gentle disposition which was loved by all who were lucky enough to call her a friend.

Agatha and Pru leaned forward as they waited for the punchline to this story. For once, it seemed, Sausage was going to relate a story all the way through from definitive beginning, by way of a relevant middle, towards an end without any needless circumnavigation to incidental observations or reflections.

'Anyway, he's just told me that his father, the earl, is demanding that he find a career.'

Agatha and Pru sat back with a little relief. This seemed an entirely reasonable request. There were too many shiftless younger sons, idling about in their clubs to no great benefit to themselves, their families or society. Agatha was on the point of sharing this point when Sausage began to speak again.

'That would be fine ordinarily, but the earl wants him to join the army. He thinks it will make a man of Tommy. He wants him to go to South Africa or India. Immediately.'

This was a problem, conceded Agatha. The Earl of Gowster had three sons one of whom would inherit, the other was in the army, albeit posted in the wilds of Kensington and now Tommy would be forced to do something altogether riskier and almost certainly beyond his capability.

'Yes, I can see the problem,' agreed Agatha. 'Tell me, has Tommy expressed any inclination to find a career to his father?'

'No.'

'I see. Well is he qualified to join a profession. Medicine, for instance?'

'He can't stand the sight of blood.'

'Has he any aptitude for business?'

'He's not good with money.'

'Could he lecture at a university?'

'He feels uncomfortable speaking in public.'

Agatha was beginning to run out of options for Tommy, so she went with the most obvious option which she'd hoped to avoid.

'What about the church?'

'Well, he is sweet, but I rather think he'd find sermons a challenge.'

'Oh yes, the public speaking. I forgot,' acknowledged Agatha. Realising that this could take forever, she changed tack. 'What are his interests?'

'He read history at college.'

'That's good. Anything in particular pique his interest?'

'Well, he likes reading about these finds of dinosaur bones.'

'Perhaps he could find a backbone,' muttered Agatha under her breath.'

'Sorry?' asked Sausage.

'Oh nothing, just thinking out loud. Look, leave this with me Sausage. I shall have a think about what you've said. I'm sure that there's something we can come up with that can spike the earl's guns so to speak and keep Tommy in the country near those who care for him.'

'Oh Agatha, do you think?'

Agatha smiled encouragingly, which brought something of the old Sausage back. Sausage had a number of firm principles which she believed in steadfastly. It was an article of faith to her that Agatha was the smartest person she would ever meet. That being so, a problem shared with Agatha was merely a solution waiting to happen.

This was sufficient reassurance for Sausage to join them in taking tea. One question did occur to Agatha, but it took a few moments to frame it in a manner that would not offend her friend.

'Of course, Tommy is keen not to join the army,' said Agatha pouring the tea.

'I admire him greatly, Agatha, but he is somewhat short-sighted, he hasn't a violent bone in his body, and he never surfaces before ten in the morning.'

'Admirably qualified for senior command,' said Agatha. Sausage looked worried for a moment before realising that Agatha was joking. She was a little too on edge to enjoy such jesting, so Agatha wisely foreswore any further comments of a light-hearted nature.

Talleyrand woke up from an uncomfortable slumber that had seen him being chased by sheep. He pootled over to

Agatha in the hope of a morsel or three. None was forthcoming so he turned to Sausage. Quite why he hadn't gone there in the first place he couldn't fathom for moments later he was happily eating a little piece of teacake much to his owner's annoyance.

Agatha stood up and walked over to the French doors. Talleyrand followed her progress unhappily. This could not be helped, of course. Mother Nature had bestowed upon him a rather doleful face. Obediently, he trotted over and followed Agatha's pointed finger outside into the cold. It had been pleasantly warm inside, but he accepted that he probably needed to have a breath of fresh air and everything else besides.

The door shut behind him and he trotted off along a route rather similar to that taken by Agatha earlier. He made his way through the gate and arrived at the lawn containing the beehives. The white structures meant nothing to him, so he pressed on towards the outer hedge. At this point he heard a sound that chilled him to the bone.

Barking. Loud, angry, barking.

Specifically, the barking of the evil-looking German Shepherd he'd seen earlier. It was growing louder and louder. This was something of a fix. He wasn't sure whether to return to the house or find a safe refuge or vantage point from which he could control matters. He chose the latter and shot past the beehives towards the fountain. Arriving at the fountain he hopped up on the perimeter wall just in time to see the malign black and brown form bounding towards him in a decidedly unfriendly manner.

Talleyrand had much in common with his namesake that went beyond a shared nationality. He was as wily as an old fox who ran advanced courses in guile. Not moving, he watched as the evil canine approached him at an impressive velocity.

Around ten feet from the fountain, the German Shepherd launched himself at Talleyrand. The Basset hound eyed the snarling assassin flying through the air towards him. This was the moment for which he'd been waiting. He hopped down just in time to leave his pursuer hurtling through time and space, teeth bared, directly into the pool around the fountain. He landed in the ice-cold water with a plaintive yelp.

The pool wasn't deep, but it was icy. The hairy beast, weighed down by his coat, could not extricate himself from his predicament. Talleyrand calmly put his head over the rim of the fountain to check on his handiwork. Satisfied, he trotted away, past the beehives, to the gate to alert everyone.

Inside the house, Agatha tried to ignore the barking of Talleyrand, but in the end began to worry there was a problem. She went to the French doors and saw her Talleyrand at the gate barking. Agatha waved him in. The hound remained unmoved. She waved once more, this time accompanying it with, 'Come in boy.'

Talleyrand stayed where he was. With growing irritation, Agatha stalked forward. In a more urgent voice she said, 'Come in. Now.'

Normally this would do the trick. Not this time. Talleyrand was not for shifting. It began to dawn on Agatha that perhaps there was a problem. Had he been hurt? She trotted forward with concern on her face. Behind her she could hear Pru and Sausage asking what the problem was. When they saw Agatha running they, too, began running into the garden.

As Agatha approached the gate, Talleyrand rose from the ground, stopped barking and began to trot away from her. This angered Agatha for a number of reasons. She thought he was playing games and, worse, was about to lead her back towards the horrible beehives. Then she heard a yelping that was definitely not Talleyrand.

'That's Bismarck,' shouted Pru, who now began to pick up the pace along with Sausage. The former players from 'the Invincibles' could shift when the occasion demanded, and this was just such a moment. Up ahead they saw Talleyrand by the fountain and Bismarck splashing around yelping.

A minute later the ladies helped the shivering spawn of Satan from the fountain. Pru put her shawl around him and began to pat his thick coat in an attempt to dry him.

'You poor thing, Bismarck,' said Pru. Bismarck was whimpering from a combination of fear and cold. Meanwhile Sausage knelt beside Talleyrand and gave him a cuddle.

'You are a clever boy, Talleyrand. Did you see that? He alerted us to his friend's difficulties.'

Pru patted the hound on the head. He was the hero of the day, no question. Talleyrand looked like it was all in a day's work. Hopefully, a reward would be forthcoming soon.

'Clever boy,' said Pru. She glanced up at Agatha, a look of gratitude in her eyes.

Only Agatha was less effusive in her acclaim. She looked at the Basset archly. Talleyrand looked back at her with his usual lugubrious expression. The one thought running through Agatha's mind was how Bismarck had ended up in the fountain. A part of her suspected that Talleyrand was responsible. Proving this, of course, would be nigh on impossible; Talleyrand would never let on.

Having saved the day and received a fair amount of commendation from the ladies, Talleyrand decided to make his exit. Country houses, from his experience, were usually home to plenty of dogs.

It was time to go in search of some four-legged fun.

11

The ladies helped carry the German Shepherd back towards the house. As they did so, a man dressed in working clothes approached them. He was tall, rangy, with weather-beaten skin that suggested he could be anywhere between forty and seventy. Hard grey eyes assessed the dog.

'Your ladyship, what's the matter with Bismarck?'

This question had probably been asked many times in diplomatic circles, but probably not in relation to a water-logged German Shepherd.

'Mason, just the man,' said Pru. 'Bismarck has had a bit of an accident. He fell in the fountain. Had it not been for Lady Agatha's dog he might have perished. Can you take him somewhere and warm him up?'

Mason took the dog in his arms as if he were carrying a pillow. It had taken two ladies at a time to carry him. He headed off with long, unhurried strides in the direction of a stone shed which lay fifty yards to the left of the house.

'That's Mason, our gardener. He's been with the house since before we came.'

'Certainly strong,' observed Sausage. 'He lifted poor Bismarck like he was a puppy.'

The ladies returned to the house feeling a little bit more reassured that the dog was in good hands. After such a traumatic experience more tea was required to calm nerves and restore warmth to mind and body.

After this, Agatha decided to retire to the library to peruse the impressive collection of books. Pru had mentioned that this was where she kept her collection of Penny Dreadfuls. Husband, John, was an equally avid enthusiast for this literature. Agatha went through the pile of magazines until she found the two that she wanted: '*The Murder Most Foul of William Pigg*' and '*The Death of a Daemon*'. She noted the author's name was, indeed, Eustace Frost.

She settled down to read through the two stories. The time passed quickly as the stories gripped her. There was no question, Eustace had a way with a story and an original, if rather macabre, mind. She'd enjoyed the stories very much. Worryingly, she could see the parallels with the two murders that Eustace had brought to the attention of Inspector Banks.

Given the subject matter, it was always possible that the similarity was merely an unfortunate coincidence. This could not be discounted, yet Agatha's mind was already whirling with the possibility of a connection. If only Betty were here. She was much more rigorous in capturing the cuttings from the newspapers as well as having a wonderful memory for the detail of the crimes they read about. She was the perfect foil to Agatha's flights of fancy on how the crimes were committed and who was responsible.

Outside, night had fallen without Agatha realising how long she'd been engrossed in the stories. The butler, Jolly, made an appearance to inquire if she needed anything. This was the first time she'd seen him on his own.

'You haven't changed Mr Jolly,' said Agatha, setting down her book.

'I hope wiser Lady Agatha, but it is very kind of you to say.'

'I'm sure it was a wrench to leave the March household after so many years,' continued Agatha. She liked Jolly and suspected the feeling was mutual.

'It was, but Lord March felt that Lady Prudence would benefit, and I was certainly not going to argue.'

There was a moment of silence between them. A shadow seemed to pass over the butler's face. Then Agatha remembered something; something important.

'Forgive me for asking Mr Jolly but...'

Jolly nodded. The smile remained as it always did, but there was a sadness in his eyes.

'Yes, your ladyship. I lost my wife two years ago; just after our fortieth anniversary. *Married in July with flowers ablaze, bitter-sweet memories in after days*, they say.'

Agatha reached out and took the old butler's hand and said, 'I'm sorry for your loss. It was inconsiderate of me not to realise.'

Jolly shook his head, a little overcome by Agatha's reaction to the news. Then Agatha squeezed his hand and added, 'Perhaps you were happy to come here Mr Jolly. I believe you would have missed Lady Prudence greatly.'

The old butler smiled at this and perhaps even a tear appeared in his eye.

'I was very happy to follow her ladyship. Yes, it was a wrench to leave. So many memories. I am delighted to be able to be with her still and his lordship too. If I may say, he is a fine young man.'

Almost to herself, Agatha said, 'They seem very happy.'

Jolly was too old a hand at his profession and too loyal to his employer to respond in any other way than an affectionate smile. Then, in a moment which was probably as unprofessional as it was human, he replied, 'It's always a pleasure to see you and Lady Jocelyn. It has been a great source of contentment to Lord and Lady March that Lady Prudence has such good friends.'

Agatha knew that he was speaking as much for himself as his former employer. This was typically self-effacing of Jolly, and she liked him all the more for it.

Jolly turned to stoke the fire a little which added warmth to the room before leaving Agatha to her ruminations. She thought about reading another story from one of the other magazines but knew it would be pointless. Her mind was too absorbed in finding parallels between the other two stories.

If there was a connection between the crimes and the stories then they were indeed fortunate that Eustace was not a prolific contributor to penny dreadful magazines. She tried to remember when the most recent story had been published. She had a feeling that it had come out just in the last week because she had not seen a copy delivered to her house. Clearly there had been no new death associated with the stories but given the recency of the publication and the time of year, then this was to be expected.

She glanced out of the window into the purplish glow of the snow on the ground. Somewhere out there were the beehives. It was interesting that the mere thought of them prompted a coldness within her, thanks to Eustace's rather effective ghost story. She tried to shrug off the thought, but it was insistent and would not leave. Was there a risk to any of them of suffering a fate similar to Dennistoun given their proximity to beehives rather like the ones described in the story?

The door opened at this point nearly causing Agatha to jump from her seat. She looked up to see de Courcy enter a trifle unsteadily at first before he realised that he had an audience, a female audience. He straightened up in the way most men do when they believe that women aren't noticing. His gait became steadier, and his eyes took on a heroic glint that had been certainly absent over the previous couple of hours spent playing brandy and drinking billiards – or was it the other way around?

'Lady Agatha, I hope I am not disturbing you?'

'No,' lied Agatha. Sober, he was quite an impressive sight to behold and enjoy for a young woman. Some of this lustre diminishes for women when the object of their attention is displaying less elan as a consequence of overindulgence with alcohol. This applies doubly when they try to disguise matters. It rarely works. There was an honesty to Eustace's lack of sobriety at James and Betty's wedding that, if not admirable, was at least authentic.

The young gentleman rather fell into the Chesterfield armchair opposite Agatha. He smiled gamely.

'I gather your hound was the saviour of that wild animal of Beefy and Pru's.'

Agatha, as related earlier, had an intuition that far from being the saviour he was, in fact, responsible for the situation. She refrained from praising Talleyrand too much. He was still in her bad books from their last visit to a country house. Apparently not one but two litters of puppies were the result of his unfettered access to the female canine residents. Thankfully, Pru had been warned and now anything remotely likely to attract his romantic interest was safely barricaded away.

'How is Bismarck?' asked Agatha. 'Have you seen him?'

'Oh yes. He's up and about and decidedly less fearsome. I wonder what happened?'

Agatha, deciding that this was not a subject she wanted explored to any degree, steered him on to other topics.

'Has John been telling you about the "ghost light" at all?'

This caused de Courcy a great deal of amusement. His laughter was good-natured which redeemed him a little in Agatha's eyes.

'That old chestnut? Yes, I'd heard. I think it's genuinely affected John and Pru. Part of me thinks that's why we've all been invited. I hear tell that you are rather a dab hand at detective work, Lady Agatha.'

An older Agatha would have taken such flattery with a pinch of a salt mine. The younger incarnation recognised it for what it was, but still, de Courcy was very good looking and there was a crookedness to that smile which she knew better than to fall for but was still worth enjoying in its own right.

'You are a sceptic then?'

'I am, Lady Agatha, but perhaps this evening we will have a chance to observe the phenomenon for ourselves.'

'What will you do if it appears?'

'John and I certainly, perhaps Lord Eustace and some of the staff, will immediately go out and look for the source of this mystery.'

'Perhaps I shall join you,' said Agatha, as much to herself as de Courcy.

'Then you are either very courageous Lady Agatha...'

'Or a sceptic,' finished Agatha with a smile that surprised de Courcy by how much it turned a handsome woman's face into one that seemed beautiful. It was a smile that could bear repeated viewings, he decided.

*

Dinner was served at eight. It was a Christmas dinner of sorts. Crackers were laid out on the table along with an array of cutlery and glasses that would have confused a cryptographer but would easily be navigated by the upper crust of English society.

They started with Palestine Soup, made with Jerusalem artichokes. This was followed by éntrées of mutton cutlets and poached meat with a rich sauce. The main course was roast turkey. All of this was washed down by a different wine for each course, although Agatha rationed her intake. No such restrictions were observed by the gentlemen who sank glass after glass with Bacchanalian abandon.

Only Tommy and Inspector Banks were more circumspect. The latter had been invited by John Parrish, keen for him to observe the ghostly happenings in the night sky. This was making virtue of a necessity. A messenger from the town had confirmed that no trains were running due to the weather conditions, thus Banks, as well as his prisoners, were stuck for the time being.

The presence of Banks in no way detracted from the conviviality. The inspector proved to be good company and appeared far from intimidated by such elevated company. In fact, suspected Agatha, the inspector would have dismissed the idea that he was among his 'betters'.

Despite the relaxed cordiality of the hosts, Agatha noted how both her friends would, from time to time, glance out of the window in the hope, or perhaps fear, of seeing this ghostly light. By ten o'clock, the lights had not yet appeared and Agatha was beginning to feel once more the effect of a long day and night. She was on the point of retiring when she heard a gasp from Pru. She looked at her friend. Her hand had gone up to her mouth. John Parrish's face seemed to fall. His eyes flickered from his wife to the window. It took a few moments and then the table fell silent. Moments later, everyone was on their feet and heading over to the window.

There, clearly and unmistakably in the night sky was a will-o'-the-wisp ghostly light. It seemed to hover rather than move, blurring in a mist over the marshes.

'Good Lord,' said de Courcy. 'You were right, John.'

Parrish was too shocked to speak. He nodded, but kept his eyes fixed on the terrifying vision in the sky. Agatha stared at the light for a few moments then made her way over to the door to ring the bell for a member of the staff.

Eustace, meanwhile, who had been riveted by what he was seeing said, 'Perhaps we should...'

Then he saw Agatha speaking to Jolly the butler.

'We need hats and coats immediately, please,' said Agatha firmly before adding, 'For everyone. Light some torches, too. You and Fish stay here just in case it is a diversion for some ne'er do wells to come here.'

Eustace approached her and said, 'Are you sure you wish to come Lady Agatha?'

Agatha's expression was somewhere in between scepticism and excitement. She said rather opaquely, 'I wouldn't miss it for the world.'

Nor would Sausage or Pru if she read their expressions correctly. Her tone was enough to dissuade the other gentlemen from pleading with them to stay safe indoors. Minutes later the Christmas party moved from the warmth and conviviality of the dining room into the searing cold of the night air and the menace of the transparent light hovering like an evil spirit preparing to descend upon them and carry them off to the gates of hell.

Or so Eustace said, as they stepped out onto the patio. For his efforts he received a frown of rebuke from Agatha for being guilty of, paradoxically, putting the wind up everybody while not appearing to take very seriously the enterprise upon which they were embarking.

They marched out towards the shed where the unfortunate Bismarck had been taken earlier to recover from his unscheduled dip in the icy water. The path to the shed took them around the perimeter of the lawn where the beehives were located towards a bog that was just outside the boundary of the estate and bordering the small forest.

'On no account move beyond the hedgerow,' warned Parrish to his guests. Agatha considered this unnecessary, she had no intention of venturing beyond the hedge without the support of a battalion of infantry and at least one cannon. By the sound of it Eustace was in no mood either to test the ground that led towards the bog.

'Probably best if we don't get caught in a swamp, I agree,' said Eustace in a light tone which only just disguised his nervousness.

Agatha made a mental note not to allow Talleyrand too free a rein around the estate. He'd already caused one near disaster even if he had redeemed himself in its resolution. The last thing she needed was for him to be lost in a swamp.

The further they ventured from the house, the further the light seemed to be. Then, slowly it sank into the mist and disappeared.

'Looks like we scared it off,' said Eustace to no one's amusement but his own.

They were now standing at the edge of the estate, freezing cold and sobering up at an unfortunate rate of knots. A plan was needed. Inspector Banks came up with one.

'Is there any path through the bog?'

'There is,' said Parrish, 'and I have been through it many times myself, but not at night.'

'Do you think you can take me through it?' asked Banks.

'I can, I'm sure, but the ladies?'

'Will return to the house,' said Agatha firmly.

'I agree,' said Pru. 'It's rather chilly and I don't think you should venture farther either.'

Parrish, however, disagreed. He looked at Banks and said, 'I shall show the inspector, my dear. We cannot continue to live like this.'

'I'll come with you,' offered de Courcy.

The men turned to Eustace who smiled.

'Perhaps I should accompany the ladies back to the house.'

Agatha would have felt safer with the more powerfully built de Courcy but decided against pointing this out.

'Good man,' said Parrish, in a manly way. He then slapped de Courcy on the arm in a manner that might have sent Eustace sprawling.

Agatha and the others turned to walk back. The gentlemen kept their eyes on the women and Eustace for as long as they could before they set off to investigate further the mystery of the light.

The walk back to the house was expedited with a haste not noticeable on the trip out to investigate the vaporous apparition in the sky. One might have been forgiven for thinking that they were glad to return in one piece. Eustace headed straight for the brandy and held it up to the others.

'A few snifters should clear the mind and allow us to sort the old wheat,' he said pouring the first glass.

The ladies needed no second invitation for something to warm them inside. The extent of the cold suffered was such that a second and then a third glass of Napoleon was necessary to restore some semblance of composure to the intrepid group. It was Pru who spoke first. There was more than a hint of triumph on her face as she addressed Agatha.

'Are you still so sceptical? What do you think we saw?'

Agatha felt all eyes upon her.

'A more interesting question for me is how it got there,' replied Agatha in a manner which suggested that she was not yet ready to concede the possibility of otherworldly explanations for the phenomena they had just witnessed. As it was clear Agatha was in one of those moods, the others decided further discussion was useless until the gentlemen returned.

Jolly appeared in the room to ask if the ladies required anything. Sausage was holding the bottle of brandy, so the answer was 'no.' Then Agatha had another thought.

'Could you go down to the prisoners and see if everything is all right with them?'

Pru looked at her friend with concern on her face.

'You don't think?...'

'No, but best to be careful,' replied Agatha. The ghostly light pre-dated their arrival at the house. In no way could it have anticipated the arrival of the two criminals. Something else had to be the cause. 'Take Mr Fish with you, Mr Jolly.'

'Mr Fish has retired for the evening,' said Jolly with just a hint of amiable disdain.

'Very well, I shall join you,' replied Agatha rising from her seat.

The butler was too surprised to say anything and the fixed look on Agatha's face suggested the ladies would be best advised not to argue the point. Jolly bravely followed Agatha down the stairs to the cellar after the butler had retrieved the keys. Without any hesitation, Agatha marched into the cellar. Despite her apparent courage, Agatha was, in fact, feeling distinctly nervous. The events of the evening had not passed without some toll being extracted on her normal composure.

She held out her candle, followed by Jolly and swung her arm gently around to see better into the remotest parts of the cellar. The only thing that perturbed her were the four empty wine bottles which suggested that, for Eustace and Banks, the time before dinner had passed in a companiable fashion.

Moving over to the door of the makeshift cell, she put her ear to the door. She was greeted with the sound of snoring coming from within. Satisfied she nodded to Jolly that it was time to leave. They both turned away and moved back up the stairs. When she reached the great hall, male voices could be heard. The men had returned. This was a relief.

Agatha marched forward and entered the room. She was greeted by the sight of three men. Their clothes muddied, their faces dirty and all registering shock.

'What on earth has happened?' exclaimed Agatha.

'Inspector Banks is missing,' said John Parrish. His face was stained by dirt, with rivulets of perspiration making him resemble an exhausted zebra.

Pru immediately went to Parrish. He put his arm around her protectively. Tommy was too manly at that moment with his unkempt appearance for Sausage to pass up the opportunity to be similarly comforted. Had the situation not been so worrying, Agatha would have congratulated her friend for such an uncharacteristic display of enterprise. As it was, Sausage clinging to Tommy passed without comment as the group decided what to do next.

A tall figure suddenly appeared at the French doors giving everyone a mild fright. It was Mason the gardener. Parrish nodded to the new arrival.

'Good, can you go to Jolly and Mr Fish. They will need to help us find the inspector.'

Agatha caught Eustace's eye at this point. His face looked amused, but then it always did. Agatha suspected he knew that Fish would be less than pleased at being roused from his slumber. At this point, standing there, legs apart, chest out, dark hair matted by perspiration, twigs, looking every inch the romantic hero, de Courcy broke in and said, 'Someone needs to check on our prisoners...' There was a hard glint in his blue eyes.

'I have already done so,' announced Agatha. All eyes turned to her, and a few noises were made about the risk she had taken, but these were waved away. 'Nonsense. Do you need any help in the search?'

'No, Lady Agatha. I think it's best if you and the ladies return to your rooms. Lock the doors as a precaution,' said Parrish. 'Perhaps we should leave one man here just in case.'

'I agree,' said Eustace. 'Fish would be best as he does not know the area as well as Mr Jolly.'

'You're right, Eustace,' acknowledged Parrish and he turned immediately to Jolly who had remained in the room with the others. Nothing on Jolly's face suggested enthusiasm for the venture, but he was clearly concerned for the plight of the inspector. There was more than a trace of admiration from Agatha for the manner in which Eustace had skilfully managed to ease Fish out of doing anything more arduous than somnolence.

'Can you get your coat, light a torch and put on some stout walking boots. We must institute a search,' ordered Parrish. 'Ask the Gooch boys to patrol the area between the house and Little Recton, just in case he has wandered off in the wrong direction.

Jolly skipped out of the room to change while de Courcy and Parrish butted proverbial heads in their efforts to be decisive. Tommy, meanwhile, kept a hold of Sausage in case any intruder should break in suddenly or the lights should go out. Eustace, meanwhile, surreptitiously reached for his brandy glass.

'We should search in groups of two. John, you and Eustace take the area around the east side of the forest. He has to be in there somewhere. That's where we last saw him. I will go with Jolly to the west side; Mason, you take Pilbream and search around the middle. We will meet you there.'

'Agreed,' said Parrish with a stiff nod of the head. 'Are you with us Eustace?'

Eustace was mid sip at this point but managed a nod and an embarrassed smile. He held the glass up.

'Take a little; it'll warm you up,' suggested Eustace.

'Good idea,' said Parrish, decisively.

Good rescue thought Agatha. She was amused, despite herself, by the deft way he'd turned an awkward moment into something resembling a helpful contribution. Not an easy man to catch out. She was beginning to see how such an agile mind would prove valuable when dealing with unfriendly nations in the diplomatic corps.

Eustace did the honours for the men including Mason and Jolly which Agatha thought was a decent touch. After all, the two men were also taking a risk in facing a potentially unknown danger. They drained their glasses then de Courcy snatched one last opportunity to look resolute.

'Ladies, I suggest you immediately retire and lock your rooms.'

Agatha glanced over at Tommy Pilbream who gave every appearance of preferring to stay locked up in a bedroom also. Ideally, with Sausage. However, to his credit he released Sausage to join the others.

The ladies sighed, clutched their hearts and urged the men to be careful. Even Agatha. It was impossible not to be moved by the plight of the police officer. Banks had seemed to be a decent man with a strong sense of duty. Yet Agatha feared greatly for him. This trip was proving to be a series of accidents or incidents. The loss of the other policeman, the ghostly light, the murders that bore a remarkable similarity to Eustace's stories and then Talleyrand's recent heroic rescue of a dog that appeared to have no goodwill towards him.

It was with a troubled heart that Agatha helped Pru lock the French windows and check that the other doors were secure before trudging up to bed. It seemed almost callous to fall into a warm bed while the men were outside in the cold searching for the lost policeman. Yet she recognised that the actions taken by the men were the most that could be expected from them.

She fell asleep the moment her head touched the pillow.

12

Polly woke Agatha the next morning around eight. At first the events of the previous night, days even, seemed like a dream then she saw Polly's face. She was barely out of her teens, pretty as one can only be at this age, yet her face was drawn, and tears had recently filled her eyes.

'What's wrong Polly?' asked Agatha, yet she knew the answer already.

'They found Mr Banks, your ladyship. He's...' Polly couldn't finish the sentence. Agatha was out of her bed immediately to comfort the young girl. A few minutes later, after donning a dressing gown, she came down the stairs to find the house in uproar.

The first person she encountered was Eustace. He was dressed with all the elan of someone who had been locked out in the rain. For a week. His eyes were bloodshot with tiredness, and, like Polly, his face was tight.

'We found Banks.'

'Dead?'

'I'm afraid so.'

'What happened?' asked Agatha. Eustace paused for a moment to consider how exactly he might answer the question. 'Please don't worry about my sensibilities, Lord Eustace. I can assure you I am not prone to fainting fits or anything else you may associate with my sex.'

Eustace shook his head and replied, 'No, I'm sure you are not so weak-minded, Lady Agatha.' He sighed before continuing. 'He appears to have been bashed over the head with a heavy object. He's quite dead.'

'I'm so sorry. The poor man. He seemed a good sort.'

'The very best,' agreed Eustace. He paused for a moment as if unsure of how to say what was on his mind. Agatha immediately read his face. There was something else he hadn't mentioned.

'Where did you find him?' asked Agatha, frowning.

Eustace's eyes had a faraway look. He was seeing an image he knew that he would never see the like of again.

'Where?' said Eustace. Then he fixed his eyes on Agatha answering, 'We found him in the garden draped over one of the tables. His head had been buried in the beehive. The bees took a rather dim view of this.'

Agatha gasped. Someone had arranged the murder to look like the death of Dennistoun in Eustace's story.

'But this is extraordinary,' exclaimed Agatha.

Eustace could not have agreed more at that moment. He nodded his head in mute astonishment. He seemed to be in the middle of a nightmare, but Agatha's mind was whirling too much to notice. Something else had occurred to her.

'The prisoners.'

She turned to go down the stairs when she felt a hand grasp her arm gently.

'They've gone, Lady Agatha. They've escaped.'

*

Breakfast brought two things that Agatha needed badly: tea, and lots of it, too, as well as more information on what had happened during the night when she and the other ladies had retired to their rooms.

'We found him when we all were on our way back from the forest,' explained de Courcy. 'It was Pilbream, who saw him first.'

'Oh Tommy, you poor thing,' said Sausage, grasping the arm of her hero.

Tommy looked like a man who'd seen a ghost and a murdered man on the same evening which, to his mind, he had.

'It was awful Sausage. I shall never forget the sight of his legs dangling out of the beehive; it was awful,' said Tommy. Sausage looked at him in the manner of a woman who intended spending a lifetime to help him overcome this trauma.

Agatha's brain, thanks to the tea, had now gained a firmer foothold on the here and now. Some questions were forming in her mind which needed answers.

'You and Mr Mason found him?' asked Agatha.

'No, I became separated from Mr Mason. I came back on my own. By mistake I came through the lawn with the beehives. I'd forgotten they were there otherwise I'd have gone another way. That's when I came across him. I immediately alerted the others.'

This alert had taken the form of screaming, but even Tommy was unprepared to admit this in front of the ladies. He looked meaningfully at the other men in the hope that they would back up his story.

'Yes, we heard Pilbream shout,' said de Courcy gallantly thus earning Tommy's undying friendship, 'Naturally we responded immediately.'

'You were all together?'

'Yes, we met up as arranged in the middle of the wood. That's when Mason informed us he'd lost contact with Pilbream. As we'd scoured the wood for the inspector without any joy we then became worried that something had happened to our friend here. That's when we heard the ...' he paused for a moment before adding, 'The shouts. Naturally, we ran towards the sound of Pilbream's voice.'

'I see,' said Agatha. 'And when you took the body of Inspector Banks down to the cellar you discovered that the prisoners had escaped.'

'Correct,' said Parrish, keen to re-establish primacy. 'The lock had been picked and also the outer cellar door lock. They had obviously been waiting until we retired for the evening before making good their escape.'

'I would like, if I may, to go out to the scene of the crime,' said Agatha. 'Perhaps after breakfast. Has anyone been sent to the town to inform the authorities of the tragedy?'

'I believe Mason has gone,' said Eustace hopefully. 'Am I right?'

'Yes, I sent him away first thing,' replied Parrish.

Pru had been quiet throughout all of this. She turned to Agatha.

'Agatha, I remember how you saved the day once at school. What do you think is happening?'

Despite her evident anxiety, Pru still managed to maintain her composure. She was not a woman who submitted easily to irrational fears. Yet the death of Inspector Banks, unlike the phenomena of the ghostly light, was all too real. Agatha sensed that her friend really believed that she could uncover the truth of what had happened; of what was happening. Despite the sense of certainty that Agatha radiated, this was not always the case. Feelings of self-doubt were rare for Agatha, but they occurred all the same. They often coincided with those moments when most was expected from her. It was then that another aspect of Agatha's character stepped forward.

She refused to be beaten.

'We will find out, Pru,' said Agatha with more confidence than she was feeling. Yet, despite her anxiety and the sorrow she felt for the death of the inspector, something had stirred within Agatha that was always a good sign, as far as her friends were concerned: anger. She wanted to get to the bottom of the two mysteries not only to bring justice to those responsible for the death of a good man, but also because she was intrigued.

Agatha turned to Sausage, 'The case you mentioned when we were at school. Do you remember you questioned the serving staff to find out where everyone was?'

'Oh yes,' said Sausage proudly.

'Can you and Pru do the same here. I want an account of the whereabouts of each member of staff from the start of our dinner through to when they went to bed. We need to know who can verify this.'

'Their alibi,' said Sausage, warming to the task.

'Precisely. The police will need this anyway and we cannot assume they'll have the...' Agatha paused at this moment to calibrate the sentiment, 'manpower at this moment. They may need to call upon the resources of Scotland Yard. We don't know when such an officer will be able to come here if problems with the line remain.'

Both Parrish and de Courcy were studying Agatha intently. She was aware of this, but her mind was too busy whirring through what needed to be done to feel concerned by their scrutiny. If they were sceptical, so be it. She would prove them wrong. For all their heroic posturing, they were when all was said and done, only men. She treated them as well-intentioned but dull-witted children. Of course the sex was not completely devoid of capability. Certainly, Eustace, when he was not deporting himself with all the dignity of a court buffoon, displayed some promise.

Eustace.

She glanced over at Eustace. His face, as ever, displayed that amused, lopsided cocksureness which irritated her greatly. Yes, unquestionably he had a shrewdness alluded to months previously by her friends which occasionally flashed before realising its mistake and running back into the shadows.

'I shall go for a trudge now.'

'Where to?' asked de Courcy. 'It's snowing quite heavily again.'

Agatha steeled herself to answer, 'The beehives. The scene of the crime.' She rose from her seat, along with the other ladies and left the dining room. Pru led the way to locate Agatha's hat, coat and walking shoes. As they walked along the corridor, Agatha stopped at the painting featuring the ghostly light. For a moment she could not quite believe what she was seeing. There, in the ground floor window, was a light that had not been there yesterday when she had first gazed upon the painting. She was just about to comment on this when Pru interrupted her thoughts.

'Here's your coat, I don't know where Polly put your shoes.'

Agatha turned away from the painting and went towards her friend. She thought to say something, but a fear of looking foolish stopped her. She felt her friend's hand on her arm leading her towards the stairs that led down to the kitchen where they could locate Polly.

*

'Are you sure this is a good idea?' asked de Courcy. 'I think it could be quite traumatising for such a young woman.'

The only remaining people in the breakfast room were Parrish, de Courcy and Eustace. Parrish seemed equally sceptical. Eustace's smile was beatific as the other two men spoke.

'What do you think Eustace?'

'I think you know what I think. She's really rather perceptive. I'm quite convinced she can hear paint drying.'

The other two men chuckled at this. When in doubt, men will always default to making humour about women behind their backs and then humouring them when face to face.

'She can certainly wipe the smile of a chap at sixty paces,' said de Courcy. The men gazed in companiable silence out to the lawn at the side of the house. Then de Courcy mused out loud, 'You know John, you're the only one of us married. To bachelors like Eustace and I, women are a mystery.'

Just then Agatha appeared in the lawn. She was wearing a coat and stout boots. She stood with her hands on her hips and stared back at the men staring out at her. She gesticulated angrily for someone to come out and join her.

'She's certainly very spirited,' acknowledged Eustace, rising slowly to his feet. 'Probably best if they think they're in control.'

There was no argument from the other two men in the room.

13

Eustace trudged out the French doors to join Agatha on the lawn at the side of the house. He was wearing a tweed jacket buttoned up against the cold with a walking stick under his arm. From one pocket he fished out a tweed cap which was planted firmly on his head. From his other side pocket he extracted brown leather gloves. He looked up at the snowflakes darting around him. It had been snowing heavily for half an hour, but it seemed that the weather was, at last, improving.

'Are you warm enough?' said Agatha. He mused how a question about how well he was coming from this woman sounded like a criticism rather than an inquiry.

'Oh yes. I rather like the cold weather. I spend so much time in tropical climates; this makes for a pleasant change.'

They began to walk alongside one another towards the lawn with the beehives. Agatha realised that she had never asked Eustace what he did. Perhaps now was the time.

'What exactly do you do?'

The ever-present look of amusement on Eustace's face seemed to grow in intensity so much so that Agatha immediately added, 'Perhaps I should rephrase that.'

Eustace chuckled, utterly charmed by the brusqueness of his companion.

'Well the question is not unreasonable, Lady Agatha. While I can certainly make a strong case for what I do, I'm not sure the same could be said for quite a few of the embassy staff in the locations I have been posted.'

'May I ask where you have been posted.'

'Mostly the Mediterranean: North Africa, Palestine and the like.'

Agatha stopped for a moment and then resumed walking.

'I presume you speak Arabic.'

'I do, plus a few others.'

'Such as?'

'Oh a bit of Spanish, French, German.'

'How much is a bit?'

'Fairly fluently.'

Agatha was not sure if she was irritated by the idea of someone being 'fairly' fluent when one either was, or one wasn't. Or perhaps it was the fact that he spoke more languages than her. Then it occurred to her that he'd had the opportunity to go to university and learn these languages before being able to deploy them in the service of something useful. It angered her that she had been denied such an opportunity.

'You are very fortunate that you are able to use your skills, Lord Eustace. Do you think that one day men will allow women to be of similar service to their country beyond bearing children and homemaking?'

Eustace glanced shrewdly at Agatha, 'Would you like such an opportunity, Lady Agatha?'

Whether it was the light breeze blowing on their faces or something else, but tears formed unexpectedly in Agatha's eyes. Eustace saw this and looked away for fear of being seen to witness this moment of emotion.

Agatha had stopped which forced Eustace to halt too. He turned back to face her. She fixed her eyes on his and said with a determination that was all the more intense for the muted tone in which she spoke.

'I should love to have had such an opportunity as you.'

The pain in her eyes was too real for Eustace to bear. He looked away. Never in his life had he felt such shame. Never again in his life would he feel this. A silent promise was made to himself and the woman he was facing. Her life would not be wasted; that mind would be freed, that spirit liberated. If he could achieve nothing else except this then his life would at least claim some victory of which he could be proud.

He looked back at her. She was still gazing at him, her face as bleak and white as a snowdrift. The pain and embarrassment of having revealed so much of herself was etched proudly across her face. For a moment there was silence between them and then Eustace nodded. He turned towards the direction in which they had been heading and pointed with his walking stick.

'This way, I believe.'

They walked together, but no words were spoken. Perhaps the power of the moment just shared had drained Agatha, then Eustace noticed she was looking around her. They were now on the lawn with the beehives. Once more, Agatha seemed more interested in everything around her rather than the beehives. Finally it occurred to him what had attracted her curiosity.

'Interesting,' said Eustace, glancing down at the ground around the beehive. Aside from footsteps, the only other sign of life were bird prints in the snow. Agatha looked up in the air and then back to the ground as if assessing the impact of the snowfall on the scene around the beehive. She made a circuit around the smashed beehive before stopping, but only for a moment. A bloodhound came to mind for Eustace as he watched her in fascination. Agatha frowned for a moment then resumed walking away from the beehive that had played host to the late inspector. She stopped just a few feet away and gazed towards the gate then back to the beehive.

'You all came from that gate, Lord Eustace?'

'Last night?'

'Yes.'

'We did,' confirmed Eustace whose eyes, like Agatha's were focussed on two sets of footsteps which came from the side.

'Do you know much about bees, Lord Eustace?'

'Only when they attack me at picnics.' This was greeted with a sigh, but Eustace saw a smile lurking in her eyes. 'Of course the wasps in Egypt quite put ours to shame. Monstrous things. You should see them.'

'I'm not sure I want to,' observed Agatha tartly. 'I've had quite enough of the blessed things in this country without being attacked by the beasts you describe. I can think of nothing worse.'

'Try having the flu in Arabic,' muttered Eustace, but Agatha was too engrossed in examining the ground leading from the beehive to the gate at the top of the lawn which led to the forest. A bee buzzed nearby but, for once, Agatha ignored it. Eustace stood ready to offer any defence in case the bee's temperament took a turn for the worse.

'Shall we?' said Agatha, pointing her umbrella towards the gate. With that she took off, retracing the footsteps from the previous night. Eustace scurried after her. On the other side of the second gate they marched towards the forest.

Reaching the point that they'd all stood the previous evening to gaze up at the ghostly light, Agatha then pointed towards the bog to the left of the wood. She gazed out across the hushed white emptiness that lay prostrate before her. To Agatha the Fens looked raggedly beautiful at that moment under the sullen sky; quietly dramatic, but with a brooding sense of something about to happen.

'Did you negotiate a path through here last night?' asked Agatha suddenly.

'We did, although I'm not confident I could do it now,' said Eustace hoping that his tone was sufficient to discourage Agatha from attempting to navigate it now.

It wasn't.

She forged on with Eustace once more trailing in her wake. Despite Eustace's worries, Agatha managed to find the path through the bog without much difficulty. At the other side they both stood and looked back towards the house.

'Interesting,' said Agatha. Eustace suspected, rightly, that such enigmatic comments could be very irritating. The only thing that held him back from commenting thus was the realisation that he was probably equally guilty of this. Experience had taught him that at some point the desire of the individual to be understood and appreciated would overcome any need to be mysterious. Agatha said nothing and began walking away from the house. Eustace supposed it was the exception that proved the rule. Not that he'd ever really understood what this meant.

'What did you see, Lady Agatha?'

Agatha kept on walking, but did reply, 'Oh nothing. It just seemed to me that the painting of the ghostly light in the house would have been painted from around about here. Eustace turned and walked backwards for a few moments.

'D'you know, I think you may be right.'

He turned back and saw that she was now quite some way ahead. He jogged along the meadow to catch up. On more than one occasion he almost slipped on the snow. At a certain point she stopped, turned around, not for Eustace, but to stare once more at the house. She spun left and began marching along towards the adjoining field.

'Careful Lady Agatha,' warned Eustace. 'I believe there is another bog nearby. The locals seem to have cunningly ensured that it remains hidden when it snows.'

There was another bog and Agatha nearly fell in it. Luckily, she stopped just in time. She looked around at the flatness. In the distance, she could see some sheep moping around looking for patches of grass to eat. Yet again, her restraint in sharing with Eustace what she was looking for proved almost too much for a man who had a reputation for patience.

A few hundred yards up ahead she noted there was a small stone bridge which traversed the first bog. She turned to Eustace, at last including him in her plans.

'Shall we?'

Eustace smiled, but inwardly was groaning. The absence of an overcoat was beginning to seem like a hasty decision. He'd badly wanted to join Agatha on this reconnaissance, but icy tendrils were enfolding his body. Agatha was off without waiting for an answer. He jogged towards her and then matched her step to the bridge.

'Have you seen enough?'

'Yes, I think so,' said Agatha glancing at her companion archly. 'Perhaps we should return before one of us dies of exposure.'

'I'm sure you'll make it back safely, Lady Agatha,' said Eustace, desperately hoping she could not hear his teeth chattering. Agatha had the grace to chuckle at this.

'May I ask what you were looking for?' asked Eustace.

Agatha smiled at this. Seeing her smile made asking the question seem like a defeat to Eustace, but oddly he did not mind.

'I had no preconceived idea of what I was looking for,' replied Agatha, deftly avoiding answering him directly. Eustace nodded in appreciation hoping that Agatha would accept this response as an indication that he was satisfied by her answer.

They trudged back to the house. Agatha was lost on her own thoughts while Eustace was content just to walk alongside her, occasionally permitting himself a sideways glance to gaze at her face. As they approached the house, they heard a low rumble of barking.

'That sounds like Talleyrand,' said Agatha, suddenly concerned.

'It seems to be coming from the side of the house where we began our walk,' replied Eustace. As ever, he was a split second too late. Agatha was already running in that direction. With an inward groan, Eustace began to follow.

*

If Talleyrand had ever heard or understood the phrase "a dog's life" he would have been the first to challenge its veracity. There was nothing difficult, boring, or unhappy about the life he led. This is not to say that, on occasion, life, or should that be love, threw him crumbs rather than a bone. But by and large, Talleyrand was as content as any canine had a right to be. He had mastered the art of studied indolence, he could wangle food out of almost any human when he so chose and the ladies, mostly, loved him.

He knew he was not the finest looking dog in the world. His ears were a trifle long, his expression perhaps too melancholic and his proximity to the ground meant that great raking strides would never be attempted when he chased and failed to catch pigeons. Yet, for all that, he had a manner and a style that helped bring him the only thing that mattered: *l'amour*.

Not all dogs took to Talleyrand, though. They mistakenly believed that his lack of height, his apparent diffidence and a distinctly affable appearance made him a pushover. This was a grave mistake. Many dogs were to regret the day they underestimated this Basset. One such canine was Bismarck, now fully recovered from his bout with the icy water. The German Shepherd had only one thought on its mind: revenge.

As Talleyrand was taking his morning constitutional, he spied the black demon similarly engaged. For a moment, a long moment in fact, the two dogs stared at one another. The only noise in the garden was a rustle of leaves on the Cedar tree near the gate. Talleyrand began to move towards the wooden fence a few yards to his right. The sudden movement seemed to galvanise the big German Shepherd. Teeth bared he began to trot towards his quarry. Seeing this, Talleyrand upped his pace, but not too much.

He had a plan.

The wooden fence was around six feet high and certainly not something the Basset could ever hope to scale. However, Talleyrand had noted that a hole had been made underneath by a fox. Earlier reconnaissance had confirmed that he could fit through it. He picked up the pace, again not sprinting and headed for the hole which led directly into a rose garden.

Bismarck saw what Talleyrand's intentions were. He increased his speed, barking a threat to his canine Nemesis. Talleyrand paused at the hole to check on the approaching black and brown devil. It was time to make good his exit, so he scurried under the fence and waited at the other side.

The fence seemed to shake as the beast hurtled against it. Talleyrand flinched but waited. Moments later the head of his enemy appeared, snarling angrily and there it stayed. Bismarck was stuck. It took a few moments longer for this to register with him than it did Talleyrand.

Silence.

Growling, Bismarck tried to push through. No use: he was stuck. He knew it. Worse, Talleyrand knew it too. The Basset watched Bismarck's effort with a disdainful raising of his nose. Panic gripped Bismarck. He began to bark with more than a hint of yelp. All this time he kept his eyes trained on the Basset.

Finally, Talleyrand turned his back on the marooned mutt. The German Shepherd stopped barking for a moment, wondering what was going to happen now. He didn't have to wait long. Talleyrand began scuffling snow into the face of Bismarck. He stopped just as he heard the sound of people approaching. Then he began to bark to attract their attention.

'It looks like Bismarck's trapped,' said Eustace who was the first to arrive on the scene. 'Well done, Talleyrand. Awfully good of him to stay with his friend.'

Talleyrand wasn't sure what was being said, but he knew a pat on the head from the man was a good sign. He risked a look at Agatha. She seemed less impressed than her companion. Something of the curl in the mouth and the frown suggested it was time he retired to a warm spot in the house for a nap. Eustace and Agatha watched Talleyrand trot off towards the house, tail up with something approaching a swagger.

'Well, I suppose we'd better try and free this chap. Remarkable dog of yours Lady Agatha.'

'Indeed, remarkable,' said Agatha drily.

14

Agatha returned to the house to search for Sausage and Pru. She found them in the drawing room which was now functioning as a makeshift centre of operations. It is a truth universally acknowledged in English detective novels that tea acts as a stimulant for cells of a greyish hue. Particularly if the sleuth in question is amateur, female and a member of the aristocracy. In this, Agatha, Sausage and Pru were as one on its miraculous properties.

'I'll pour,' said Sausage as Pru readied her notes from their inquiries earlier with the staff. Of course, amateur detection is merely the art of looking for clues, disproving alibis, drawing the wrong conclusion before blaming the butler.

Agatha studied her friend as she sipped her tea. Pru, or Prudence Winifred March, had been the great beauty of the school. Tall, willowy, elegant, with fair hair and sparkling blue eyes that glittered with a sharp sense of humour. Men stood as much chance of not falling in front of her as cavalry charging at guns. Surprisingly, for one so blessed with beauty and wealth, she had been remarkably unaffected by the good fortune bestowed by rich parents and Mother Nature. She was a team player, through and through.

'Are you ready?' asked Pru, leaning forward, eyes shining.

'I'm all ears,' replied Agatha.

'They all have alibis,' said Pru, sitting back, satisfied with her report.

Agatha raised her eyebrows then burst out laughing. All three were in mild hysterics. It was a moment that transported them back over ten years to night after night in their dormitories: co-conspirators, rebels, pirates and detectives all. They had fulfilled many roles in their time at school and, just then, just when they all needed it very much after the last few days, Pru took them back to that time when their lives were simpler, the road ahead promised untold excitement and love was a whispered conversation after summer breaks.

'I know a police inspector who would greatly appreciate such clarity in assembling evidence' observed Agatha.

'It's true,' said Sausage. 'We spoke to everyone, and they were either in bed or seen going to bed.'

'What about Eustace's man Fish?'

'He was seen by Polly. Apparently he looked very sleepy. He asked what all the commotion was, then, when he heard, he rolled his eyes and went back to bed,' replied Sausage.

'Sensible man,' agreed Agatha. There was a hint of a smile on her face.

'So that means it was only Mason and the two boys, from the staff, who were out during the night. I meant to ask you about Mason, Pru, but is he the estate manager?'

'Yes, he manages everything within the grounds. He looks after the gardens himself but usually hires men from the town during summer to maintain the estate. Good man.'

Pru pushed forward to Agatha a piece of paper which had a list of all the staff, their names, the times they went to bed and who would have seen them. It was a model of simplicity and Agatha nodded approvingly.

'Do you think we can discount the staff from any involvement in this business?' asked Sausage.

'Oh I would say so,' said Agatha vaguely. 'May I keep this?'

Pru nodded in response. They spent a minute or two looking out at the view. Agatha could see snow, but her mind was somewhere else. Her reflections were interrupted by noises in the corridor. Hearty male voices making hearty conversation about hunting probably. In fact, it was knitting. Agatha's eyebrows shot up as she listened more closely. Eustace appeared to be explaining that the pullover he was wearing had been knitted by his Aunt Griselda. His two companions had been making none too gentle fun of Eustace's attire. Just as Agatha began to feel her blood boil on his behalf she heard him reply.

'Oh I know it's a ghastly thing. She was bit of a harridan, I remember. Taught me wrestling. Tough lady, I'd have backed her against Jem Mace. Although to be fair to Mace, he was only a middleweight.'

The men laughed at this, causing Agatha's sympathies to switch immediately and, oddly, towards the unknown aunt. The men appeared in the room to be greeted by looks that would have made the frost outside seem positively warm.

'Any tea left?' asked Parrish, hoping to break the icy atmosphere.

'No,' said Pru stonily.

Silence followed this. The women continued to stare down the men who were, as ever, utterly mystified as to what they'd done wrong. Eustace and de Courcy glanced at Parrish to see if his greater experience of living with the distaff side could shed light on matters. His face registered utter bewilderment which tended to be how he normally looked so there was no help forthcoming there.

'How are your investigations progressing ladies?' asked Eustace.

Pru decided it was time to let them, temporarily, out of the doghouse.

'We've established that all of the staff can account for their whereabouts,' said Pru. 'That leaves only a handful of people who need to explain where and what they were doing,' said Pru.

This was an opportunity for Parrish to reassert the control he'd sensed had deserted him these last few minutes. He stood to his full six foot plus height, expanded his chest and said, 'Well, we must find these people and they must explain themselves.'

Silence followed this unarguable and impressive statement of the obvious.

'I think she means us, Beefy,' said Eustace, greatly enjoying the moment.

'Oh,' said Parrish, 'Oh, well, that's a different matter then. Quite right too. Who's first?'

Agatha rose at this point and began to leave the room. The men parted like the Red Sea as she made her queenly progress to the door.

'Pru, Sausage, can you do the honours with the men. I have some matters to attend to in the library.'

Everyone, bar Sausage and Tommy, stared at Agatha, whose petite figure was framed by the doorway. Pru seemed surprised that Agatha did not want to handle the interviews personally. Sausage was just happy to be with Tommy again. The two would-be lovers stared at each other in rapture.

'It's snowing again,' said Pru with a groan.

This was greeted with dismay by the others around the table. All except one. Agatha suddenly and without warning began to chuckle. All eyes turned to her. She gave no indication as to what had amused her. Instead, she smiled and departed, making sure to close the door behind her.

As much as Agatha would have liked to stay at the door a few moments after she had left the room, this was rendered impossible by the appearance of Mrs Gallagher the housekeeper. She bowed to Agatha and asked if she needed anything.

'When will lunch be served?'

'Another hour I should think,' replied Mrs Gallagher.

'Then I shall wait until then, thank you.'

Agatha hurried on to the library. She paused a moment at the picture of the house. Just for a moment her heart stopped beating. The light she had certainly seen on the ground floor of the house had been extinguished. Furthermore, Agatha was certain that there was a dark figure standing near the house who had not been there before. She was on the point of putting her finger up to touch the painting when she had the feeling that someone was standing behind her and turned around: no one was there.

She continued on to the library. For the next few minutes she scanned the bookshelves looking for something that would be of use. She picked out two books, the second of which was *Lady Paulina's Passion* by Onya Bachnow. Agatha had no more interest in the latter book than she had in the finer points of bricklaying. It served a secondary purpose. Moments later she heard footsteps outside the door. She rose from her seat immediately, just as the door opened. It was Mrs Gallagher again. She was holding a duster.

'I'm sorry your ladyship, I thought the room was unoccupied.'

'That's no problem, Mrs Gallagher. As you can see I was just leaving.' Mrs Gallagher eyes drifted down to the books in Agatha's hand. Agatha had made a point of holding the romance face out so that the housekeeper would only see it and not the other book that Agatha was borrowing. 'I shall go to my room and rest before lunch.'

'Very good your ladyship.'

Walking back up the corridor, she paused by the painting. Moments later Eustace appeared, thereby preventing her from analysing the house and grounds too much.

'A little light reading,' said Agatha holding up the romance for Eustace to see.

'I think I read it last year,' said Eustace with a smile.

'Is it any good?'

'Oh love conquers all, Lady Agatha, love conquers all.'

'It usually does.'

They parted and Agatha swept past Eustace, trotting up the stairs to her room. She locked the door behind her before settling down on an armchair by the window. The romance was hurled carelessly onto the bed. Then a thought struck her. She went over to the book and placed a bookmark on page twenty-seven. Returning to the chair, she opened up the second book and began to scan the contents more closely.

Agatha read for around three quarters of an hour, engrossed. When the clock on the mantelpiece read twelve forty-five, she closed the book and rose from her seat. Opening the door she checked that the corridor was empty before speeding out. She reached the library half a minute later and replaced the book she'd been reading just as the door opened again. Mrs Gallagher reappeared with a cloth.

'Windows,' said Mrs Gallagher pointing to them lest Agatha be in any doubt as to what she was referring to.

Agatha smiled and nodded before going through the motions of perusing the shelves for more books to read. One of the books attracted her interest, *History of the Decline and Fall of the Roman Empire* by Edward Gibbon. She stared at the book for a minute. All six volumes were present, so she took the first book down and leafed through it. An idea formed in her head. She replaced the book and looked for other historical tomes. Thankfully, the library was well-organised with clear groupings for fiction and non-fiction books. Alongside the work by Gibbon were other tomes covering ancient Greece and the history of Britain.

It was so simple an answer it made her smile.

A noise behind her suggested that Mrs Gallagher was becoming increasingly irritated by the need to clean the windows while, at the same time, spying on Agatha. It was time to release her from this burden, although the temptation for Agatha to point out that she'd missed a spot was only just overcome.

Agatha smiled, but said nothing, as she left the room to make her way to the dining room. On her way she met de Courcy who was standing by a suit of armour, holding the sword that had once been used by the knight.

'Are you going to a duel, Galahad?' inquired Agatha.

This brought a smile from de Courcy.

'My lady, I lay before you my heart, my life, my sword.'

'It's certainly a long one.'

'It has seen much action, Lady Agatha,' replied de Courcy.

'Looking a little rusty if I may say.'

Bringing the sword up to his head, de Courcy bowed slightly, 'I pledge my troth.'

'Very noble,' replied Agatha. 'You definitely have potential as a Lord of the manor.'

Black tendrils of hair draped lazily from his forehead. He pushed it back, running his hand through his hair. The smile on his face would have been considered "dangerous" had Miss Bachnow been around to describe it for her next romance. Certainly, the jaw was looking particularly chiselled at this moment which doubtless would not have escaped the attention of Miss Backnow's pen, nor the bulging shoulder muscles as he was no longer wearing a jacket.

Unquestionably, he was an enjoyable specimen of the sex to gaze upon and Agatha was woman enough to enjoy the gazing. He looked every inch a rogue. But what kind was he? A murderer? The gong was banged enthusiastically by Jolly, interrupting any other thought on this subject.

Lunch was a muted affair. Agatha said little, content to sit back and enjoy not listening to the men talk about the weather, Disraeli and romance in literature. The latter was a sop to the ladies, but Agatha had never liked the genre, Pru was oddly pensive, and Sausage was too engrossed with Tommy Pilbream.

Thankfully, lunch was a relatively short-lived affair. When the gentlemen left, Pru and Sausage were able to update Agatha on their conversations regarding the events of the night before. There was unquestionably a worried look on Pru's face. Agatha smiled in reassurance and gripped her friend's hand.

'After we left the gentlemen,' said Pru, 'They skirted around the edge of the marshland where it borders the forest. Unfortunately, the mist was so bad that John decided it was not worth the risk to venture further out into the marsh itself. The others agreed. At this point the inspector claimed that he saw a torch in the forest. This could only have been a man. Neither John nor Freddie saw it, but before they could say anything, the inspector began running in the direction of the torch.'

'Did John or Freddie see this torch?'

'That's the strange thing. They didn't see it and before they knew it, the inspector was away from them. They tried to follow him, but it's rather thick in there. The torches weren't much use as they do not project light.'

'Wasn't the inspector carrying a torch?' asked Agatha, rather surprised.

'No,' said Pru. 'That's the problem.'

'So presumably they shouted for him,' probed Agatha.

'Yes. At first he replied, then they thought they heard a cry, but it might have been a bird.'

'After that they saw no more of him?'

Pru shook her head and buried her face in her hands. 'It's all too terrible, Agatha,' she exclaimed.

'Can you tell me a little of what happened when the men went searching for the inspector, after they returned here?' asked Agatha.

'As you know,' began Pru, 'John and Eustace took the eastern side of the forest where it adjoins the marshland. I think this was sensible as John knows his way around that area without falling in.'

'Yes, I went there this morning,' said Agatha. 'I imagine at night with a little mist it can be treacherous.'

'They walked as best they could around the perimeter of the wood before entering from the back.'

'Did they spend any time apart?'

'Once inside the wood, yes, but they were always within range of one another because it would have been easy to lose yourself.'

'I don't doubt it,' said Agatha. 'Look what happened to poor Tommy.'

Pru nodded before turning to Sausage who had conducted this interview. Her questioning must have been rigorous because it took her as long to elicit answers from Tommy as it took Pru to speak to Parrish and de Courcy.

'Indeed,' said Sausage, eyes widening in imagined horror at Tommy's traumatic evening that had begun long before he encountered Banks sticking headfirst in the beehive. 'He and Mason walked through the middle of the wood. They saw the other torches, either side of them and from time to time they heard shouts.'

'Was Tommy carrying a torch?' asked Agatha.

'Yes,' replied Sausage. 'Mason gave him his torch. He said that he knew the woods like the back of his hand.'

'Has anyone spoken with Mason?' asked Agatha suddenly.

Pru and Sausage looked at one another. Then Pru remembered, 'He went to the town to inform them of the terrible murder.'

'Oh yes, I'd forgotten,' said Agatha, who had not. She rose from her seat and added, 'Perhaps he has returned now. I shall go and see him myself.'

She glanced down at the notes taken by Pru and then picked them up.

'We shall come with you,' said Pru, decisively.

'No, Pru, let me conduct this interview. You and Sausage should have a rest. I can see you're tired.'

Pru would have liked to accompany Agatha, but she knew her friend well enough to guess that she had her reasons. Instead, she rose with Agatha and went to the door. Mrs Gallagher was there waiting, which amused Agatha greatly.

'Can you bring Lady Agatha's coat and boots please?'

Mrs Gallagher darted off while Agatha went to the window. In the distance she could see a small stone cottage which was at the other side of the wood. Smoke was billowing from the chimney.

'Is Mr Mason married?' asked Agatha.

'No,' answered Pru. 'A lifelong bachelor. You know how some men are.'

And some women too, thought Agatha sadly. Would this be her life? Alone, self-contained, reliant on nobody. Lonely? She shook off this mood quickly. It was happening a little too frequently for her liking. She would not feed it. She turned away from the window making sure that she could see outside with the corner of her eye. Moments later she saw what she'd expected to see. A man was jogging towards the cottage from the house.

15

Agatha took several minutes to make herself ready for the walk. Wrapped up against the cold, she began the march through the snow towards the cottage. It was further away than it had seemed from the house, taking her around five minutes at her usual brisk clip.

It began snowing just as she reached the door of the cottage. She was just on the edge of the forest now. Glancing towards the wood she could see how the snow caked every crevice on the trees. Little light penetrated through the thick blanket of branches. Visibility was further limited by clumps of wood and mounds. It was easy to see how someone could be lost in the wood, especially at night.

Using the handle of her umbrella, she rapped on the door three times. From inside she heard the sound of a chair scraping in the floor. Her heart began to beat a little faster. Was she taking a risk in coming here alone? Such an action would have been inconceivable in London. Just as this thought occurred to her, the door opened. In the distance, she saw de Courcy's head appear. Perhaps it had dawned on him that the idea of a young woman visiting a man unaccompanied was inappropriate. Or was it something else?

Mason stood tall at the door glowering down at Agatha. If he was happy to see her then he made a remarkable effort in disguising his joy behind a surly mouth and angry eyes. Without saying anything he opened the door to allow Agatha through.

'Thank you Mr Mason,' said Agatha walking into the cottage. It was small and very stony. Grey unadorned stone walls and a grey stone floor. The only colour came from the fire in the hearth. It roared and crackled a warmth notably absent in the manner of her host.

'May I?' asked Agatha, pointing pointedly with her umbrella as if in warning to Mason that she was armed and ready. Her request was met with a grunt and a sharp wave of the hand. A man of few words thought Agatha. She didn't anticipate a long interview.

There was one other chair in the sitting room which, even by the standards of the male primate, was particularly rudimentary in its furnishing. The only other furniture was a table with one chair at the side of the room underneath a small window. A wooden sideboard with a couple of plates completed the home. It looked as if any cooking took place over the fire as there was an iron grill at the side of the hearth.

Agatha resisted the temptation to compliment Mason on keeping such a charming cottage. Mason settled his tall frame in the armchair across from Agatha's. He said nothing and for a few moments the only sound in the room was his breathing and the crackling fire. Then he took a pipe out of his breast pocket and tapped it on the nearby table. He filled it with tobacco from a pouch, all the while staring at Agatha.

'Thank you for seeing me,' said Agatha by way of initiating some dialogue. 'I am making some inquiries on what happened last night.'

Mason nodded but had still to register his first word with Agatha.

'What have you been up to this morning?' asked Agatha.

If there had been some wariness in the tall gardener's eyes before, it seemed to transform into something close to panic. Just then there was a knock at the door. It opened before Mason could respond. Into the cottage strode de Courcy.

'Ahh, Mason, you're back I see.' He stopped and seemed surprised by Agatha's presence. 'Lady Agatha, what on earth are you doing here?'

Agatha smiled up at the new arrival.

'I could almost ask you the same question, Mr de Courcy. I came here to ask Mr Mason some questions relating to the events of last night.'

Mason looked between de Courcy and Agatha. Then de Courcy leapt into the vacuum created by his arrival.

'Have you informed the police in Greater Recton?'

Mason nodded warily, 'Yes, sir. They said that the sergeant is ill, but they would ask for a detective to be sent up here to investigate the death of Inspector Banks.'

'And presumably start a manhunt for the two main suspects, Mr Kurr and the mysterious Sebastian,' suggested Agatha.

Mason's eyes widened almost imperceptibly.

'Yes, your ladyship, they said that too.'

'It sounds as if you were dealing with a young constable, Mason,' said de Courcy almost prompting Mason to answer.

'That's right, sir,' said Mason slowly.

'Oh good. I'm glad we're clear then,' responded Agatha happily before adding another question. 'How were they sending the message?'

Mason's face suggested he hadn't the slightest notion as to how this would happen.

'I don't know your ladyship.'

Agatha began to speculate out loud, 'Unless there is a telegraph office in town then it may be difficult for anyone to travel to a larger town, what with the snow.'

'I think I remember seeing a telegraph office at the train station,' said de Courcy. He looked at Mason with his eyebrows raised. Mason, did not see or, at least, understand the hint. This caused de Courcy's eyes to flash in an altogether charming manner from where Agatha was seated. There really was something rather dashing about the man, particularly when he was angry.

'Anyway, I was hoping you could shed some light on what you remember about last night, Mr Mason.'

Agatha knew that it was a forlorn hope that Mason could provide illumination on anything without the aid of a box of matches and three sticks of dynamite. This was particularly the case with de Courcy standing only a few feet away ready to jump in and add to the narrative gaps that would unquestionably result from Mason's lack of eloquence.

Mason paused before answering, 'I'm sure it's as the gentlemen will have told you. I was with Mr Pilbream one moment. The next he was gone. We found him by the beehives.'

If not verbose, there was no questioning Mason's commitment to sullen reticence. His story did leave some, possibly all, details tantalisingly out of reach. Agatha went through the motions of probing further.

'Why do you think you lost touch with Mr Pilbream?'

Panic once more filled the eyes of Mason. His gaze shifted from de Courcy and then back to Agatha.

'No one is blaming you,' prompted de Courcy. 'Mr Pilbream is a bit distracted isn't he?'

Mason nodded at this. It was if someone had just pointed to the exit when a fire starts.

'That's right. I was probably moving a bit fast, like. Well, I'm not one for talking. One minute Mr Pilbream was behind me.'

'And then he wasn't,' suggested de Courcy.

'And then he wasn't,' agreed Mason.

'Did you both have torches?' asked Agatha.

'No,' replied Mason. 'Just Mr Pilbream.'

Agatha assimilated this for a moment before commenting, 'You were most fortunate to navigate your way around without a torch.'

'Oh your ladyship, I could walk around that wood with my eyes shut.'

'You must know it very well.'

'I do, your ladyship.'

'And the Fens?'

'I've been round those marshes at all hours without a torch,' replied Mason with no little pride in his voice. That pride evaporated in an instant when he caught sight of de Courcy's face. Agatha did not have to look at her fellow guest. His anger was reflected in the face of Mason.

'Very impressive. Well, I think I've heard all I need to hear Mr Mason. You've been most informative'

Agatha rose from her seat, swiftly followed by the two men. She turned and marched towards the door to leave de Courcy and Mason to deal with any recrimination following the brief interview.

Outside the snow was falling lightly. The contrast with the warm interior was stark, making Agatha feel a little light-headed for a moment. But it was only a moment. Soon she was walking briskly back to the house, forcing de Courcy to trot in order to catch her up.

'Was that of use to you Lady Agatha?' asked de Courcy when he reached her.

'Oh it fills some gaps in the story. I think I can see how a taciturn man like Mr Mason might become separated from a man as distracted as Tommy.'

'Indeed,' agreed de Courcy. 'Do you want to know what I think?'

'I don't suppose a "no" would deter you?' said Agatha slyly.

This gave de Courcy pause for thought before he broke into a smile.

'You like to give men a hard time, don't you?'

'I wouldn't quite go so far as to call it a hobby but, yes, I suppose I do, now that you mention it,' admitted Agatha. 'Anyway, what do you think?'

'I think those two scoundrels escaped without us realising then they made their way into the forest and came across poor Banks and did for him.'

Agatha stopped, forcing de Courcy to do likewise. She fixed her eyes on his.

'How does that explain the noises I heard in their cell after I returned from our little expedition to see the lights?'

This was new news to de Courcy. He looked away and thought for a moment before replying carefully, 'So you went down to the cellar unaccompanied?'

'Correct,' said Agatha primly.

'Lady Agatha, I must ask you to refrain from such perilous escapades in future. Who knows what you might have encountered?'

'Indeed,' said Agatha, turning back towards the house. 'So for your theory to be true, very soon after I made my perilous journey down to the cellars, the two men escaped from their cell through two locked doors before making their way upstairs, unseen by anyone. They went outside into the snow where they headed directly to the forest, encountering on their way, Inspector Banks. I suppose it's possible,' said Agatha.

Even de Courcy realised that Agatha had made his theory sound utterly implausible. They continued back to the house in a thoughtful silence. When they reached the house, Agatha turned and gazed up at the sky. It was as grey as a dead fire. She stood back to let de Courcy through. He stopped and looked at her with a question in his eyes.

'I just want to go round to the kitchen. We shall no doubt meet for dinner.'

With that she spun around and left de Courcy standing fuming at the door, unsure whether to follow her or to give it up as a bad job. He chose the latter, stomping inside to rid himself of the snow caking the soles of his feet. He needed a brandy and some male company. You knew where you were with both.

Agatha meanwhile made a circuit round the house to the back door situated on the lower ground floor; this led to the kitchen. She knocked once then entered without waiting for an invitation. Inside the kitchen, seated round the table, were the staff enjoying either a late lunch or an early dinner. At the head of the table was the butler, Mr Jolly. At the other end of the table was Mrs Gallagher. Polly sat beside Fish, Eustace's butler and the housekeeper, Mrs Gallagher along with the cook, Mrs Reid, sat with their back to the new arrival. The Gooch boys sat opposite Polly.

Chairs were scraped back as they all rose to greet Agatha's arrival. Agatha waved her hands up and down to tell them to sit down.

'Please continue, don't mind me.'

This, of course, was easier said than done.

'Is there anything you need, your ladyship,' asked Polly responding to an amused look from Mr Jolly which, if Agatha read it correctly, meant – *Lady Agatha never changes.*

'Nothing, nothing, I just wanted to thank Mrs Gallagher for the wonderful meals she has provided.'

'Thank you, your ladyship,' replied a beaming cook. Mr Jolly looked on proudly.

'I look forward very much to seeing what you have in store for us later. Anyway, I won't delay your meal. Cheerio,' said Agatha, waving brightly. She made her escape before anyone in the kitchen had time to take in she was gone.

Mission accomplished and happily free of de Courcy's attentions, Agatha was now free to explore the next location on her agenda. How long she would be left to explore was not something she wanted to test. She quickly made her way up the steps and rushed towards her destination.

The stone shed was around fifty yards to the left of the house. It was a large building used to store equipment for the upkeep of the estate. The size of the estate had shrunk over the years due to taxes and admirably inept attempts to manage it as a working farm. The last lord of the manor had, for the most part, given it up as a bad job and focussed instead on all of the benefits of his position rather than its responsibilities. He died without issue, although there were many children in the two villages near the estate that might have claimed otherwise, had they known their true antecedents.

When Agatha reached the shed she looked around to see if she was being watched. No one seemed to be around. She pulled the heavy wooden door open and walked in. There was some light in the cavernous building, but visibility was poor. The ceiling was very high with half the shed open and the other half with a wooden mezzanine floor. This stored the straw which could be used for heating or even as a building material.

Agatha headed directly towards the straw to look for any signs that the two men might have spent time here. The area was too disturbed to draw any conclusions. If they had been here, it would take a number of policemen several hours to pick through the area to find clues. Agatha had neither the time nor the inclination to do so. There was a woodburning stove in the centre of the barn. She went over to it and touched the top. It was warm. She opened the front to look at the grate. Lying on top were the smouldering remains of a fire. Someone had definitely been here and perhaps not many hours ago. Agatha had seen enough now. It was cold inside the building, and she was beginning to feel distinctly nervous about being alone now.

A noise behind her caused Agatha to spin around. The door of the shed was open.

'Who's there?' said Agatha.

The response was a low growl.

16

'I'm sure there are greater killjoys to conversation than chess, but I can scarcely think of one at the moment,' said Eustace. He was sitting in the games room looking at Sausage and Tommy Pilbream staring engrossed over a chess board.

By the looks of the number of fallen black pieces, Tommy was on the wrong side of a rinsing. He didn't seem to mind, and Eustace felt all the more affection towards him for it. The face on Sausage was a mask of concentration. She certainly had a hitherto unrevealed competitive streak.

Had he known the young woman better he would have known that there was no fiercer competitor in the house than the former captain of 'the Invincibles'. In fact the only behaviour within Sausage more savagely intense than her competitive streak was her loyalty to family and friends. In this regard, she was a veritable tigress. All in all, there was much that Eustace would have found to admire in Agatha's great friend.

Eustace turned his attention to a fine old pair of binoculars sitting on the sideboard. He picked them up and went to the window. It was from there that he was afforded a fine view of Agatha standing at the door of the big old stone shed.

'I say,' said Eustace.

This caused Sausage to look up from her game just as Tommy resigned. Eustace did not realise he had stolen her catchphrase because his attention was fixed on the shed. Agatha had gone inside. Moments later he saw a large black and brown shape bounding up the hill to the shed.

Eustace immediately set the binoculars down. Rushing outside the room he almost clattered into Jolly who was surprised, but not too put out by the encounter. There was no time to apologise. Eustace hot-footed it outside the front door and sprinted around the front of the house towards the shed. As he drew closer he heard the sound of Agatha shouting as well as Bismarck's barks and snarls.

Years of life in the diplomatic service of country which required an injudicious amount of alcohol consumption to oil the wheels of international peacekeeping had not prepared Eustace for the effort required in sprinting even short distances. Another thought was now crossing his mind: what exactly was his plan for rescuing Agatha if she was imperilled?

He burst through the door of the shed to find Bismarck lying at the feet of Agatha, on his back, feet in the air.

'Good Lord,' exclaimed Eustace.

*

A mortal coldness fell over Agatha. Her heart began to beat harder as she saw the malevolent snarling face of Bismarck approach her slowly. Agatha was not the sort of woman to scare easily. If pressed, she would admit to not having a great fondness for spiders. She'd heard enough bad reports about snakes to take a dismal view of them, too. As she did not believe in ghosts, it was difficult to think of much else that would ruffle her unduly. However, just at that moment, it was difficult to think of anything more frightening than the sight of the black, hairy shape approaching her with teeth bared.

Suddenly Bismarck began barking. It was a fearsome sound. This was a prelude to something even more frightening. He stopped, crouched down, back rising, then erupted from this spot and charged directly at Agatha.

And past her.

Agatha spun around to see Bismarck attacking a badger that had appeared from inside the straw. If Agatha was far from keen on snarling dogs, then this went double for the badger. One sight of the charging Bismarck was enough for the badger to offer his apologies and absent himself, at speed, from the scene.

Bismarck decided against following the badger into the straw. There'd been too many misadventures of late brought on by exuberance and interaction with that Basset hound. Instead, he contented himself with giving the creature, lost somewhere in the straw, a piece of his mind.

Agatha breathed a rather loud sigh of relief. She strode over to Bismarck and stroked him just behind the ear. If anything was guaranteed to erase the last vestige of aggression from the big German Shepherd it was being stroked in this manner. Moments later, Bismarck collapsed to the ground rolled on his back and permitted Agatha to rub his stomach.

'Good boy,' said Agatha.

'Good Lord,' said Eustace, entering just at that moment.

Agatha glanced up at the new arrival in surprise, but continued tickle Bismarck who was all but purring at that moment.

'I saw Bismarck rushing up to the shed,' said Eustace. 'Thought I'd better pop up in case...' He paused at this point unsure of what to say next.

Agatha smiled. It was the sort of smile that women often bestow on men who have acted foolishly. It is not unkind, but affectionate and therefore unkind because it betokens only affection rather than anything more ardent.

'What would you have done had he been attacking me?' asked Agatha in a fetchingly teasing manner. Perhaps there was hope after all, thought Eustace. However, he was as stumped for an answer on that one as he had been on the way up when considering his options for rescue.

'I suppose I could have told it about the London Protocol with Russia. Perhaps this might have bored him into docility.'

The laugh which greeted this remark was like a balm to the most tormented soul. Then she looked from Eustace to Bismarck and said, 'My hero.' Eustace was certain that this was directed towards the dog, yet part of him hoped otherwise. 'He rescued me from a badger,' explained Agatha. She rose from her crouched position. 'Come on boy.'

Bismarck obeyed immediately and hopped up to follow her. Agatha fixed her eyes on Eustace and walked straight towards him. When she reached him she put one hand on his shoulder and stood up on her toes. She was going to peck him on the cheek however, something changed her mind, and she kissed him gently on the lips instead. Then she walked out of the shed triumphantly. Eustace, whose knees were now even weaker than when he had first entered the shed, waited a few moments to regain his composure before heading outside again.

Agatha marched down the hill towards the house without waiting for Eustace. Her mind had turned to the problem of Sausage and her potential beau, Tommy Pilbream. An idea had occurred to her which might present a potential solution to the conundrum presented by the Earl of Gowster's insistence that the young man join the army.

Only a patent fool could be blind to the obvious mismatch between personality and career. The most violent thing Tommy had probably ever done was sneeze. However, perhaps the Earl was not such a fool. There was no question that Tommy, for all his good qualities, was sorely in need of something to do. Furthermore, if he were to marry her great friend then he would also need to understand that Sausage was not the sort of girl to admire indolence even if it came dressed in such inoffensive and genial clothes. Perhaps the old earl understood this better than his son or, indeed, the smitten Sausage at that moment. If so, then it offered possibilities not hitherto considered by the lovestruck pair.

Bursting through the back door she found Mrs Gallagher looking sternly at Talleyrand. Talleyrand looked from her to Agatha and then to Bismarck. Then he disappeared. Bismarck decided to let him go. Bad things happened when he tangled with the Basset.

'Give him a treat, Mrs Gallagher,' ordered Agatha. 'He's been a good boy today.'

'Very well your ladyship,' replied Mrs Gallagher, a ghost of a smile on her face.

'Do you know where Lady Jocelyn is?'

'In the games room with Mr Pilbream, I believe.'

Agatha left the engaging Mrs Gallagher to go to the games room. She knocked on the door first. Better to be safe than sorry. The last things she wanted to do was to interrupt any declarations of love or worse.

'Hello, it's Agatha, anyone there?'

It took a few moments longer than good form permitted for an answer to be forthcoming from Sausage.

'Yes, I'm here.'

Agatha entered the room to find Sausage staring out of the window on one side of the room while Pilbream was admiring the mounted head of an antelope several feet away. Her friend's hair was distinctly ruffled in an un-Sausage-like manner which led Agatha to conclude that she was not the only one to have enjoyed a kiss in the last few minutes.

'Odd looking deer,' said Tommy looking up at the stuffed animal's head.

'That's because it's an antelope,' said Agatha before scolding herself for sounding unkind. Then she added, 'Easy mistake to make.'

'Well, I think it would look better on the animal than on the wall,' said Sausage, angrily.

'I quite agree,' said Agatha. 'Anyway, I'm not here to discuss the merits of taxidermy or hunting. I have been giving your problem some consideration.'

This was something of an exaggeration. A few minutes in the library had proved sufficient, but that was probably not for disclosing.

'Golly, Agatha,' said Tommy with hope in his eyes.

'You're wonderful, Agatha,' said Sausage, clasping her hands together as if in prayer towards a benign deity.

'I agree, Sausage,' added Tommy.

Agatha raised her hand to forestall any further comments about her perspicacity.

'Hold your fire, soldiers,' ordered Agatha, 'until you have heard what I have to say.'

Silence.

This surprised Agatha for a moment then she pressed on. She walked towards Tommy, which appeared to slightly unnerve him. It confirmed a lurking suspicion within Agatha that men were, fundamentally, afraid of her.

'Tommy, I want to ask you some questions.'

'Jolly good,' replied Tommy not sounding like he meant this in the slightest.

'Who is our Prime Minister?'

'Uhhh, is it that chappie, Disraeli?' offered Tommy hopefully.

Agatha seemed surprised that he'd answered correctly. Time to toughen things up a bit.

'Which party does he belong to?'

Tommy looked stumped. He offered a weak, 'Whig?'

'No, he's a Tory. Now, think about this one very carefully. What are your views on the South African question?'

'That is a question.'

'It is Hamlet. Thoughts?' persisted Agatha.

Tommy's face scrunched up a little and his eyes shot upwards to the left. He looked like he had just consumed half a bottle of a particularly vile emetic. Finally, after a few moments, he shrugged in defeat.

'Not a clue.'

'I thought not,' said Agatha, but not unkindly. 'Very well, one more question.'

Tommy grimaced at this, but he was a Pilbream and a Pilbream never shrank from any challenge, or so he'd been told.

'What do you think of Livia Drusilla?'

Tommy's eyes lit up and shone with intelligence, or if not that, then something closely approximating the right answer.

'Oh she was a bit of a harridan, but you know, I've always had a sneaking admiration for her. I mean killing the relatives of Augustus was a bit rum. I wouldn't have wanted to be on the wrong side of her, but those were the times, I suppose.'

'I agree, Tommy,' said Agatha. 'Men fear strong women. Reminds them too much of their mothers I suppose. Or aunts. Well, I think that clears things up, don't you?'

'It does?' chorused Sausage and Tommy in unison.

'Yes, of course it does. Tommy you have no more future in politics or the army than I have in pugilism.'

Sausage and Tommy were not quite so sure that Agatha was being unusually modest but held their counsel. You could never tell with Agatha.

'Augustus Franks is a family friend,' announced Agatha.

'I say,' said Tommy, impressed. Sausage said the same, but evidently had no idea who he was.

'I could, if you like, speak to Augustus and establish if there is any role at the British Museum that he could use an enthusiast in Roman history such as yourself.'

'That would be marvellous, Agatha,' said Tommy, positively overcome with emotion. 'Do you think that he would take me on?'

Agatha could think of several thousand reasons why her friend would be taken on. but this would require a separate conversation with Tommy's father, the extremely wealthy Earl of Gowster.

Agatha patted him on the arm and said, 'Leave it with me, Tommy. I'm sure we can arrange something to your mutual advantage.'

There were tears of joy at this point and not just Tommy; even Sausage was crying. Agatha decided that she should exit at this point lest she succumb to the outbreak of emotion engulfing the room. On her way out she saw the binoculars that Eustace had been using earlier. These would be useful for what she planned later. Picking them up she made her farewells and escaped the room to allow the lovers to share their excitement at the potential solution to their travails. Or something like that.

17

Councils of war work best when you know who to invite. As she left Sausage and Tommy to the business of sharing their joy at a potential solution to their problem, Agatha pondered how she should move forward with the plan that was forming in her mind. She needed an ally. The question was, who?

The great unspoken fear she had, which seemed not to have occurred to anyone else, was the possibility of there being a murderer or murderers in their midst. Who could she trust? The answer was both obvious, but nonetheless alarming for being so: herself.

This was not to say that she distrusted her friends, Sausage and Pru, but with each passing hour, she was growing in the conviction that she had the answer to a number of the problems they faced. To prove it, though, would require an act of either madness or extreme courage. While Agatha would certainly not have characterised herself as mad, she would equally have disdained being branded courageous. This was merely madness dressed in the clothes of a good cause.

What she intended doing was a risk, she knew. Yet she *had* to know. She had to know what was going on and show the others. It was what they were expecting; for what they were waiting. The expectation both angered and emboldened her. She wanted to prove to them that their trust in her abilities was merited while feeling resentment at having to prove this. The more she thought about it, though, the more the anger receded. The challenge had been set.

And she would be equal to it.

Agatha went to her room and sat by the window. She stared out over the back gardens to the forest in the distance and the Fens. Under the snow they lost some of their wild remoteness but took on another form of flat monotony. The waterways were like black veins running through the landscape. Somewhere out there lay an answer to a question. Would she be prepared to venture out and find it? Then another question occurred to her.

Is this where she needed to look?

The answer to this question was greeted with a smile. She shook her head in amusement, but then stopped herself. There was a complacency enveloping her now that could pose a risk. Yet what other answer could it be?

If she were wrong, her life would be in danger.

Just as she was on the point of drifting off to sleep, Agatha heard a scratching at the door. She rose from her seat to let Talleyrand in before settling back on her chair. The warmth of the room, in addition to the sight of the icy whiteness outside, soon began to weave its magic over the two occupants. Soon both were asleep: Agatha in the chair, Talleyrand by the fire.

An hour or so later, Agatha awoke to the sound of barking inside. She glanced down to see Talleyrand happily snoring, oblivious to the sound downstairs. The curtain of night was falling slowly. Agatha reached down to the floor and picked up the binoculars she had pinched earlier from the games room. She put them up to her eyes and scanned the area from the open fenlands to the wood. This was as much as her view could take in. She thought about opening her window, but this would only let the cold air in.

The barking continued. Curious, Agatha rose from her seat and strolled over to the door. Opening it, she heard Parrish with Bismarck. He was saying he would take the dog for a walk.

'Damn snow never stops,' said Parrish putting on his boots. 'At this rate we'll all be stuck in here until Christmas.'

Agatha heard Pru laugh. She always saw the funny side of any situation. Then she heard Parrish laugh also. She was glad to hear this. Although she was closer to Betty and to Sausage, Pru was someone she cared for deeply. After leaving school their lives had taken them in different directions. Had it really been three years since she'd last visited Pru's family home? Where had the time gone? The realisation had only hit her when she'd heard of poor Jolly's loss. In this time Pru had met and married a man she did not know well. Hearing Parrish's unaffected laughter at the ridiculousness of their plight was a great reassurance to her that Pru was with someone that understood and valued her.

Agatha waited until Parrish had left to take Bismarck for a walk before leaving the room to go downstairs. She left the door open so that Talleyrand could come down also if he ever awoke from his snooze. Descending the stairs she saw Mrs Gallagher overseeing the maid dusting in the entrance hall. She smiled to the housekeeper.

'Mrs Gallagher can you tell me where Lady Jocelyn is?'

'She's in the games room. I believe Mr Pilbream is showing her how to play billiards.'

'I suspect it's the other way around, Mrs Gallagher.'

The housekeeper broke into a grin at this. It was probably the first time she'd seen the lady smile. She should do this more often, thought Agatha. Then she wondered if people thought the same about her. Probably, was the sad conclusion. Agatha nodded to Mrs Gallagher before continuing down the hallway pausing briefly by the painting of the house. She peered closely at the painting.

The downstairs light was back on.

Agatha moved on, aware that Mrs Gallagher was looking at her. Reaching the games room, she knocked on the door then entered when she heard Sausage's voice a few seconds later. Quite a few seconds later as it happened.

Agatha entered to find Sausage standing over the table with the billiard cue in her hand. This was certainly a relief to Agatha. Sausage expertly potted the ball with an assured cueing action learned from years of playing the game at her own home.

'I say Sausage, you certainly are deadly with the stick,' said Tommy.

'Cue,' corrected Sausage, just beating Agatha to that particular punch.

'Where are the other men?' asked Agatha, fully aware that Parrish was walking the dog.

This was met by a collective shrug from the would-be lovers. Agatha suspected that the men in question, Eustace and de Courcy, had been forced to flee from the games room, perhaps on the orders of Pru, to give the blossoming romance a chance to flower fully. If this was the case then it was a sound idea and one that Agatha felt she should follow too.

'I shall leave you in Sausage's capable hands Tommy. You'll be racking up big breaks in no time.'

'I'll need to improve my cue action,' said Tommy guilelessly.

'Practice makes perfect, Tommy,' replied Sausage with a wink towards Agatha who exited the room immediately before breaking out into a fit of giggles. She ran into the toned body of de Courcy who was just about to enter the room.

'Is everything all right Lady Agatha?' asked de Courcy. He could see plainly that it was but thought he should ask anyway.

'Yes, quite all right,' replied Agatha. She glanced towards the games room and added, 'Sausage and Tommy are in there. You have been warned.'

'Still?' grinned de Courcy. 'Pru did say something about leaving them alone. I hope matters are progressing satisfactorily.'

'They are, but I hold out little hope for Tommy's billiards game.'

'He doesn't strike me a sportsman, but I like him very much.'

Agatha smiled and realised that she did too. Sausage would mould someone like this rather than herself be moulded to fit in with a man. This was the best possible foundation for a stable marriage, felt Agatha. Too many marriages, reflected Agatha, descended into a desire to understand what spouses disliked and then expose them to it frequently. If Sausage were to marry Tommy this would not be the case. Both would be too grateful that Cupid's arrow had not missed them entirely to waste time worrying about the other's faults.

Agatha felt no guilt at thinking this because she knew this was one of her greatest worries for herself about marrying someone. She was exactly the sort of person to pick up on the fault of another. She knew it was one of her less agreeable character traits but was almost powerless to stop herself. Marriage was as much about compromise as it was about love.

Was there anyone out there who would really wish to take her on, knowing how critical she could be and accept her for this? Could she, in turn, put up with either the faults or, indeed, perfection, of another?

Eustace appeared in the corridor at this point.

'Are we still *persona non grata* in the games room?' asked Eustace with that curious amused look of his.

'Billiard practice,' replied Agatha, straight-faced.

This was greeted with a manly laugh from de Courcy.

'Good old Pilbream. Making his assault on the citadel.'

Agatha wondered if he had things the wrong way round and, by the sardonic look on Eustace's face she suspected he thought likewise.

'Where have you been Frost?' asked de Courcy.

Eustace's eyes widened slightly then he replied, 'Taking some air before dinner.'

'How was the air?' asked Agatha with just a hint of irony in her voice that she knew Eustace would pick up on.

'Cold.'

'I saw John go out,' said de Courcy.

'A brave man who would go out on a night like this,' said Agatha. 'Better to be indoors, where it's warm, I imagine.'

There was just the merest hint of a frown before Eustace smiled. Meanwhile, de Courcy sensed that Agatha was talking about something else and glanced from her to Eustace to gain a foothold in the unspoken conversation. None was forthcoming.

'I'm sure you're right, Lady Agatha,' replied de Courcy as Eustace was curiously uncommunicative on the point. Like nature, de Courcy abhorred a vacuum. 'Well I, for one, shall go and change for dinner.'

When he had left, Eustace, who had not moved, spoke to Agatha. His mood seemed more sombre although the infuriating smile remained landlocked on his face.

'Do you feel you are any closer to solving the mysteries we have encountered, Lady Agatha?'

'I think the weekend is coming to an end, Eustace.'

Eustace. She'd called him Eustace.

His head began to swim. Already his heart was hammering in a manner that he had not experienced since entering the tent of Muhammad Ahmad a few months earlier. Then he thought he was going to lose his life. Now he knew he had.

Everything he'd heard about this remarkable woman had barely begun to describe her. She was impossible and he, happy fool that he was, just wanted to escape time, logic and all else besides, to inhabit the orbit of this brutally intelligent, obliviously beautiful sun.

'I suppose it is,' replied Eustace. He could do little to hide the sadness in his voice at this prospect nor the look of gratitude on his face for the time they still had left together. They walked past the painting of the house. The light in the bottom floor window was still on.

Agatha almost laughed.

'Where are you going?' asked Eustace. He wasn't sure if he were asking about which room or where she would spend Christmas or, perhaps, the rest of her life.

'The library.'

'Do you mind if I join you?' asked Eustace.

'Not at all. Is there any book in which you are interested?'

'Yes, I saw something by William Rankine that caught my eye earlier on thermodynamics,' responded Eustace. He was rather pleased by the shocked reaction on Agatha's face.

That was the book she'd read earlier in the morning.

18

The gong for dinner went at eight that evening. Jolly, as ever, executed his duties with the relish of a five-year-old and bashed it heartily. Despite his three score plus years, some things remained fun, even for highly experienced butlers. Agatha left the room accompanied by Polly. She handed her maid the binoculars and said to her as they reached the stairs.

'Remember, come up to the hallway around ten and wait. If Mrs Gallagher says anything, tell her that I asked you to meet me then. Have my coat ready.'

'Yes, your ladyship,' said Polly with an excited grin.

They reached the bottom of the stairs. Agatha's footsteps echoed off the parquet floor until she remembered to walk more softly. Thankfully, she was the first to appear, so no one noticed. She walked into the dining room to find Jolly somewhat flushed from his efforts with the gong putting out some more Christmas crackers.

'That fork looks a little skew whiff,' said Agatha pointing at an offending utensil at Parrish's place at the head of the table.

Jolly leaned over and moved the fork a quarter of an inch to the left. He glanced at Agatha over his half-moon glasses and raised his eyebrows hopefully. Agatha frowned angrily before breaking into a grin. Jolly smiled back at Agatha.

John Parrish and Pru appeared just then, soon followed by de Courcy. Sausage floated into the room looking radiant in a new dress that Agatha had not seen before. Pilbream followed her, openly besotted. Last to arrive was Eustace. His black tie was undone which required Pru's help to tie properly.

There was a hint of melancholy among the group as they knew the next day would see the guests returning home, weather permitting. There had been no new snowfall since the morning and the late afternoon had brought a hint of sunshine. There was also, thought Agatha, the unresolved tension around the various mysteries and the loss of the inspector. Sensing that the mood was rather gloomy, Eustace manfully stepped up to the crease and tried to raise spirits with a story.

'I'm told this story is true. A friend in Dublin who is a judge heard it from a colleague, so the source is impeccable. If we believe Judges that is.'

A few smiles broke out around the table.

'Anyway, there was a court case in Cork taking place, a dispute between two neighbours: both elderly ladies. One of the elderly ladies was in the witness stand and the barrister approaches her and asks, "Mrs Lynch, do you know me?" To which the lady replies, "I do Mr Hamill. You were a horrible little boy I remember, and you've turned out just as I thought you would. You drink, you gamble, and I've heard you cheat on your wife." This was greeted with stunned silence, so the poor barrister sat down to recover his composure.'

The table began to chuckle at Eustace's telling of the story.

'The opposing barrister approaches the lady, carefully, I might add. "Mrs Lynch, do you know me?" he asks her. The old lady looks him up and down like a general inspecting a deserter and says, "Yes Mr Carson, I do know you and as bigoted a man I have never met. You've cheated on your wife with many women, one of them was Mr Hamill's wife." Well, if her first comment had caused shock this one nearly induced a heart attack in Mr Hamill.'

'Moments later, the judge called the two barristers over to the bench. In a voice barely louder than a whisper he says, "If either of you two eejits ask her if she knows me, I'll send you to the gallows." The trial resumed without any further revelations I gather.'

Eustace dabbed the side of his mouth with a napkin while the rest of the table laughed heartily at the story.

The story had the desired effect in picking up the mood of the table. The murder and the ghost light, while not forgotten, ceased to dominate the mood of the people at the table. Yet Agatha could see the eyes of both Parrish and Pru darting off sometimes to check outside the window.

Agatha was once more sitting beside de Courcy. As ever, he was dressed impeccably. There was not a so much as a hint of lint on his black dinner suit. His collar was starched to within an inch of its life and his tie was a symphony of symmetry. Agatha glanced across the table at Eustace. Neither he nor Fish appeared to have the first idea of how to do a tie and his shirt could have benefitted enormously from having the same sure hand that had helped de Courcy.

Just at that moment, Eustace caught her eye. It was if he had read her mind. He glanced down at the sorry looking black silk tie and smiled.

'In peace negotiations I've often found that it's best not to look too smart. Undoes the best of us.'

Agatha looked unimpressed by this and replied, 'I think the only thing likely to be undone in the near future is what you are wearing around your neck.'

'I can assure you Lady Agatha, it takes much practice to make it look this bad,' said Eustace with as much of a straight face as he was able to offer.

It was not a surprise that Agatha surprised him once more. She broke out into a fit of giggles. A few of the others at the table stopped talking and turned, amused, to Agatha. When the fit had subsided she looked Eustace directly in the eye.

'I imagine it would be easy to underestimate you.'

'I certainly hope so,' replied Eustace with a wide grin. 'I put as much effort into this as almost anything else.'

'Successfully,' added Agatha knowing that an ostensibly unkind comment would be greeted as something akin to flattery.

Just then, Pru said in a hushed voice, 'Look, it's starting again.' Her hand went instinctively to her throat as she said this.'

Everyone turned to look out of the window, except the men of course who were instantly on their feet. Parrish and de Courcy strode over to the French doors forcing everyone else to do likewise. It's difficult to see out of a window when it's blocked by a man of six feet or more built to, admittedly, not unpleasing dimensions.

'Ten o'clock,' said Parrish in a voice that was barely audible. 'Extraordinary.'

'What should we do?' asked Pru.

Sausage looked fearfully at Tommy. The last thing she wanted was for this man, thinking not of himself, but only of his friends, bravely volunteering to go out and investigate.

'I don't want you to go out John. Look what happened last time,' said Pru.

Sausage felt like giving her great friend a hug of thanks for this observation which chimed so much with her own way of thinking.. As it was she contented herself with saying, 'Quite right Pru. The risk is too great. There are criminals and all manner of things out there. We are quite safe here if we stick together.'

In fact, coincidentally, Sausage had taken this thought and applied it quite literally as she was at that moment all but glued to Tommy. The only risk facing Tommy just then was asphyxiation.

'We can't just stay here and cower like whipped dogs,' said de Courcy puffing his chest out.

'You're right Freddie,' said Parrish, realising that his cousin had opened the bidding in this particular trick and had gone quite high. 'I say we bring out the shotguns and put an end to this matter once and for all.'

This suggestion certainly upped the ante considerably, but de Courcy was not a man to be outdone in wild posturing.

'You're right Beefy. I say you, me and the boys go a-huntin'. I don't believe in ghosts. This is man-made I'll warrant. Let's see how this ghost responds to some well-aimed buckshot heading in its direction.'

Sausage did not like where this was heading. She did not like it one little bit. After nearly twenty-seven years on this planet she had finally found someone that she could love and would love her too. As much as Sausage loved Tommy however, she was in no way blind to where his strengths lay. Toting a gun in order to go hunting ghosts was not one of the qualities that had first recommended Tommy to Sausage as potential marriage material. Quite the opposite. Tommy's strength lay more in the planning rather than the execution of dangerous missions. And if this was not the case either, then she was not about to sanction any rash expeditions that might reveal exactly where his talents could be best deployed.

'I don't think I like this idea, Tommy,' said Sausage. 'Both John and Freddie have had experience with guns, you don't.'

'I'm sure Tommy knows how to handle a gun,' said de Courcy turning to him and clapping him on the back with enough manly affability that it almost sent him careering across the room.

Tommy, who barely knew one end of a gun from the other, wisely decided to say nothing. Instead, he hoped that the common sense of the ladies would carry the day ahead of the reckless adventurism of the gentlemen.

'Well, I don't think any of you should be running around at night with shotguns,' said Sausage in a hurt voice. Then inspiration struck her. She turned around and said, 'Agatha, don't you agree? Agatha? Agatha, where are you?'

Everyone stopped looking out of the window and turned back to the room. It was true. Agatha was nowhere to be seen.

19

A few minutes earlier, the Parrish and de Courcy instigated exodus to the window had acted as Agatha's cue to put into operation the plan she had formulated earlier. As the dinner party guests went in one direction, Agatha went in the other. Outside the room she was met by Polly who was standing in the hallway clutching Agatha's hat, coat, a lit torch and a bag containing a couple of items that would be important over the next few minutes.

'Thank you Polly,' said Agatha quickly putting on her coat. 'Not a word to anyone. That will be all.'

Polly grinned conspiratorially at Agatha before disappearing downstairs. Agatha, meanwhile, strode past the Christmas Tree and to the door. Seconds later she was outside and my goodness it was cold. At least that's what she said to herself as she began to shiver. Then she began to run in the direction of the ghostly light far in the distance.

For a few consecutive years, she was the school champion over the fifty-yard dash. This was the perfect distance for her. She had mastered the art of starting quickly. By the time her longer-legged rivals had begun to close the ground between them and the race leader, the matter was as good as settled. Agatha, wisely, avoided the longer distances. Aside from being too much like hard work, her smaller stride worked less well in these races. Ahead of her lay a couple of hundred yards of snowy terrain. This was not her favoured distance. She knew it well, though and felt completely comfortable negotiating her way despite the darkness. And why shouldn't she be able to? The ghostly light represented a clear target for her nocturnal excursion.

Notwithstanding her natural speed, Agatha kept a steady pace as she navigated her way through the snow towards the wood and, beyond it, the marshy Fens. The ground snow was turning to sludge now and on more than one occasion she felt her feet nearly give way. Her plan had no room for a twisted ankle. Nor, for that matter, did her ego.

The effort was beginning, at least, to warm her up. Heart beating fast, one arm pumping, the other clutching the torch, Agatha flew towards the edge of the marsh. Finally, as she neared the spot she'd identified earlier, she slowed down. This was not without some relief. It had been a while since she'd run so far and so fast. She bent over and took in great swathes of icy air.

Finally, she looked up and stared at the strange, hovering light in the far distance. As ever, it seemed to float just at the top edge of the mist hanging low over the bog. Agatha began to shiver again. Standing alone, in the middle of a field, just near a marsh with traps that could pull her down below the black mud, lost forever, she felt real fear.

She took out of the shoulder bag the pair of binoculars that she had pinched from the games room. Placing them carefully to her eyes she trained them on the ghostly light. A slight adjustment of the focus and she saw what she needed to see.

Somewhere in the distance she heard shouts coming from the direction of the house. Immediately, she extinguished the torch by throwing it on the ground and kicking snow over it. The only light that she could see was the malevolent presence drifting over the distant fog. She looked in the distance and saw the torches. She only had a few moments now. Turning back towards the marsh, she began to run towards it and the strange light in the sky.

*

'Agatha where are you?' asked Sausage looking around the room.

'Good Lord,' said Parrish, 'She's not here.' This was certainly true. Agatha was not among them. The group looked at the empty space and then at one another.

'You were standing beside her Sausage, did you see where she went?' asked Pru, concern etched over her face.

Sausage had been rather too tangled up in Tommy to notice her friend's movements. She shook her head. Eustace meanwhile turned back and stared out of the window. He saw the torch and a figure running towards the ghost light. At that moment he wasn't sure whether to feel proud or afraid by the extraordinary actions of this woman.

'She's outside. She's running towards the light,' said Eustace calmly. He wasn't feeling so calm. The idea of her running out in the night, so near the marshes of the Fenlands terrified him.

'We can't let her,' exclaimed Pru. 'She doesn't know the marshes. She could be killed.'

This galvanised the group in an instant. Within seconds they were all racing for the door. Jolly appeared in the hall, concerned by the shouts coming from Parrish and de Courcy. He was despatched immediately to obtain coats and boots.

'I'm coming too,' said Sausage gamely. The idea of her friend out in the wilderness alone was enough for her to loosen her grip on Tommy. All fear for herself was forgotten. There was only Agatha.

Pru nodded to her friend. Soon the whole group was outside, coated and booted, clutching torches which provided light and some badly needed warmth. Pru started the shouting, followed by Parrish and then de Courcy.

'Agatha, come back!'

They were all running now towards the torch in the distance. And then, much to their astonishment, the torch was extinguished. The lead runners in the group, de Courcy and Parrish, came to a halt immediately, almost causing a pile up behind them with the less fleet-footed Tommy.

'Good Lord,' exclaimed Parrish. 'What's happening?'

They began running again. A minute later, a gunshot echoed through the night air. Pru and Sausage were too dumbfounded to scream. Everyone stood still for a moment then they all began to shout.

*

Agatha was running once more: directly towards the marsh. She arrived seconds later at the spot she'd been earlier that morning. Rather than try to cross, however, she turned right and jogged towards the large wood. Soon she was skirting the edge of the forest. She stopped for a moment when she heard the shouts from her friends. She didn't respond. Instead, she started running again. A minute later she was at the other edge of the wood. Finally, she stopped to get her breath back. She'd probably done more running in the last few minutes than she had in the last eight years. There was a fallen tree in front of her. She went over to it and sat down.

Her friends were still shouting which only made her feel guiltier for not letting them know she was safe. Yet she knew this was not possible. They might find the torch which could prompt a search in the bog, but with John Parrish there they should be all right. Once they realised she was not around they would have to return to the house and find Mason to commence a proper search.

This was their best course of action. Even with Parrish and de Courcy butting heads to be leader, common sense would surely prevail. She hoped so anyway. The thought of her friends heading out into the marshes was always the part of her plan that gave her the most concern. A million thoughts like these ran through her head while she waited to get her breath back.

For the first time she became aware of the darkness. It was like a separate, unwelcome presence. She felt the cold seep through her coat, her dress and onto her skin like an icy hand. When the shouts subsided she became aware of other sounds. The slight rustle of branches. The light rain that was now falling. A drop fell from the branch of a tree onto her cheek. It rolled down to her jaw and dropped onto her lap. Agatha did not move. She closed her eyes and listened to the sounds of the wood, of small animals scuttling about the mossy ground. An owl almost made her jump of the log on which she was sitting. Still she sat there in silence. Waiting. Watching.

She stayed almost five minutes. Then she saw what she wanted to see. It was enough. Agatha was now almost certain she understood the mysteries that had occurred at Campbell House. It was time to return. Thankfully, there were enough lights on in the house for her to navigate the return journey safely. She was in no rush. There was still shouting somewhere in the distance, but there was nothing she could do about that. The gaps between the shouts had grown in duration. They would make their way back soon to organise something more extensive.

Agatha reached the front door, which was open. She walked in and was greeted by a rather shocked looking Jolly.

'Lady Agatha!'

'Mr Jolly, would you be so good as to have the brandies served in the dining room. I believe my friends will surely need one.'

'Very good your ladyship. You've had a bracing walk?'

'Run, Mr Jolly. I could do with a brandy myself.'

Jolly's smile returned. It was something that rarely left his face. He left Agatha while she made straight for the dining room. She opened the door and was greeted by a familiar voice.

'You're back. I wondered how long you'd be.'

*

'She can't have gone far,' announced Parrish.

'Not out into the marshes surely,' replied de Courcy. There was genuine concern in his voice.

'We have to look for her,' said Sausage. Years of being around Agatha meant that she had as low a tolerance for shilly-shallying as her friend. The group were spending too much time discussing the unknowable. It was time to act.

'Come on Tommy,' said Sausage, all but yanking her young man in the direction of the marshes. This forced the rest of the group to follow and then overtake her. They reached the edge of the marsh. In front of them was a low mist hiding the treacherous marshes.

'The light has gone,' said Pru.

This was the first time that anyone had noticed this.

'Good Lord, you're right,' said Tommy, pointing to the dark sky.

'Do you think it was Agatha who fired the gun shot?' asked Pru.

'I'm almost certain it was, Pru,' sad de Courcy. 'She must have taken a revolver from the house.'

'Where can she be?' said Sausage, unable to hide the worry in her voice. She shouted 'Agatha.'

The others joined her in shouting for their friend. There was no answer.

'What can we do?' asked Sausage.

'I think we should return to the house,' said Pru.

'Good idea,' said Parrish. 'We can find Mason and the boys and organise a proper search.'

'If we need to,' said Pru enigmatically. She looked around the group and said, 'Where's...'

*

'Hello Eustace,' said Agatha with a smile. She went to the table and sat down opposite him. A part of her was happy to see him although it was troubling too. She addressed the latter part first.

'You didn't feel the need to search for me then?'

Eustace proffered the bottle of brandy, but this was met with a shake of the head. Agatha's eyes bored into Eustace's.

'Well, it was rather cold outside,' said Eustace ungallantly.

Silence.

Then Agatha erupted into laughter. Once more, Eustace reflected that he could stand very much to hear this sound. He was also a very relieved man given what he'd said. As ever, the gambler in him had ripped away the safety net without it resulting in serious injury.

'I had a feeling you would come back sooner rather than later. Did you find out what you needed to?'

'Not quite. Almost there.'

'Was that you who fired the shot? I presume it was.'

Agatha took a revolver out from her bag. She pointed at Eustace. This was greeted with a smile. Just at this moment Jolly entered the room carrying a tray with a bottle of Napoleon and seven glasses. He glanced at the gun then at Eustace.

'Will there be anything else your ladyship?' he asked in the manner of someone who saw guns being pointed all the time at one another by members of the nobility.

'No thank you. I'm sure we can serve ourselves. You should retire, Mr Jolly. It's been a long day,' replied Agatha.

Jolly absented himself from the room quietly while Eustace reached over to the bottle.

'Would you prefer brandy?'

'No thank you, it's bed for me,' said Agatha putting the revolver on the table. 'It wasn't loaded, by the way,' added Agatha taking the bullets out from her bag as well as the binoculars. 'I think this will be the last night. It was beginning to rain when I was outside so I imagine the trains will be running. Are you returning home tomorrow?'

'No I am here for Christmas. Where will you be this Christmas?'

'At Cleves with my family.

'You have a couple of brothers don't you?'

'Yes, Lancelot and Alastair.'

'I think I met Lancelot. Handsome young man. I daresay he would give John and de Courcy a run for their money.'

'Yes, he is rather good-looking. Sadly, he is all too aware of this.'

'It's turned his head, somewhat?'

Agatha almost snorted at this. She shook her head and replied, 'Not only his, alas.'

'A problem I will never have to deal with,' said Eustace ruefully. Agatha smiled back.

'Oh, I don't know.'

As she said this, her eyes flicked towards the window which led Eustace to turn around. They could see several torches heading their direction. This was Agatha's cue to rise from the table leaving Eustace on tenterhooks as to what she meant. Then, glancing towards the window she said, 'Pass on my apologies. I think if we convene tomorrow morning I will have organised matters in my head.'

'I'm intrigued.'

'Intrigue is certainly the word I would use. Goodnight Eustace,' said Agatha as she left the room.

Eustace watched her leave and felt a wave of emptiness surge through him. A minute later he heard the voices in the corridor. Parrish and de Courcy were issuing orders like a pair of duelling sergeant majors. This made him smile. The door of the dining room burst open to reveal the startled faces of his friends.

'Brandy?' asked Eustace.

20

Agatha did not join the others for breakfast, preferring instead to have it sent up to her room. She had been up since first light and been for a walk with Talleyrand. Then, while everyone was still in bed, she'd returned to her room and spent the early morning looking out of the window lost in thought, only some of which was devoted to the mysteries she'd encountered.

Everything about the weekend had proved unexpected. More than this, she conceded that she had never experienced anything quite like it. The nature of the events she'd faced and the people whom she'd met had left a mark. It was profoundly unsettling. No, that wasn't right. It was something else. Her great fear was that she was feeling excitement. This would not do.

She was hungry, yet when the breakfast arrived she found she could not eat. This would not do either. As ever, she felt anger. It was a little known by many, even by her closest friends, that her greatest source of impatience was with herself. Where everyone saw strength she felt weakness, where everyone saw courage she knew fear. It was what drove her on. Yet, it was tiring to be like this. The effort of being Agatha Aston was often overwhelming.

The walls were closing in around her. Sometimes it became too much, and she wanted to disappear from the world. To vanish as if by a conjuring trick so that all that was left for the many people who knew her was the memory of a rather odd woman or, for the very few, a good friend. The problem, she realised, was that the person she wanted to run away from was the person she would be alone with.

It was at these moments she felt at her loneliest, but then something else would happen. The anger would return bringing with it the one thing she needed most at that moment: energy. She leapt up from her chair. For a moment she stood and looked out of the window at the rain creating black spots on the snow. The trains would be running today.

There was a knock at the door.

'Your ladyship, it's Polly.'

'Yes, come in Polly.'

The young woman came in, thought about curtsying, but changed her mind. Agatha was not one for such formality.

'Thank you for coming up, have you finished your breakfast?' asked Agatha.

'Yes, would you like me to start packing up?'

'Not yet, Polly. There's one task that I would like you to do this morning. Is the bedroom at the end of the corridor still empty?'

'Yes, I believe so.'

'Good. I want you to go there and stay by the window. Whatever you hear going on downstairs, ignore it. Stay by the window and keep look out over the back garden. It may be an hour; it may be less. Would you mind doing this for me?'

'Of course,' said Polly eagerly. Then a frown crossed her face. 'But what is it I'm looking for?'

Agatha told her.

Having communicated her instructions, Agatha watched Polly leave. She took a deep breath and left the room accompanied by Talleyrand. Her destination was the drawing room. Ignoring the chatter from within the breakfast room, she headed towards the corridor that led to the games room. She took one look at the painting of the house and smiled to herself. Then she quickly skipped across the hall towards the drawing room. She opened the door and found it was empty. She took a seat by the window. The ground was still white but dark patches were appearing. The sky was a leaden grey with a low mist hanging over the Fens in the distance.

This was the last day. The thought was bittersweet. The emptiness inside her was only partly due to the missing breakfast, a mixture of apprehension and regret. This was unusual. Was she coming down with something?

The door of the drawing room opened a minute later. Talleyrand growled from his position by the window. It was Mrs Gallagher. She seemed surprised by Agatha's presence in the room. Talleyrand, realising it wasn't the black and brown demon, returned to lying at Agatha's feet.

'Hello, Mrs Gallagher. Would you mind letting the others know where I am. When they are all assembled here could you and Mr Jolly join us also? And Mr Mason, of course. Let's not forget about him.'

If she was surprised before then, Mrs Gallagher was now thoroughly confused and not a little bit worried. She hurried out of the room leaving Agatha to her thoughts on what she was going to say. Her heart was certainly beating at a faster rate than normal. She tapped her fingers on the arm of the chair while she waited. Yes, she conceded. I feel nervous. Perhaps this was a good thing. It would give what she had to say a certain fervency. Yet, of course, she might be wrong. It was always possible. There was one occasion nine years ago when she had been wrong. The thought of it still chilled her. That case had turned out well, as the true villain had been uncovered, but it had been a close-run thing.

Sounds in the corridor suggested that the group were moving from the breakfast room to the drawing room. Her heart was beating like a drum now. So were her fingers. The door exploded open.

Pru entered followed by Sausage then the gentlemen. There was an amused look on Pru's face, but Sausage seemed a little sore following last night's events. The look of hurt accusation was there in the downward tilt of her eyebrows. Agatha felt a stab of guilt at engineering her own disappearance the previous evening and hoped that all would become clear in the next few minutes. But where was Polly? She couldn't be wrong, otherwise this would be the first and greatest humiliation of her life.

'I'm happy you are recovered from your nocturnal excursion,' said Pru, but there was no hint of accusation in her voice. She seemed to be enjoying herself, but there was a wistfulness too in her eyes. A memory of long ago when they had all been free and adventures came upon them at school like sunshine breaking out from the clouds.

'I am, thank you, Pru,' said Agatha and then she raised her voice slightly for the others to hear. 'We shall wait a moment for Mr Jolly, Mr Mason, and Mrs Gallagher to join us. This concerns them too.'

'May I ask what all of this is in aid of?' asked Parrish, a trace of irritation in his voice. Pru glanced at her husband and smiled.

Agatha could see just how much she was looking forward to this. This emboldened her: the confidence of a true friend. It was as if she was showing her friend off. *Look at what she can do.* She watched as Pru leaned over to husband and whispered in his ear, 'You'll see.'

A surge of energy flowed through Agatha. She risked a glance at Sausage. There was a hint of a tear in her eyes and a frown, but it was not of anger. Agatha smiled sympathetically to her. An apology passed between them, unspoken, as it can only do between old friends.

The door opened moments later revealing Jolly, Mason and Mrs Gallagher. Agatha stood up: everyone was in the room. The nervousness returned. This time it was not because of what she had to say, she knew she was right. It would just be easier if Polly were to appear.

'Good morning everyone,' began Agatha. She smiled a little guiltily and got the apology out of the way first. 'I'm sorry if I gave you a fright last night. It was not my intention to worry you, only to uncover the truth of the mysterious events of the last few days. I hope if I explain myself this morning, you will find it in your hearts to forgive the little, albeit necessary, escapade from last night.'

She looked meaningfully once more at Sausage. She received a smile of encouragement back. This was familiar ground for Agatha and for Sausage. Eustace, meanwhile, seemed captivated. As with Pru's smile of encouragement earlier, she felt heartened by this.

'I think we can all agree, the last few days have been extraordinary. It started at St Pancras for us when some thieves stole my bag. Thankfully, Lord Eustace was on hand to save the day.'

The reminder of this drew a frown from Sausage which amused Agatha. Eustace beamed shamelessly with pleasure at the pats on the back he received from de Courcy and Parrish. Agatha glanced at de Courcy and felt her heart beat a little faster again. He really was quite magnificent. It was almost funny.

'Yes, Eustace was our hero on the platform. It was there that we first saw poor Inspector Banks and his colleague with their prisoner, Mr Kurr, boarding the train. And so we left on our journey, quite late because of the snow. If the theft had been a frightening experience it did give us the benefit of being able to make the acquaintance of Lord Eustace on the journey up from London. We discovered that Lord Eustace is not just involved in the publishing business, but that he is also a writer of some ability. We were able to read his latest story which I enjoyed enormously. Grammar and punctuation aside, you are rather good; much as it pains me to say it.'

Such acclaim could not go un-blushed by Eustace. He smiled, he reddened, he waved Agatha to move on to save him further embarrassment.

'In fact, it was quite a shock to find that in one aspect it seemed to have drawn inspiration from Campbell Hall: specifically, the beehives. It was on our way up that we lost one of the policemen. Mr Kurr claims that he was thrown off the train by his associate, Sebastian, who apparently joined the train at Bucknell. He suggested that the worst he would have experienced was a little bit of bruising. I am sure we will hear more of this soon.'

Agatha gestured outside where the rain had stopped, but it was clear from the dark patches on the ground that it had helped clear some of the snow.

'Yes, I am sure we will be seeing the police very soon,' continued Agatha. She hoped so otherwise what she was about to say would look rather foolish indeed. Where was Polly? A creeping anxiety filled Agatha, but she forged on regardless.

'The arrival of Sebastian set in motion the chain of events that has led us to this moment. As you will recall, although they managed to overpower the policemen at the station we managed to regain the initiative.'

'Brava Agatha,' chipped in Sausage at this point. A murmur of 'here, here,' followed this, but was ignored by Agatha.

'And so we arrived at Campbell Hall somewhat bedraggled, bemused and bewildered by what had happened. Yet, we had our men. They were imprisoned in the cellar. All was fine. Yet, as I was to find out, this was not the case. We had the mystery of the ghostly lights and then worse was to follow: the tragic death of poor Inspector Banks and the breakout by the two criminals. I wonder where they are now? Were they responsible for the death of Inspector Banks?'

'They had to be,' said Parrish. He was sitting with his legs apart, a hand on each knee. 'Who else could have done such a ghastly deed, Agatha. Surely you're not suggesting it was one of us?'

A hush fell on the wood-panelled room. A few eyes flicked nervously this way and that. The grandfather clock ticked aggressively in the hallway. Agatha, ever the performer, let this last a couple of beats longer than decorum, even detective stories, normally permitted.

'Why John, that's exactly what I am suggesting.'

Parrish's mouth fell open like a drawbridge. Sausage, meanwhile, gasped at this and looked around her. Well, to be precise, she looked in horror at Tommy, who had been staring out of the window. Then she turned fearfully to Agatha. Anything but this, she thought.

Agatha's thoughts were also bordering on a different form of panic. Where was Polly? She was reaching the dramatic conclusion of her story and her coup de theatre was inconveniently absent.

Still, she had more than one dramatic surprise to pull out of the hat. The order, fundamentally, of the revelations did not matter.

'I went for a walk this morning with Talleyrand. It really is quite lovely here, isn't it? So remote. So quiet. I only had this boy,' said Agatha glancing at the snoring Basset, 'and the birds for company. I must say we went for quite a hike. We even ventured into the Fens. With the snow cleared, the pathways were really quite visible.'

Parrish looked uncomfortable at this, he sat up and said, 'Really Agatha, that was quite a risk.'

'I agree,' said Eustace, plainly unhappy at what he was hearing. Or was there a trace of guilt, wondered Agatha? There was no question that this revelation had erased the smile that was normally a fixture on his face.

'Oh I don't think so John. I had no problems walking deep into the marsh area. Whoever laid the tracks did an excellent job. I was able to explore the area for close to an hour. Most enlightening. It's astonishing what you can find.'

At this point Agatha bent down forcing all of the others to lean forward. She extracted from a bag a few pieces of rubber and threw them on the table before them.

'What's that?' asked Sausage, now thoroughly confused by what was happening.

Agatha picked up the two pieces of rubber and held them up for everyone to see.

'What's left of the ghostly light. Or balloon. The William Rankine book in the library was most informative on balloons and thermodynamics. I was relieved to see I wouldn't cause a small explosion when I shot it. I wouldn't have wanted to kill anyone by accident.'

'Such as?' asked Eustace.

'Well Mr Mason has wisely chosen to remain silent. I believe he is responsible for the ghostly light which has been entertaining us for the last few nights.'

Everyone turned to Mason who was standing alongside Jolly and Mrs Gallagher at the back of the room. He said nothing. His face retained its normal aspect of benign hostility. This was greeted with gasps. Well, two gasps: Sausage and Tommy. Sausage's face began the long process of formulating a question. Agatha decided to put her out of her misery and explain.

'Yes, Mr Mason is responsible. I went out last night with a pair of binoculars to confirm this suspicion. Alas, I could not see Mr Mason, but I saw the balloon hovering in the mist. I must congratulate you Mr Mason on the effect that you produced. It wasn't an easy shot so I'm rather pleased that I managed it first time.'

There was a half-smile at this praise from Eustace. Oddly, noted Agatha, no one had said anything to Mason about what might have been considered a vile act on the one hand or a joke in poor taste on the other.

'Of course, Mr de Courcy, I don't think the finger of blame is meant to be pointed solely at Mr Mason, do you?'

This had de Courcy not only sitting bolt upright, but on his feet in an instant.

'What is the meaning of this?' he said.

Agatha said nothing to this and chose instead to smile back at him in silence. It was rather an odd feeling as no one else was saying much either, so he sat down as feelings of foolishness began to ascend into his face making him turn quite red.

'Well, I think the story here is that you bribed Mason to recreate the ghostly light from the painting and, of course, the legend surrounding it. I imagine the next steps would have been in no short order to dispose of John Parrish and, if you have any sense, which I think you do, to marry Pru and take up your position as next in line to the position of Lord Recton. I think that about sums it up, don't you?'

'This is outrageous,' said de Courcy, but something in his tone suggested that his heart was not quite in it.

Agatha's heart, meanwhile, was beating faster and faster. Where was Polly? She needed Polly to arrive at that very minute. Things were reaching a head now. It was imperative. Agatha paused for a moment. Prayed for a second and waited.

The door burst open. Everyone turned around.

It was Polly.

She nodded to Agatha.

Agatha nodded back. Then she blew her cheeks out and audibly sighed in relief. She and the others watched a rather red-faced Polly depart after her dramatic entrance. Everyone turned back towards Agatha. Before she could say anything, de Courcy was on his feet again.

'This is intolerable. You can't seriously suggest that I would be a party to anything so underhand. I would never do this to John, and I certainly did not have anything to do with the death of Inspector Banks.'

Agatha made a motioning gesture for him to sit down.

'No, I'm not suggesting for one moment that you had anything to do with the death of Inspector Banks, Mr de Courcy.'

This appeared to work in mollifying de Courcy, so he sat down. He was only on the seat for a few moments though as Agatha's next comment shocked almost everyone onto their feet.

'No, Mr de Courcy, you didn't kill Inspector Banks. It was Eustace.'

21

'It was you, Eustace, wasn't it?' said Agatha. There was a smile on her face as she said this.

'An interesting theory, Agatha,' said Eustace who looked not in the least put out about being accused of murder. It seemed the most natural thing in the world to him, as if he'd been praised for his wit. 'May I ask what proof you have?'

This was greeted by a smile from Agatha. She rose from her chair and moved over towards the Christmas tree while Eustace stood up, too. They faced one another like two duellists which is what they were; words and ideas were their weapons. Eustace put his hands in his pocket while he waited for Agatha to unwind the events of the weekend.

'I believe the strange events of the weekend were planned by you and staged by your accomplices in the room.'

Agatha heard a gasp that was all too recognisable. She quickly moved to correct this statement.

'I would exclude Sausage of course and, I think, Tommy. Both were important foils for the rest of the group, or should I say, team?'

Eustace seemed most happy at this description.

'Polly's rather dramatic entrance was to confirm to me my suspicion that Inspector Banks has made a most miraculous recovery. For all I know he may be in the garden as I speak smoking with his two friends, Mr Kurr and Sebastian. I'm not sure who these gentlemen are, but they are certainly not who they profess to be. Are they friends of yours?'

Eustace shook his head.

'An actor and a medical student, as you ask. Unfortunately, the weather and the lack of trains has meant that I will be somewhat more out of pocket than I had planned. How did you arrive at your conclusions? Congratulations, by the way. You are every bit as remarkable as I was led to believe.'

Agatha glanced out of the window. She loved praise, but it was best not to show just how much this was the case. It was raining again; the sky was dreadfully overcast, yet Agatha felt as happy as she could remember being in a long time. She turned back to Eustace and fixed her eyes on his. Eustace gripped the armchair as he felt his knees weaken.

'You wanted me to find out, Eustace. You left enough clues.'

'Did I?'

'Yes. The first clue that this was going to be an unusual weekend was when you staged the robbery and the rescue of my bag. This was obviously a ruse to become acquainted, yet, later on, I realised it served other purposes. For example by travelling with us in the carriage it meant you were able to give us your story to read. This was another, crucial part of the process of unsettling us, well me and then suggesting that there was a connection between your stories and other murders. I must confess, I'm still chuckling at the manner of the death you chose for Inspector Banks although I'm sorry for poor Tommy.'

'Yes, it was horrible,' said Sausage with a frown that was aimed with deadly precision at Eustace's heart.

Eustace bowed and replied, 'Forgive me Sausage and you, too, Tommy. Perhaps it was a little macabre.'

'A little macabre,' fumed Sausage. 'That's one way of putting it.'

Agatha held her hand up to Sausage. Matters were getting out of hand, and she was loving the attention.

'It was macabre and, if I may say, makes me worried for how that mind of yours works.'

This was greeted with a snort and laughter from de Courcy. Eustace seemed perfectly unworried by the praise or criticism or both.

'I was told by a friend that you have an unusually Byzantine way of thinking. His exact words were that there is always another straw to Eustace's machinations never mind a final one.'

Eustace waved away the praise once more. Agatha, however, noted the affectionate smiles in the room.

'I couldn't be sure that the dearly departed Inspector Banks was no longer with us as I knew that you or the staff would do their utmost in preventing me searching the cellar. His would-be killers were another matter. Staging their escape was always your plan of course but, as with Inspector Banks, what to do with the men was a challenge given the enforced extension to their stay here? So you made a virtue of necessity by using the painting which Pru drew my attention to as a means of communication not only between you and the staff, but also as a clue to me that something was afoot. It was only when I started to disbelieve that Inspector Banks was actually dead that I began to view the mysterious light in the window in another way. The staff were signalling to you when the men were in the cellar, weren't they?'

Eustace bowed saying nothing.

'Then the men would divide their time between there and the large shed. I found signs of their fire there. It must have been rather miserable for them the last few days.'

Eustace shrugged at this before replying, 'They will have been well rewarded, trust me, Agatha. Very well indeed. Just in time for Christmas.'

'I'm relieved to hear this,' replied Agatha. 'Anyway, the painting was the biggest clue that this was some sort of practical joke. The artist's name was the confirmation of this. Renato Lima.'

Agatha laughed to herself at this. Sausage, meanwhile, looked on dumbfounded. Noticing this Agatha said, 'It's an anagram.'

'Ahhh, I see,' said Sausage with a smile before turning to Tommy, scrunching her face up and shrugging.

Agatha noted that de Courcy had not worked out the anagram although both Pru and Parrish appeared were smiling.

'To save you working it out on paper, Renato Lima is an anagram of "I am not real",' said Agatha.

Pru stood up and went over to Agatha. There was a smile on her face, but the sense of wistful sadness remained in her eyes.

'I'm sorry about all of this Agatha, it feels as if we have played a horrible trick on you. But I'm so proud of you too. You never disappoint us.'

'Thank you,' replied Agatha who far from being offended by the events gave every appearance of having enjoyed the challenge. 'It does rather feel as if I have attended an unusual party.'

'A murder party,' laughed Pru. 'Very unusual.'

'A murder mystery party,' corrected Agatha. 'Don't forget about the 'ghost light', too. Yes, I've never heard of such a party before. There is, of course, only one mystery remaining to which I have no answer. Why?'

Just then the door opened, and three men entered. The first man through was Inspector Banks. He looked in remarkably good health for a man who had met his end as a result of a bash over the head and a thousand bee stings. His erstwhile murderers, Mr Kurr and Sebastian entered. All were given a round of applause to which the three men gave rather extravagant bows.

Tea soon followed the arrival of the three men who were given a chance to meet everyone under their true guises. Eustace did the honours of introducing them as it was he who had engaged their services.

'May I introduce Inspector Banks or as he is in real life, Mr Cedric Fletcher.'

Banks / Fletcher nodded to everyone. Although the group, aside from Sausage and Tommy, had been in on the deception, no one had been formally introduced to the actors.

'My friend Fletcher,' continued Eustace, 'Is an actor of no small reputation on the London stage. I think we can all agree that he played his part with distinction.'

Everyone clapped once more causing Fletcher to modestly wave their acclaim aside. Eustace then stood beside the man everyone knew as William Kurr.

'This, ladies, and gentlemen, is Mr Arnold Donahue who made a wonderful William Kurr. I have to say the resemblance is quite remarkable.'

Kurr / Donahue laughed at this and replied, 'Perhaps I could make a career of this.'

A few of the group nodded and de Courcy said out loud, 'You should. The trial of the policemen would make a very entertaining play. I, for one, would love to see it.'

The second criminal stepped forward and Eustace put his arm around him and beamed proudly.

'This young man is not an actor never mind a murderer. He is actually a medical student from Edinburgh. A few months ago, he sent my magazine some of his short stories and I must say they were very impressive. I think a career beckons in literature if he ever decides that medicine is not for him. You knew him as Sebastian, but may I introduce you all to young Arthur. Arthur Conan Doyle.'

More applause followed from this announcement. Soon everyone was tucking into tea and a selection of buns and cakes created by the indefatigable Mrs Gallagher. As ever, Agatha remained the focus of everyone's attention.

'Tell us Agatha, how on earth did you come to understand that it was all one great hoax?' said Pru.

Agatha smiled at her friend and the rest of the group who were crowding around to listen.

'Well, I should have realised at the outset when I found Eustace asleep while he was meant to be guarding the prisoners.'

There was a cheer from Parrish and de Courcy who proceeded to jest with Eustace affectionately. Agatha was laughing also.

'I thought I'd witnessed the nadir of male incompetence before, but congratulations, Eustace, you surprised me that night. Utterly useless. I'm referring to myself, though, not Useless, sorry I meant Eustace.' Agatha blushed at her mistake, but Eustace did not seem to mind.

'I think Useless is rather accurate, actually,' he admitted with a self-deprecating smile. Agatha nodded to him before continuing.

'Anyway, with each new mystery I was quite overwhelmed at first. It was a rank impossibility, yet there was no other explanation. I had eliminated all other impossible explanations. What remained was the truth.'

Conan Doyle seemed transfixed by the young woman he was listening to. He leaned forward to catch everything she was saying.

'Making a case without evidence is like building a house without bricks. The first hint of wind and it falls apart. I had nothing to build my theory on, beyond the observations of trifles and occurrences that made no sense whatsoever. It left me in the invidious position of developing a theory without first having facts. But this was liberating also. Had I not done so, I would not have risked everything last night. Induction and deduction both have merit. I'm undecided which is superior. But there you have it.'

Eustace smiled proudly, 'In other words, you gambled.'

'It rather appears I did.'

'And you won,' said Sausage putting her arm around her friend. This was greeted with a raised eyebrow from Agatha and flick of the eyes towards Tommy Pilbream. Sausage blushed immediately, but there was no denying the hope in her eyes.

'What were the trifles?' asked de Courcy, genuinely curious.

'Well,' responded Agatha, 'I was troubled by how few footsteps were around the beehive the next morning. Also, the murderer could only have come from the forest, which meant it had to be one of you. Of course, as we know, it was not. Mr Mason struck me as an ideal person to use in the ghostly light.

His self-confessed knowledge of the marshes, day or night, suggested that he could easily navigate himself into a position to fly the balloon.'

'But what about the other policeman Agatha?' asked Sausage, still trying to catch up. 'We saw him. Polly saw him and then he was gone.'

'Oh that was Mr Doyle. He and Mr Fletcher were the original policemen. Mr Doyle stepped off the train as the policeman at Bucknell and came back on as Sebastian.'

'Oh,' said Sausage.

*

After an early lunch, it was time to part company. The weekend was at an end. While Eustace was staying on with Pru and John Parrish for Christmas, de Courcy was heading across country to Liverpool while Tommy was going to South Yorkshire. The three men who had so realistically performed their roles were to join Agatha and Sausage, at their insistence, in the first-class carriage for the trip to London.

Mason sat atop the landau while the luggage was loaded onto the top by Fish and the Gooch brothers. The rain had stopped long enough for the partings to take place outside. Sausage and Tommy held hands and could think of nothing to say to one another. It was all in their eyes. Pru hugged Agatha and they both smiled affectionately in the direction of their friend.

'Let's hope,' said Pru.

'Well, now that I've taken to gambling,' said Agatha, 'I'm willing to bet the house they'll be married next year.'

'I want better odds than this,' grinned Pru.

Agatha went over to Mr Jolly and gave him a hug. She could not say anything, but his smile and the moistness in his eyes was all that was needed. She shook hands with the rest of the staff.

Everyone was momentarily distracted by the sound of barking from inside the house. Not Talleyrand, he was up and inside the carriage in an instant. He slumped in the middle with no little relief that he was safe from the black demon.

Eustace was standing a little away from the main group. He looked on with that quizzical smile. At last, Agatha made her way over to him. Once more she felt the strange emptiness that had assailed her earlier that morning.

'Well Eustace. This is farewell.' She held out her hand. He took it in his and held it for a moment. They looked at one another and then a thought struck Agatha. 'You know, I never did receive an answer to my question about why? Why did you create this extraordinary plot, because it was you, wasn't it?'

Eustace grinned modestly, but just for a moment seemed lost for words. Then he answered her, 'I hope that you have a wonderful Christmas with your family Agatha. Would you consider it an imposition if I were to call on you after you return to London? Perhaps I could explain more then.'

Agatha raised one eyebrow and looked at him archly. She thought for a moment and then replied, 'I shall be back in Grosvenor Square late on the thirtieth of December.'

'Thirty-first?'

'Yes.'

'Eleven?'

'Yes,' whispered Agatha and then she turned and walked to the carriage without looking back.

22

Grosvenor Square London, 31st December 1877

Agatha was in the drawing room at her house in Grosvenor Square reading some highbrow literature when, to her surprise, she heard a rap at the door. It was precisely eleven in the morning. Flack's footsteps echoed across the hall then he opened the door. A familiar voice spoke, 'Hello, my name is Frost. I believe Lady Agatha is expecting me.'

Moments later the aged burler entered the drawing room in all his dignity. Just as he was about to speak, Agatha smiled to him and said, 'Send Lord Frost in and perhaps bring some tea.' She set down the magazine, a penny dreadful called, '*The Sweet Smell of Death*' and looked up towards the door.

Eustace entered the room dressed in a dark morning suit that revealed some signs of lint on the shoulders, his tie seemed like an afterthought such was its distance to his collar. He strolled in with his eyes fixed on Agatha. It was as if seeing her gave him renewed energy after two weeks apart. He inhaled deeply and looked around the room.

'Does it meet with your approval?' asked Agatha rising from her seat and walking towards Eustace. There was a grace to her movement, a fixedness in her eyes that caused Eustace to cease breathing momentarily. She came up close to him joined by

Talleyrand whose tail was wagging like an overwound clock pendulum.

'Yes, I think everything looks in order,' replied Eustace before screaming silently inside at this remark. He had faced Bismarck, the young Mahdi, yet one look from this young woman severed the link between his brain and his mouth. Thankfully, Agatha seemed unconcerned. She gestured towards the sofa.

Eustace sat down and Agatha sat down beside him while Talleyrand deposited himself at their feet. Her proximity, the subtle fragrance she was wearing, the touch of her knee on his, was having a disastrous effect on his composure. There was a newspaper lying open on the table. He glanced at it then back to Agatha and felt his stomach tighten.

'I believe you owe me an answer to a question I posed at Campbell Hall. Shall I remind you of the question?'

'No,' smiled Eustace, finally recovering some of his respiratory capability. 'I believe I remember. I, too, have a question for you, Agatha.'

This had the desired effect on Agatha. Her eyes dilated, although outwardly she seemed calm. Seeing this relaxed Eustace somewhat. If he was feeling nervous and, for the first time in a long time he acknowledged this was the case, it was a relief to see that Agatha might be experiencing the same flux. This gave him some hope.

'Pray continue,' said Agatha.

Eustace inhaled deeply. Perhaps he should have planned this part a little more thoroughly. It always seemed so easy in books.

'Well, to begin with, I would like to apologise again for the hoax that we perpetrated on you.'

'I enjoyed it,' pointed out Agatha with a grin.

'Even so, I must still apologise. Particularly to Sausage, I doubt she'll ever trust me again.'

'Nor will I.'

'Quite right too,' agreed Eustace. 'Anyway, I was assured by all I spoke to that not only would you be up to the task of working out the conundrum set, but that you were also the sort of person who would enjoy the challenge and appreciate the joke. I was worried about this.'

'Please do not. I'm glad I met the expectations of my friends.'

'You did and you exceeded mine, Agatha. You see, this was not just a juvenile prank, it was a test.'

Agatha frowned at this. Whatever she had been expecting, it certainly was not this.

'Yes, I see this rather surprises you. Let me explain. As you know, I work for the foreign office. Diplomatic Corps and all that. My role combines a little negotiation with, shall we say, information gathering to assist in those negotiations.'

'Spying?' exclaimed Agatha.

Eustace was feeling a little uncomfortable now.

'It has been called this, yes. But you see, if we are to protect our country, our national security depends on the work that we do. It is not as unseemly as you may have been led to believe. I might add that in my work I have been greatly assisted by de Courcy, by Parrish and by your good friend Pru.'

Agatha was nearing a state of shock now, so it was as well that Flack chose this moment to enter with a trolley of tea. She waited until the tea had been poured before leaning more closely to Eustace. It was all he could do to stop himself...

'Are you telling me that Pru is a spy?' she whispered, conscious that Flack's ears were undoubtedly pinned to the door.

Eustace glanced towards the door then back to Agatha.

'Campbell Hall has been used on a number of occasions recently to host conferences with some of our allies and some who are not yet allies.'

'Enemies?'

'Let's be a little more optimistic Agatha. If you are to join us then you must be more flexible in your approach.'

Agatha sat back, much to Eustace's disappointment.

'Join you?' she exclaimed.

Eustace met this with a shrug and a nod. Agatha looked away. Outside the window she saw a young woman with a black perambulator. In the park young children were playing while mothers sat in a group on a rug. A little bit cold for that thought Agatha. She looked back to Eustace.

'So you would like me to be a hostess for conferences and the like?' There was a noticeable edge to her voice now. It was harder. Eustace had expected this though. He took another deep breath. It was time. There could be no more beating around the bush.

'Agatha, I want you to be my wife. Will you marry me?'

Silence.

Eustace, despite the feeling that his question had been unambiguous, felt that he might have been a little better to add a little bit more ardour to the proposal.

'I want to spend the rest of my life with you, Agatha. I'm in love with you, you see. In fact, I think I fell in love with you long before I met you. Your friends painted quite a picture, believe me. It's just that I must be honest with you about what my life is like. You will, by necessity, be part of what I do.'

Agatha was still in shock by the turn the conversation had taken.

'Are you recruiting me or proposing to me?'

'I suppose it's a bit of both, really,' admitted Eustace sheepishly.

The unexpected was Agatha's normal way to react. She burst out laughing. It was too funny. Only this man could say such a thing, no one else was, what was the word, so useless. Marry me and become a spy. It was not exactly something from a Jane Austen novel. Perhaps it was more Onya Bachnow. Who knows? She stood up from the sofa, still laughing and began to walk towards the drawing room door. Finally, she was able to speak.

'I'm not sure what to believe anymore with you Eustace. I mean you haven't even admitted anything about what happened at the rail station. Can I trust you? I'm not sure I can.'

Agatha could see the confusion on Eustace's face as she opened the door and walked out, stopping only for a moment to say, 'Look at the newspaper. I knew there was something about Little Recton that was familiar.'

Agatha walked out of the room and shut the door behind her. He could hear her laughing in the hallway.

Eustace picked up the paper and gasped. A mortal coldness descended on him as he read the headline.

FIRE AT RAILWAY STATION KILLS SIGNALMAN

His eyes flicked from the headline to the date. The newspaper was a year old. He cast his eyes over the story.

There was no question in his mind that the signalman described in the story was the man they had met that night. Bewilderment and fear gripped him. He looked away from the paper to the door.

'Agatha, that wasn't me. It wasn't...'

The words died in his mouth. It was unfathomable, yet it was true. What had they seen that night? He was shivering now despite the warmth of the room. It might have been minutes, but it was probably only a few seconds before he was on his feet and striding to the door. He opened it to find Agatha standing in the corridor. There was something in her eyes he could not read.

He walked towards her. Moments later, her hands came up behind his head. Instinctively, his arms encircled her waist. They paused for a moment then their lips met. For what seemed like a blissful eternity they stayed in this embrace before they parted.

'So, this is a "yes," my love?' asked Eustace, hopefully'

THE END

If you enjoyed this story – please consider leaving a review on Amazon. They really help sell my books which means I will write more of them!!

About the Author

Jack Murray was born in Northern Ireland but has spent over half his life living just outside London, except for some periods spent in Australia, Monte Carlo, and the US.

An artist, as well as a writer, Jack's work features in collections around the world and he has exhibited in Britain, Ireland, and Monte Carlo.

There are now seven books in the Kit Aston series.

A spin off series from the Kit Aston novels was published in 2020 featuring Aunt Agatha as a young woman solving mysterious murders.

Another spin off series is features Inspector Jellicoe. It is set in the late 1950's/early 1960's.

Jack has just finished work on a World War II trilogy. The three books look at the war from both the British and the German side. Jack has just signed with Lume Books who will now publish the war trilogy. The three books will all have been published by end October 2022. See taster after this section.

Research Notes

This is a work of fiction. However, it references real-life individuals. Gore Vidal, in his introduction to Lincoln, writes that placing history in fiction or fiction in history has been unfashionable since Tolstoy and that the result can be accused of being neither. He defends the practice, pointing out that writers from Aeschylus to Shakespeare to Tolstoy have done so with not inconsiderable success and merit.

I have mentioned a number of key real-life individuals and events in this novel. My intention, in the following section, is to explain a little more about their connection to this period and this story.

Sir Augustus Wollaston Franks (1826 – 1897)

Augustus Franks was a part of the British Museum for 45 years. He became administrator in 1858 and was the leading authority in England on medieval antiquities of all descriptions including: porcelain, glass, and other artefacts of anthropological interest as well as works of art later than the Classical period.

William Kurr

William Kurr was at the centre of the horse racing scam outlined in the story. Part of their successful operation was their ability to avoid arrest by means of prior warnings from Inspector Meiklejohn, and Chief Inspectors Clarke, Druscovich and Palmer. The policemen were arrested and later stood trial for corruption.

Sir Conan Doyle (1859 – 1920)

Arthur Conan Doyle studied medicine in Edinburgh between 1876 – 81. It was during this period he began writing short stories. He submitted "The Haunted Grange of Goresthorpe", was unsuccessfully submitted to *Blackwood's Magazine*. His first published piece was, "The Mystery of Sasassa Valley", set in South Africa. It was printed in *Chambers's Edinburgh Journal* in 1879. The first Sherlock Holmes story, A Study in Scarlet, was published in 1886 for which Doyle received the princely sum of £25 (£2,900 in 2019).

Acknowledgements

It is not possible to write a book on your own. There are contributions from so many people either directly or indirectly over many years. Listing them all would be an impossible task.

Special mention therefore should be made to my wife and family who have been patient and put up with my occasional grumpiness when working on this project.

My brother, Edward, has helped in proofing and made supportive comments that helped me tremendously. Thank you, too, to Debra Cox who has been a wonderful help on reducing the number of irritating errors that have affected my earlier novels. A word of thanks to Charles Gray and Brian Rice who have provided legal and accounting support.

My late father and mother both loved books. They encouraged a love of reading in me. In particular, they liked detective books, so I must tip my hat to the two greatest writers of this genre, Sir Arthur and Dame Agatha.

Following writing, comes the business of marketing. My thanks to Mark Hodgson and Sophia Kyriacou for their advice on this important area. Additionally, a shout out to the wonderful folk on 20Booksto50k.

Finally, my thanks to the teachers who taught and nurtured a love of writing.

TASTER FOR UPCOMING NEW SERIES BY JACK MURRAY

If you enjoyed this and my other books, perhaps you will consider a new WWII trilogy that starts with 'The Shadow of War' in June followed by 'Crusader' in August and 'El Alamein' in October 2022. It features some of the characters from the Kit Aston series. This will be available on Amazon and is published by Lume Books.

If WWII is not a genre that interests you perhaps you can share this with someone who enjoys war books!

Thanks!

Jack

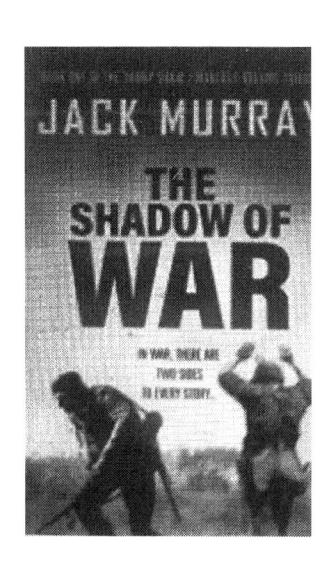

The Danny Shaw / Manfred Brehme WWII Trilogy

Two Boys.

One English. One German.

They will meet at the battle of El Alamein. Only one of them will walk away...

Danny Shaw, the son of a blacksmith, is growing up in the idyll of the English countryside. Manfred Brehme, the son of a policeman, is growing up in a Germany that has turned towards the Hitler and the Nazis. When the shadow of war falls over their lives, they both volunteer and join their country's tank regiments.

Shipped out to North Africa, they are destined to meet at the battle of El Alamein. Follow them as they encounter friendship, death and love in this thrilling new series set in World War II.

This is the first novel in a new WWII tank series by Jack Murray.

Perfect for fans of David Black, Alistair MacLean, Jack Higgins, and Jeffrey Archer.

CHAPTER ONE

Little Gloston: February, 1933

The air was cold and green with shadow under the trees hinting at the first bloom of spring. The brightening sky had lifted Danny's mood of despondency as he pounded up the road. Blood pulsed through his veins. Ribs vaulted with every stride. Muscles drew and flexed and pumped through the morning ground mist and his head jerked from side to side until he finally darted clear. His adversary gave up the chase with the shake of a fist accompanied by a few words unlikely to be repeated in front of the congregation at St Bartholomew's on Sunday.

Danny grinned, gave a mock military salute, and slowed to a trot. He made sure to maintain some momentum lest his pursuer find a second wind. The sound of the lad's voice receded into the distance. The lad in question was Bert Gissing. Eighteen and at least as many hands in height: over six feet anyway. Large, too. He liked his food. Perhaps too much. Quick enough over thirty yards but if you could evade his massive paws then you could outlast him even when weighed down by a couple of dozen apples.

Safe at last, Danny turned around and saw Bert trooping dejectedly back to the farm where he worked.

For a moment, Danny felt a stab of guilt. Would Bert find himself in trouble, he wondered? He wasn't a bad sort really. He had his job to do. It wasn't made easier by Danny or his chums who periodically raided the orchard for apples. The farmer could afford it. Still, he'd tell Bob and Alec to lay off old man McIver's farm for a bit.

Reaching into his canvas bag, he extracted a red apple. Moisture glistened like tiny jewels on the skin. He admired the product of his criminal efforts for a moment. Filched fruit seemed to have a fragrance and a sweet taste all its own. The first crunch released watery juices that overran his mouth and oozed down his chin. He wiped it away with his sleeve and continued back to his house, dodging puddles of water on the muddy path as he went.

Eleven years of age, Danny should really have been in school but, of late, his interest in academic life had petered out. He and his friends regularly mitched off for a day if the weather was clement. By early summer they would have abandoned school altogether. Most of the boys left at fourteen, anyway, bound for field or factory. Danny saw no reason why he should not plough the same furrow.

Danny's attendance had decreased with each passing year following his move to 'the big 'uns' side of the partition. He could read well, he thought. There wasn't much more to learn there. He could write, although the neatness was not quite at the same level as the girls in the class. And he could count. Geography seemed pointless, if the folk around him were anything to go by. Everyone tended to stay in the village. Well, except those who had gone to France.

Like his dad.

He had no yen to travel after seeing what it had done to those who had left. Many had not come back. Most never spoke of their time during the War. His dad for one. No, travel was not for him. He ambled along the road enjoying the freedom. The run had warmed him up and he was in fine fettle. He stopped at a clearing in the forest to look down over the valley at the twenty or thirty houses scattered around the slope. Behind them, on the flatter areas, lay the farms. In the distance he could see Cavendish Hall.

The rising sun had cast a shadow over a portion of the valley. He looked up. The sky was cloudless. A few birds fluttered around. He finished his apple and threw the core onto the ground in front of him. Getting up, he made his way towards the brook where he had agreed to meet his pals to share the booty. His feet pushed through the fallen leaves.

As he picked his way through the forest, he thought about the future. He would soon be expected to start earning his keep. There was work out there on the farms. It wasn't well paid, but Danny didn't care if it meant he was out of school. Then, of course, there was the forge with his dad and brother. Neither had mentioned about joining them yet. Anyway, there were choices. But the choice would come soon. He would suggest leaving school this summer. Once you left school you were a man. This was Danny's somewhat limited view of the world.

Physically he was getting there. He'd grown at least two inches in the last year. In two or three years he'd be as tall as Bert, although his body had not filled out so much. He was lean but not gangly. If Bert had caught him, it would have been a one-sided affair even with Danny's special 'throw'. Thought of his earlier adventure prompted the desire for another of the apples. He grabbed one from his bag and took a bite. It had been a near escape. This made the apple taste all the better.

As he munched the apple, he passed a youth sitting against a tree. The youth was a little bit older than Danny. His clothing was like Danny's; worn, patched up and a little too small. He looked at Danny and then the apple. It was difficult to say if there was hunger in those eyes.

'Morning, Ted,' said Danny with a smile.

Ted Truscott was a bit daft; all agreed. Harmless, but not all there. He rarely said much. Education had been attempted and abandoned with little regret on either side. His life was spent wandering in the forest. Danny went over to him and offered him an apple. Ted looked at Danny and then the apple. He took it and began to eat. Perhaps there was gratitude in the boy's eyes, it was hard to say. Their hooded emptiness was its own story.

Conversation over, Danny left him and continued his way to the brook.

Bird song echoed around the trees providing Danny with a musical chorus as he tramped towards the arranged meeting place. He couldn't see any birds, though. Just squirrels scuttling up trees. Some stopped for a moment to return his gaze before boredom set in. The only other sound in the forest was the crunch of twigs under Danny's boots.

This was the life. He knew it would not last forever. The prospect of joining his dad and older brother at the forge was something he neither welcomed nor wanted to avoid. It didn't occur to him there was anything else. That was it. Life in a village was like this. The future was written in the seasons.

The family were the village smiths. They always had been as far as Danny could tell. Always would be, probably. There was no reason to change this way of life. There was no reason, ever, to leave. His father had left. Not his choice, mind. Much good it had done him, thought Danny. Still, he'd survived. He thought of his friend Bob. His dad had survived the War. In a manner. Injured at Cambrai. One leg went that day. Gassed, too. Danny's dad had seen what had happened. He lived just long enough to see Bob walk.

Up ahead he saw a gap in the wood. Through the branches light danced on the flowing brook. No sign of his pals. Maybe they'd run into trouble. The milk raid was the most difficult of their plundering activities. They took it in turns. Two would do the milk: one as look-out, one to break in. Danny was on apple patrol. They rotated the farms they stole from so as not to raise any suspicions. They didn't take much. Just enough to feed them through the day.

A few minutes later, he broke through some foliage and arrived at their meeting place. Looking around he found a flat spot to sit on and waited. The brook ran fast a few feet away. He listened to it gurgling nearby where it hit the rocks. Further upstream it was deeper. They would probably go for a swim. A few months ago, Alec had fastened a rope from one of the overhanging branches. They could swing from it for hours on end.

Finally, he heard two voices. They sounded full of vim. A successful mission guessed Danny. He hoped Bob had brought some of his mother's bread. She worked in the bakery and the boys loved the fresh bread she dispensed every day from her iron oven in the cottage Bob shared with her and his sister.

'Oy,' shouted Danny, as the boys neared.

'Oy' shouted Alec by way of response.

Danny looked up as the two boys appeared. Alec was carrying an old bucket full of milk. It would have been quite heavy so they would have taken turns to carry it. As Danny had hoped, Bob was carrying the bread. Two hours out of the oven. His mouth began to water in anticipation as the warm smell enveloped him and caressed his senses.

They sat down and Danny poured the contents of his bag out onto the grass. Neither boy said much but the grin on their faces was pure and grateful as they gazed upon their ill-gotten bounty.

'Any trouble at McIver's?' asked Alec.

Danny nodded.

'Bert?' asked Bob.

'Bert,' confirmed Danny.

Alec looked serious for a moment, and they voiced what was on everyone's mind, 'We should avoid McIver's maybe for a while.'

For the next half hour, the conversation, such as it was, took second place to the grub. Bob had brought a veritable feast and feast they did. He liked his food and food liked him. When the last drop of milk was drunk and the last apple demolished, the boys lay on their backs and stared up at the cerulean sky, broken only by a solitary puffy white cloud floating, almost in embarrassment, looking for some companions.

'What shall we do next?' asked Danny.

'Swim?' suggested Bob.

This was greeted with a biff over the head with Danny's empty canvas bag.

'I meant who will we do tomorrow?'

'Why didn't you say?' complained Bob, but not angrily.

They discussed potential targets for the morrow. Each farm had advantages and disadvantages. Dogs were a no go. Farm boys less of an issue. The three boys had developed a set of ruses that could distract anyone likely to interfere with the commission of their crimes. The discussion lasted around an hour before the boys felt ready to amble down to the pond for a swim.

Predictably, Bob charged forward first, stripping off as he ran and taking a running leap onto the rope swing before completing his splash into the water with a poorly executed somersault. His ample frame caused a deluge of water and the two other boys laughed hysterically.

'Belly flop,' shouted his friends in unison.

'Let's see how you do it, then,' replied Bob, brightly, as he surfaced in the pool.

Ladenburg (nr. Heidelberg): February, 1933

The leaden grey sky was heavy with cloud. Rain and who knows what else was coming. The prospect did little to improve Manfred Brehme's mood as he stared out of the window. Rage coursed through him. Rage and a desire to inflict violence. He kept his attention on the window. Just in front of him a man was on his feet. He paced to and fro, footsteps echoed in the sullen silence of the classroom. He was speaking a heavily accented English, although Manfred was not to know this. The man tapped the blackboard crisply and read to a class that was as bored as he was.

Manfred continued looking away from the teacher, the blackboard and, critically, the person beside him. Normally he liked English class, and why not? He was probably the most accomplished speaker in the class. Second most accomplished. Diana Landau was better but then again, she had the advantage of being half-English so that didn't count.

No, the problem was the boy beside him: Erich Sammer. What had started out as a few playful punches before the class, had escalated steadily during the class. Now they carried real venom and neither boy was prepared to give way until they had struck the last blow. A glance at the clock on the wall confirmed there was another fifteen minutes of this war of attrition left to run.

A few classmates were aware of the undeclared conflict and would no doubt press for a more explicit resolution to the hostilities at the next break.

This was now a problem. He and Erich were nominally friends. However, these episodes happened from time to time. Rarely did they reach a point where a fight would end the quarrel. If they stopped now, the issue could be resolved, if not amicably, then at least without bloodshed.

Manfred felt a stab of pain in his shin. He turned around quickly. The two boys looked at one another. Erich was clearly angry. The look in his eyes suggested he wanted to get another blow in. Manfred widened his eyes slightly and then shifted them behind to indicate others were looking. Erich paused for a minute while he tried to assimilate the communication. A voice from the front of the class interrupted them both and caused the rest of the class to giggle.

'Silence,' shouted the English teacher. 'Herr Brehme, I asked you a question. Will you answer it please?'

Manfred reddened; he had absolutely no idea what had been asked such was his intense focus on ending the fighting with Erich. He had to think quickly now. Risking all, he plumped for the least embarrassing response he could think of.

'I'm sorry, sir,' he replied in English, 'I didn't hear the question.'

'Was that because Herr Sammer was hitting you?'

'No, sir,' lied Manfred. His face reddened as he said this. Burning shame and anger rarely stay hidden long.

An angry glint appeared in the eye of Franz Fassbender. He was a man renowned for a very un-Teutonic lack of self-control. His nickname was Franco due to this Latin-like volatility. His skin even seemed to take on a darker sheen when he lost it. That, and a rather unattractive eye-popping anger, gave a diabolic quality to his outburst that was, by turns, frightening, violent and comical, depending on your proximity to its original cause.

'Stand up,' ordered Fassbender. The voice was quiet. A sure sign that violence was imminent. Manfred shot to attention like a soldier. 'Both of you,' snarled the teacher in a voice that resembled an animal growling.

The situation was now deteriorating, realised Manfred, and he wasn't sure if he should blame himself or Erich. The post-mortem would identify the causes. For now, they were in trouble. Serious trouble. It was a mess that would extend beyond the classroom.

Any hope that his obvious linguistic capability and a previously unblemished record would stand him in good stead was swiftly put to rest by the malevolent look in Fassbender's eyes. The teacher stalked forward like a hunter about to seize its prey. His arm lashed out so fast that Manfred could not avoid it. Moments later, an index finger and thumb hooked around Manfred's left ear and proceeded to drag him to the front of the class. Nervous giggles were stifled. Fassbender deposited Manfred in front of the blackboard and then spun around. A worried-looking partner in crime joined Manfred at the front of the class.

Rage mixed with humiliation for Manfred as he stood at the front of the class. He and Erich were to be made examples of. This happened very rarely for Manfred, more often for the less-academic Erich. Fassbender was notorious as a disciplinarian. The ordeal the boys were about to face was an almost daily ritual for some poor soul. The eyes of the class all looked up at the two boys. The same thought hung in the air over their heads: thank God it's not me.

Manfred risked a glance at Diana Landau. She looked horrified. Manfred reddened a little as their eyes met and he looked away in shame. She stood out from the other girls and not just for her intelligence. Her hair was shorter, with no attempt to tie it into pigtails or platted in the manner of the other girls. He'd never spoken to her in the two years she had been in his class. This was odd as he liked what he saw of her. Such thoughts ran through his mind as he held out his hand.

A swish in the air and a stabbing pain. Manfred grimaced but uttered no sound. He kept his hand out. Experience had taught him that, if you removed it, this merely served to invite a second helping. Fassbender was moralising as he inflicted violence on the children, but Manfred had stopped listening. He moved outside himself and observed the situation as if from a seat in a

Roman amphitheatre. This crowd bayed in silence. Blood lust in the eyes of the boys. Horror in the eyes of the girls.

Erich stayed silent, too, as the cane lashed his hand. The pain was almost unbearable. The hatred kept him silent. Like Manfred, his hand remained outstretched. One question was now front and centre in both their minds. Would Fassbender make it two lashes? There was more than enough precedent to suggest he would. However, perhaps conscious of time, or maybe Manfred's previous good behaviour, Fassbender ordered the boys back to their seats.

The class ended soon after and the two boys trooped out. Rather than renew hostilities, they called a truce and compared their injuries. Both had a vicious-red pulsing streak across their palms. Their classmates crowded around to see the damage. Whether due to the humiliation or guilt, both boys decided not to mention the event again.

When the school day ended, Manfred walked back along the village street towards his family house. He followed the same route to and from the school every day. The market Platz in the centre of town was full of children and a few older boys in brown uniforms. Many were dotted around the war memorial in the middle of the square.

A few minutes later, he arrived at his house. It was large by the standards of the village. White plaster and wooden beams painted a vivid red greeted the visitor and left them in no doubt as to what country they were in. Inside, his feet clumped noisily on the wooden floorboards. The furniture was also wooden and seemed pre-war in its antiquity: the Franco-Prussian War. The house had a forest of such furniture but felt empty, in Manfred's view. The high ceilings seemed to create a sense of vastness in the smallest, most cluttered of rooms.

His mother greeted him with hardly a smile. He walked up to her and kissed her proffered cheek. He said nothing about the events of the day because he was not asked. The housemaid smiled at him, but she tended to speak only when addressed.

'How was your day?' asked his mother after a few minutes of silence, more out of duty than actual interest.

'Fine,' said Manfred, glancing out the window, or was it an escape route? The rat, tat, tat of rain suggested any request to go outside would be denied. He looked up at his mother for inspiration. Her face was drawn. She rarely smiled these days. It had not always been so. But now her eyes looked empty, like a dry well. The chill and the grey seemed to have seeped into the house, inhabiting the foundations, the walls, and the people.

Manfred left her and went to the drawing room. It was full of books with characteristic bindings. He thought about reading but realised he was in no mood. The events of earlier had left an impression and not just on his hand. It still throbbed. He went to the sink in the kitchen and bathed it. As he did so, his mind wandered again. He thought of Diana Landau.

She was twelve and generally considered the prettiest girl in the class. Dark haired and dark-eyed, she was exotic not just because she was half-Jewish but also because her mother was English. Lots of the boys had cast eyes in her direction once but, of late, this had ceased. Manfred knew why this was so; it was impossible to ignore and yet still a surprise. He found it difficult to imagine why politics should matter when it came to boys and girls and love.

The tap must have been running for an age when his reverie was broken by the echoing clump of footsteps outside the kitchen. In the doorway stood his father, Peter.

His father was tall and forbidding. He was a serious man doing very serious work as head of the town police force. Whether by way of conversation or, more likely, interrogation he asked, 'What are you doing, Manfred?' The muted tone was the most unsettling part. His father rarely raised his voice. Instead, it was like a liquid whisper. The sound of it wrapped around your ear and invaded your mind, enfolding, compressing and then suffocating it until you screamed your confession.

'I hurt my hand, Father.'

His father stepped forward and looked at his son's hand. He could see the red welt across the palm.

'How did this happen?' asked Peter Brehme in a low voice. Why do adults do this? Why the low voice. Don't they know we're frightened enough as it is? Fear was now strangling Manfred. His father's glare was hot enough to melt snow. He had a choice now: full disclosure or an outright lie. Neither alternative held much appeal, so Manfred told him the truth. And then held his breath. He didn't have to hold it long. His father's eyes hardened.

'Come with me.'

THIS CONCLUDES THE TASTER FOR 'THE SHADOW OF WAR'

Printed in Great Britain
by Amazon